WACKO'S
CITY OF FUN
CARNIVAL

WACKO'S CITY OF FUN CARNIVAL

by Jeff Metcalf

Printed in the United States of America

ISBN: 978-1-5323-5339-0

TKE Ink
www.kingsenglish.com

1511 South 1500 East
Salt Lake City UT 84105
www.kingsenglish.com

To Alana, Bailey, John and Susan Palmer and to my grandchildren Jack and Finn for their constant support.

To all the carnies who ever worked the midway and especially those I worked with as a young man.

I offer a special thanks to all the marvelous teachers who believed in me during my wild days.

Chapter 1

I should have seen it coming but thinking back on it, all of it, it was a chain reaction, pure and simple. Sort of like one of those "perfect storms" where nobody could see the little things adding up to a disaster. I mean really. The individual stuff was no big deal but when you lumped them together it told a different story.

It went something like this: 1. I got caught trying to steal a couple of bottles of whiskey out of Lucky Jake's Gas-o-Rama. I could've gotten away with it if the new owner hadn't pulled a shotgun out and pointed it directly in my face. When that happened, my buddies peeled out of the parking lot and left me there alone. I'd have done the same thing. 2. The cops came to take me home to my parents. 3. My parents weren't home so they took me downtown to put me in holding. 4. Lindsey Sweet told me she was going to the 10th grade dance with Bullet Ruweidel because I never asked her to go and she really wanted to go in a big way and 5. I'd been officially kicked out of Pershing High School. All in one day.

And then things went downhill from there. In a hurry.

Chapter 2

A couple of things you need to know about the other crap I told you. I lied to the cop about my name and I didn't let the him take me to my parent's place. Told him my name was Benjamin Lynch and I acted real polite and scared. Secretly, I thought it was pretty clever of me. Mr. Lynch was the assistant Principal at Pershing High and we didn't get along really well. So, I directed the cop to a house on Lincoln Lane, a couple of blocks from school, where the people had gone on vacation. I only knew that from my buddy Smitty who had a newspaper route before school. I knew that fact because he told me the people'd put a vacation hold on the paper and we were going to break into the place and kind of look around. Maybe take a couple of things.

The cop's name was Officer Broadhead and he fit the name. I almost started to laugh when I saw the name embroidered on the shirt because he fit his name. You know people like that, don't you? I mean, he had a really broad head. Bigger than anybody I think I've ever seen except the one kid in the sixth grade that had water on his brain. I think he eventually died.

So, Broadhead is talking to me about, "How come a young man like you would be inclined to steal whiskey."

Broadhead went on about how a guy like me was on the verge of making a serious mistake with my life. One that I couldn't turn back on and this was the first step to a life of crime. It sounded like a bad television series. Plus, I was way ahead of that curve. I'd already started down that road but this was the first time I'd been accused of *stealing*. And that was all bullshit in the first place. I hadn't left Jake's. I put the whiskey in my jacket, walked up to the counter and told the guy what I had. Those were the rules at Jake's because we were underage. We'd been told that if you hid booze under your jacket, then maybe bought some gum or something small, he'd charge you for the booze and gum and you were in business. Everybody knew that. Kids at Pershing had been doing that for years. The problem was, he'd sold the liquor store to a guy who didn't know the rules and how the hell were we supposed to know about that? That's when the guy pulled out the sawed-off and told me I could drink it in jail. Honestly, I could have been killed.

When Broadhead said I reminded him a lot of himself at that age, I almost gagged to keep from laughing. But, when he said maybe if I found Jesus, my life would change, I said the stupidest thing .

"I didn't know that Jesus got lost and needed to be found."

Broadhead ripped into me calling me a smart ass and adding on some other things I really don't feel like writing about. You get the point.

My sister says that I'm my own worst enemy. Sometimes I'm thinking about stuff in my head and it just comes out of my mouth. Like the filter isn't working.

So, when we got to the police station, Broadhead grabbed me by the back of my neck and marched me into the station. He more or less slammed me down at a desk out of the way, told me not to move and keep my 'pie hole' shut and wait until he could get hold of my parents. He made three phone calls but I'd given him a phony number. He could call that number until he turned blue in the face but the phone number belonged to a telephone booth and the chances were that nobody was going to pick it up.

A couple of drunks were brought in and were getting booked for intoxication. I think they were a husband and wife team or a boyfriend and girlfriend. But they were both flat ass drunk and screaming and swearing at each other like a bunch of sailors. It took Broadhead and couple of cops to get them separated. Smelled like cheap booze, sweat and anger.

It was kind of funny and kind of sad too because it made me think of my parents. Not that they swore at each other like that but they'd get staggering drunk and slobber talk. Always sent my brother and sister off to their corner of the house and sometimes it made me cry. I'd wait until they'd finished up and had fallen asleep on the couch or bedroom before I'd turn in. Just to make sure they didn't choke to death and die in the middle of the night. Crazy stuff for a kid to have to deal with, huh?

And then it struck me. There, in a nutshell, was the problem. I had no way out of this night. Sooner or later Broadhead would figure out I'd been lying to him and I knew that wouldn't go down well with a man of Jesus who was trying to throw me a raft of salvation that I'd punctured with my smart-ass mouth.

I knew I couldn't get out of here until I fessed up and told him who I was. Unless I did that, I couldn't be released into the custody of my folks which meant they'd probably end up having me picked up by Social Services and dealt with as a runaway.

I knew the drill because this wasn't the first time I'd been here at the station. Sooner or later somebody would recognize me and all hell would break loose. If I stayed with my phony name and was shipped off with Social Services, I'd probably end up in Juvenile State School. And there was nothing good about that.

A couple of hookers were brought in and booked. I recognized them from over by Peter Pan Pool Hall where they hung out and pedaled themselves. They looked at me and shrugged and then one of them said, "Hey doll, don't I know you?"

"Nope," I replied, but I knew who she was. She'd gone to the same school I did and was a couple of years older than me. She came from a big family and lived over by the copper mine. Her old man was a complete drunkard, a brawler and a nasty drunk. "Funny thing is," she said once, "The old man never missed a day of work in his life. Never."

We'd hung out in the parking lot a couple of times. I was the youngest of the parking lot gang and didn't have a car so I usually wasn't interesting but she kept looking over at me while she was getting booked. Broadhead was doing the paper work on her and I was afraid she might catch onto my name and ask Broadhead what I was doing in here. I tried not to make eye contact with her but I couldn't help looking over at her. Even all painted up like she was, she was beautiful. It was a rough kind of beauty. Her name was Rhonda and that was pretty cool because the Beach Boys had written a song called *Help Me Rhonda* and she said they'd actually written it about her. We all called *bullshit* on her but she said she'd met them when they played a concert at the Copperhead Amusement Park and had partied all night with them after a concert. And honestly, she might very well have done that. She carried that sort of mystery about her.

But having Rhonda there at the precinct presented a problem for me. She'd figure out where she knew me from, and she'd probably mention my name to Broadhead. So the only play I figured I had left was to go up and confess to Broadhead and maybe he'd go easy on me. I mean, I knew more about him than he knew about me and I could bullshit him out of handing me over to Social Services if I apologized about my earlier comment regarding *Lost Jesus*. I could tell him that I thought he was right...that in fact I was heading toward a life of crime...and maybe I needed some help.

I got up and headed toward Broadhead when I saw Rhonda nod her head in acknowledgement. There it was; she was raising the stakes of the game. She sort of lifted up her hand as if to say, *Hey, I finally got it. Aren't you...* and instead of letting her finish, I walked out of the room and out to the station's parking lot just as easy and calmly as anything I'd ever done.

And that's when I saw the keys in Broadhead's Ford Galaxie 500 just sitting there.

Chapter 3

"Lynch! Get your sorry ass back in this building you ungodly piece of shit!"

It was Broadhead. I opened the door of the Galaxie and briefly marveled at the fact that there were leather bucket seats in a cop car. I hadn't noticed them from the back seat when we were headed to the precinct.

I could see him standing outside the door. I wasn't going to wait around and shoot the shit with him because we'd already done that and it didn't work out so well. So I jumped in, fired up the Galaxie, slammed it into drive, screeched gravel all over the place and sped toward the exit.

I did a quick adjustment of the rear view and saw Broadhead push something up against the wall just outside the exit door to the precinct. A siren blast came on, and red lights started blinking all over the place underneath the parking lot lights. The squawk box crackled on inside the squad car and a lady's voice reported, "All units, 10-31. Crime in progress. Stolen vehicle."

When I looked back from the rear view I saw the chain-link fence rolling closed. If I didn't make it out of the parking-lot, I was pretty certain Broadhead would rip my arms out of the sockets and beat me to death so I stomped on the pedal. It would be close. Real close.

I was totally amped up. I was slamming my hands down on the steering wheel and wishing the Galaxie through the gate and for some reason I thought of Steve McQueen in that scene from the movie *The Great Escape* where he's in a Nazi prison camp that was supposed to be impenetrable and he steals a motorcycle and makes a run for his freedom. The thing is, you don't know if McQueen makes it or not but he did it because he had to be free. It was all or nothing.

And I became Steve McQueen as I roared through the gate tearing off the passenger side mirror.

Chapter 4

I knew I couldn't stay in the Galaxie. It was too hot and so was I. I was screaming along the roads and then I turned down Central Street. I knew I'd have to get off that pretty quick because it would be the most obvious route for a stupid punk kid. I was running stop lights, and I had the lights on but no siren. That would have been pretty amateur. On 5th Avenue, I swung a hard right, peeling rubber on the turn and almost losing control, and headed toward the Rio Grande Railroad Depot. There was a place there in the bone yard where a bunch of hobos hung out, and I could dump the car there.

The squawk box came alive and it sounded like a roll call. "Car 28 in pursuit. Out." "Car 16 following. Out." "Car 13 in pursuit. Out." The dispatcher asked for locations and they called in their locations one by one. None of them were headed toward me. Then I got shivers when I heard the next squawk. It was Broadhead.

"Broadhead and Talbot here. Suspect is a white, teenage male approximately 5'9", jagged scar below left cheek. Biker boots, Levi jacket, slicked back hair. Alias: Benjamin Lynch. Earlier booking pleaded out for information on suspect. Offered up the name Hubert Walker. Currently following the lead. Considered armed and dangerous."

Hearing my real name on the radio was a game changer. And the *armed and dangerous* crap!!! What was that all about? I had nothing on me at all. Not even the switch blade I usually carried in my boot for protection. I wanted to pick up the radio and tell the dispatcher in no uncertain terms that I WAS

NOT ARMED AND I WASN'T DANGEROUS!!! Because that sort of thing would get a person...oh, say like me...KILLED!!!

A Browning pump shotgun was tucked in a scabbard in the center of the front seat. I realized that was what made me armed and dangerous but I wasn't dangerous. Stupid *yes,* but not dangerous. There is a big difference. Breaking down the pieces, I could see how Broadhead would make the call he did. I attempted to steal some whiskey which would become *attempted robbery.* I'd lied about who I was and where my parents lived. I'd escaped the precinct. I'd stolen a squad car and there was a shotgun on board.

On paper, they had a pretty compelling argument against me. Once they found out that I had a juvenile record it was not going to get any better. I could only imagine what my parents would be thinking when the cops went to the house. Of course, they'd also show up at school and talk to the vice principal and probably my teachers. The vice would like to see me fry in an electric chair as would a few of my teachers. So that wouldn't help me out. I only hoped they'd talk to my English teacher because she'd be that lone voice who would defend me.

But that would look pathetic, right? Like when the FBI catches a Russian spy in a quiet neighborhood and the neighbors are shocked because *he seemed like such a nice man.* No question, this would make the news and I could not imagine what it would be like in the living room of Lindsey's house. Mr. Sweet sitting in *his* wingback chair smoking his pipe and his wife and Lindsey sitting on the couch when the news unfolded. It would be the top story and when they mentioned my name and showed a yearbook picture, Lindsey would probably burst into tears and her parents would turn on her and say *didn't we tell you so, Lindsey?* After a few minutes, her mother would probably comfort her but her dad was the kind of guy that couldn't let go. But the winner in all this would be one of my biggest rivals at Pershing, Bullet Ruweidel, the guy who was taking Lindsey to the dance because I hadn't asked her. That was stupid on my part and her girlfriend, Rita, told me so because Lindsey said yes to Bullet only because I'd never asked and there was less than a week before the dance.

I could see Bullet working it now. He'd call her up and act like he was really concerned and worried about her. Probably go over to the house and polite himself to death around her parents. He was smart that way and then he'd do something really smart like not put me down but act concerned like it *just didn't seem like Hubert.* He'd use Hubert because it's such a stupid sounding name and it sounded like somebody stupid enough to do what I'd done. Then he'd maybe ask if Lindsey wanted to go somewhere and *just talk* and she'd probably be allowed to go with him because he was the sort of young man her parents liked and then they'd go down to the Arctic Circle and get a burger and fries and sit in the car with Lindsey and they'd talk. Then they'd go to Gravity Hill and park and he'd hold her and tell her he was really sorry for what she was going through and who knows what would happen after that. I didn't like the situation but I was in no position to do anything at all and it was the least of my worries.

I passed Burton Lumber and, going through the intersection, I caught sight of a squad car two streets over heading the opposite way. I didn't know if I'd been seen or not, but if I stayed in the squad car, sooner or later they'd find me and I'd be in a wild chase and maybe a shootout.

I wasn't far from the Rio Grande Depot and there was a spot in the yard that I could dump the car and it wouldn't be found for a while. I knew the place well and I knew where to go where I'd be safe. In the meantime, I'd have to come up with some sort of plan. Maybe I'd hitch a ride on one of the trains and head out to California because if I stayed around here I'd end up in State School. That was a given.

It was getting dark when when I pulled into the yard. In the distance, I could see a couple of small fires burning where the hobos would get together before hopping a train. There was a spot known as the boneyard where old out-of-commission locomotives and carriages had been abandoned and left to rot. It would be a perfect place to dump the Galaxie.

I found an out of the way spot and parked the Galaxie, got out, took off my jacket and pulled my t-shirt over my head and wiped off every place I thought I might have touched. I'd watched enough cop shows on TV to know not to leave any fingerprints around. I locked the Galaxie and left the keys on the front tire of the passenger side.

In a couple of days, after I'd figured out a plan, I'd make an anonymous phone call to the precinct and let them know where it was. I started off along the tracks when it occurred to me that I had to go back and do something with the shotgun. If the car was in the boneyard more than a couple of days, it'd be busted into and stripped. The first thing to go would be the shotgun and whoever stole it would rule the yard. And the way things had been going for me, I could just see some bum drinking Busthead hooch and getting into a fight, firing the shotgun and killing somebody and the cops would more than likely tie it back to me. Why not? I opened the Galaxie back up, took the shotgun and locked it in the trunk. I also kept the trunk key before putting the other keys back on the tire.

Across the yard and back toward the station was a 24-hour café called the Lonely Caboose for the workers and a few daring souls from the city who liked pretending to be part of this world. The food was cheap and hot and I needed something to eat and to make a plan. Cautiously, I made my away over the tracks while keeping a keen eye out for the bulls. I didn't need to get beat up and turned over to the authorities.

The Lonely Caboose was made out of two railroad cars butted end to end and connected by a short passage between the two cars. The kitchen sat in the center of the first caboose and it was busy with cooks slinging hash, flipping flapjacks, cooking bacon, sausage and with plenty of counter seating. I sat at the counter on a parlor stool, the kind that are bolted to the floor and spin around, next to a couple of big beefy looking guys. I felt pretty puny alongside them. The counter was some sort of pounded out tin and it was all scratched up from use. About every four seats and there was one of those Seebury Automatic juke boxes where you could select a tune without having to get up and walk over to the jukebox. You could get 6 plays for a quarter, 2 for a dime and one for a nickel.

The place was packed and almost everybody was smoking. It had a comfortable feel to it and all the men in there were probably eating during the evening shift. There were about a dozen booths all filled with railroad workers, a phone booth by the hallway that led to the dining car and a couple of restrooms off to the side. I studied the menu scratched out on a chalkboard and decided to go with the hash and eggs and a cup of coffee. A waitress came over to take my order. She had red hair and a dirty waist apron smudged with grease and probably ketchup. Her makeup was kind of orange and her eyelashes were thick like bristles and I guessed she'd probably done this work all her life. You could tell she barely tolerated people by the way she kind of stood there, anxious, like if you didn't order immediately she'd just walk away from you and never come back. I'd heard her greeting customers along the counter asking them if they wanted the *regular*. She called them *dears* or *darlings* mostly out of habit because I couldn't feel any real interest in the response. It wouldn't have been hard to imagine her saying, *How you doin' Butch?* and Butch would reply with something like, *Not very good, Pearl. A couple of guys got crushed in the yard and died.* And Pearl would probably reply, *Want those eggs over easy with extra bacon?* like nothing in the world had happened. So, when she came for me, I was ready.

"What do ya' want, kid?"

"Hash and eggs. Over easy and coffee."

"Cream?"

"Yes, ma'am."

I dropped a nickel into the juke and selected *Light My Fire* by the Doors. Before it started, Pearl was already back with my hash and eggs and dropped it in front of me and topped off my coffee.

"Anything else, kid?"

"No, ma'am. Thank you very much."

"Ain't he sweet, Mel?" she said to the guy sitting to my left. "Ma'am and thank you very much."

"He don't know any better," Mel said, laughing with a mouthful of food, "but he'll learn."

Pearl sort of smiled, looked at me like she was going to say, *You're welcome*. But she didn't. Instead she slapped the bill in front of me and disappeared.

"She almost smiled," Mel said to me. "Almost."

"Doesn't she smile? I thought it was me."

Mel laughed and shook his head. "I been coming here for 12 years and I don't ever remember her smiling. She's a hard lady. Tough life."

"You can see it in her eyes. Like she had dreams once and now they're gone," I said. Mel just looked at me like he didn't get what I was saying so I just nodded my head and got down to eating and making a plan. The meal was good, really filling, and I started to slowly come down. Like after a fight's over. You're so pumped up when it's happening you don't really feel any punches until it's done and then it's like you just crash and things slow down and level out. Like you're out of adrenalin and there's nothing left in the tank.

I started putting the pieces of the puzzle together and began to form a plan. I'd call my sister Soup just to get a feel for how things were going at the house. Find out the important stuff. I got the check and paid the bill then left a good tip for Pearl. Then I got up and went to the bathroom. When I was done with my business, I washed my face with warm water, wiped it off with a dirty towel and stared into the mirror. I looked tired. Not like the wanted fugitive

I'd become. I had a couple of dimes in my pocket so I went directly to the payphone to call my sister. I dropped a dime into the phone and started to dial our number when something made me look over at the counter. Maybe it was because I wanted to see if Pearl had gotten her tip. Maybe it made her smile. I don't know why, but I'm glad I did because standing at the hostess stand were two cops talking to the girl that seated you when you came in. The tall cop handed her a picture and she studied it.

I never finished the call. Left the phone hanging there, turned around and headed back towards the bathrooms. The men's room had three guys in there so I knocked on the door to the ladies' crapper and called in, "Janitor. Anybody in here?" There wasn't so I went in, locked the door and immediately went over and tried to open the window. It was stuck and I began to panic. I tried a couple of more times and it finally creaked open. Not by much but enough to get the upper part of my body through but that was it. The drop out the window was about 10-12 feet and if I went out head first I'd surely break my neck. Worse if I had to go out by trying to shimmy out on my back and then try to do a back-flip mid-air. The other play was to simply try to walk out behind the two cops and high tail it out of there.

After all, what made me think they'd be looking for me...here...already? Of all places?

Think about it Sherlock. You stole a cop car from their yard. It was embarrassing for them so it became personal. Real personal. Walking through the Lonely Caboose in front of the cops was not a good plan so I went back into the men's crapper and there was a guy sitting on the can doing his business. I went over, turned on the water right by the window and let it run like I was washing my hands and tried the window. I gave it a mighty push upwards and almost caught my fingers between the rail and upper sash. The man in the can called out.

"Hey, you okay? What's going on out there?"

"Nothing," I replied, trying to figure out what to say next. "The boss wants me to do the windows?"

"Now?" he asked suspiciously, "In the dark?"

I had to think of something quick. "Right...(*pause*)...you know how bosses are, huh?"

"Ain't that the truth," he replied, laughing hard enough to start coughing and that gave me just enough time to pull myself up onto the window sill and drop out the window. My landing was pretty rough and knocked the air out of me. I went to stand up too quickly and fell back on my ass. I finally got up and headed deep into the shadows and dark corners of the yard where a person could disappear and become invisible. And right now, I needed to become invisible.

Chapter 5

I carefully made my way through the yard and, every once in a while, I looked over my shoulder to see if anybody was following me. When I felt nobody was after me, I took a whiz, found a wooden milk crate all busted up but good enough to sit on and then lit up a smoke. The smoke calmed me down a bit to the point where I could collect my thoughts. I had a plate full of problems and none of the answers I could come up with were any good. I knew one thing, I couldn't go back home and live in my house anymore. My acts were big and stupid with some pretty serious consequences. None of which I felt I could handle now. I needed to get some distance and some clarity.

I felt like the actor, David Janssen in this really killer television show called *The Fugitive*. See, Janssen plays a doctor, Dr. Richard Kimble, who gets wrongly convicted for killing his wife. The deal is, you know in the first episode that he really, really loves his wife. But here's the catch, nobody believes him because there are just enough unanswered questions and too many fingers pointing at Dr. Kimble so he's really in a tight spot. Kimble tells the police and anybody who will listen to him that he saw a one-armed man running away from the scene of the crime. He knows it was the murderer but the cops don't find anybody fitting that description so he is tried, convicted and sent off to death row. Kimble is seriously screwed and he's going to the electric chair and there is nothing he can do. Right?

It's something we all did as a family. Watched *The Fugitive*. We never missed an episode. Mom, Soup, Sparky and me would be sitting on the couch watching and my old man would be sitting in his wingback chair smoking Marlboros like a fiend. All of us on pins and needles. During this one episode I inadvertently reached for one of the old man's cigarettes to light one up and he grabbed my hand. I was totally busted and he just looked at me and said, "I don't think so."

The Fugitive opens up with this train screaming along the tracks at night. You hear the clickitty-clacking on the rails and a deep lonely sound of a whistle blowing into the night and then the narrator, with a really deep voice, breaks in saying.

"Name: Richard Kimball. Profession: Doctor of Medicine. Destination: Death Row, State Prison."

And then you cut to this hard-ass cop, Lieutenant Gerard who is on the train escorting Kimble to death row at the state prison. Lieutenant Gerard hates Kimble and you'd have to be blind not to see that hate in the lieutenant's eyes. Anyway, neither Kimble or Gerard are saying anything. They're handcuffed together and then Kimble reaches up to get a smoke but realizes he doesn't have any and Lieutenant Gerard pulls out a pack and offers him one. The credits to the show haven't even rolled yet but we're all at the edge of the couch because Kimble has got to escape or the series is over, right? Is Kimble going to punch Lieutenant in the throat and then strangle him and escape? Then you hear the narrator's voice again.

"Richard Kimble has been tried and convicted. But laws are made by men and carried out by men. And men are imperfect. Richard Kimble is innocent, but proven guilty. What Richard Kimble couldn't prove was that moments before discovering his wife's dead body he encountered a man running from the vicinity of his home. A man with one arm who has not yet been found. Richard Kimble looks out at the world and ponders his fate for the last time but sees only darkness. But in that darkness fate moves its huge hand......"

It's got you hooked, right? I could leave you hanging there but that would be mean. THE TRAIN DERAILS!!!!! And Dr. Kimble manages to escape and he vows to hunt down the one-armed man, bring him to justice and clear his name. But following him and trying to do the same thing is Lieutenant Gerard. Only Lieutenant Gerard is not looking for the one-armed man...he's on a manhunt for Dr. Kimble and HE won't stop until he's found him. What a cat and mouse game!!!!

The crazy part is that all of this takes place in 2 minutes or less and then the credits roll and the heavy voice of the narrator introduces the show, **"THE FUGITIVE"** starring David Janssen with special guest stars so and so.

I lit another smoke and thought how my life was kind of like *The Fugitive*. I was on the run from the law for something I didn't do. And Officer Broadhead was to me like Lieutenant Gerard was to Richard Kimble. Okay... not quite. Technically I didn't steal the whiskey. I hadn't left the premises of Lucky Jake's Gas-o-Rama so *technically* I hadn't actually stolen it. I did take the Galaxie and there was no way to get around that but I was not armed and dangerous. I had no doubt that if Broadhead caught me he'd work hard to make sure the full weight of the law would come crashing down on me. In that revelation, I knew what I had to do. I had to leave the state and the sooner the better. I stood up, ground my smoke out with the heel of my boot and buttoned up my Levi jacket. The night air was beginning to cool off the valley. I noticed a broken shovel handle a couple of feet in length and picked it up for no particular reason.

The first thing I'd do is call Soup and get a feel for what was going on at home. I'd have her pull together my clothes and some other things and shove them in a duffel bag. Then I'd give my best friend Smitty a call and see if I could crash at his family's funeral parlor for a couple of days while I got a plan together and finally, and most importantly, I really needed to make contact with Lindsey and try to explain.

Chapter 6

I doubled back through the rail yard and headed toward the Jordan River where I could walk unnoticed along the worn path into town. There was a small convenience store called Mel's Market at the edge of town with a pay phone I could use to call Smitty and Soup.

The river stretch I walked was sketchy. There were two or three camps of drifters along the Jordan that were pretty well known to rail hoppers. The camps had their own unwritten codes. It was supposed to be neutral ground and there were really only two rules: No fighting and don't do anything that would bring the cops into the mix. For the most part, it worked. It was a place where people'd camp, cook and share food, if there was enough, and exchange information about who was hiring and how work was across the states. And you'd learn where the yard bulls were so you wouldn't get the shit beat out of you. Those bastards were junkyard dog mean.

Don't get the idea it was romantic or a Robin Hood and his band of merry men sort of place. It wasn't. The camps were full of people who'd lived hard lives. People you don't want to see in your town because they've been lopsided by life. Plenty of nut cases and alcoholics, but enough folks who'd just fallen on hard times and had to move along. Those were easy marks to spot but, in these camps, people left them alone and even schooled them so they weren't so *green*. Looking and acting *green* could get you robbed or beat up pretty bad. Because this ragtag group lived on the fringes of town and out of sight, the cops pretty much left them alone. Every so often you'd hear about a transient getting stabbed in one of these camps and the mayor would get all upset and throw a shit fit and then the cops would come in and do a sweep, knock down the shelters and haul them all away. Here's the interesting part to me. You'd hear something on the news about it or catch something on the front page of our two rags and see people from the camps helping the cops clean up the place. It baffled me until Soup explained it was a symbiotic relationship. I must have given her one of those baffled looks because she explained it by giving me something to see.

"Remember the sharks in the aquarium?"

"Yeah, of course" I said, acting bored with the conversation.

"And the fish that attached themselves to the sharks?"

"Yeah already."

"The shark provides food and the fish keeps the shark clean."

"So?"

"They both get something from the relationship. It's symbiotic."

I nodded my head.

"The cops get help cleaning up the river by the very people that will move back in an hour after they leave the scene. Both groups know what's going on. Like most politics... A great deal of all of this is just for show."

My sister really was smart but the best part about it was that she honestly didn't know it. She never showed off or boasted about it. Soup was crazy smart and she just assumed everybody else was as smart as she was.

I was almost out of the woods when a guy stepped out of the dark onto the path. I pulled up short and he looked at me. I kept my gaze on him. He did a quick once over and probably saw the shovel handle in my hand.

"Didn't mean to scare you."

"You didn't," I said firmly.

"Where you going?" he asked.

"None of your business," I said pretty coldly.

"Got any smokes?" It was rhetorical because he could clearly see the pack in my Levi jacket.

"No," I said, gripping the handle tighter.

"Just asking," he said. He nodded his head and went down a side path toward the river. I watched him until he disappeared down the slope and into the trees. I breathed a sigh of relief and then lit another smoke. And a thought occurred to me...*If I was going to be on the run, I'd meet a hell of a lot of people like the drifter, only meaner, so I'd best be ready for anything.*

Coming off the river I crossed North Temple to Mel's Market where the phone booth was. I stepped inside and called my sister. The booth smelled of piss and there were a bunch of phone numbers scribbled and etched crudely on the glass that said crap like, *For a good time call Heidi at 388-1066* plus a load of pretty disgusting pictures of *boobs* and *vaginas* and *penises* fully erect.

My sister answered on the fourth ring.

"Bonjour, mon nom est Soup. Comment puis-je aider?"

"It's me."

There was silence on the end of the phone and then she whispered, "I can't talk. The cops are in the living room talking to mom and dad. Give me the number and I'll call you from my bedroom."

"Okay, but hurry. I'm kind of on a main street and I'm afraid somebody will spot me." I gave her the number, quickly stepped out of the booth and walked around the corner of the building where I was not so visible but could still hear a ring. The phone didn't ring immediately and after about 5 minutes I decided to call her back. I got to the booth, pulled back the door and the phone rang. It startled me and I was surprised how loud the ring seemed. I expected Mel or somebody to come out of the market to see what the noise was all about.

"Que diable se passe-t-il?"

"In English. What took you so long?"

"After I hung up mom wanted to know who I was talking to. So did the cops."

"What'd you say?"

"Told them I was talking to Bonnie Parker."

"Did they believe it?"

"I think so." Then she started laughing.

"What's so funny?"

"The one cop wanted to know if you'd try to contact me. I told him no."

"And that's funny?" I never knew what my sister found funny but it was usually the strangest stuff that nobody else would laugh at.

"No, but he wanted to know what sort of *secret code* language I was speaking."

"Any imbecile would know it was French."

"I know, right? So, I told him it was Klingon from Star Trek."

"Then what?"

"He got serious. Told me that if I had any contact with you it was best that I let him know because if they found out I had, I'd be an accessory to a crime. I told him you'd never do anything that stupid and he just gave me this stupid look like, *Right, that's what they all say.* But Hub, he was pretty worked up. Then he gave me his card and told me to call."

"What was his name?"

"He had a really big head. He reminded me of that kid, the McVicker kid that died in the..."

"Broadhead?"

"Right, he had a big head. Not particularly broad but it was big and his name was...just a minute, I've got his card on the bed. I actually didn't look."

"Broadhead," Soup. His name is "Broadhead."

"Broadhead," she said quietly reading the card to me. "You know him?"

"I stole his police car."

My sister was very quiet and then I could hear her start crying.

"I didn't believe the stuff he told me you did."

"It's true," I replied trying to calm her down. I hated when she cried. I really felt bad because she was crying for me. "But it's not the way it sounds."

I explained things the way they happened and how bad it all looked on paper. But honestly, it was an incomplete story. After a few minutes, she stopped me.

"I believe you Hub but it's your word against his and he's a cop."

"I know. That's the problem."

"There's more to it than that, Hub."

"I know."

"The minute you stole the cop car, any chance of you getting off easy ended." She paused and I could tell she gave what she was going to say a great deal of thought before she said it, "Why did you do it, Hub?"

"I honest to God have no idea," I replied and I meant it. I felt like shit because I couldn't give her a better answer. There wasn't one. One tiny scrap of something that might have made sense, might have justified my stealing the car in even the most flawed and convoluted way, might have helped her. It wasn't going to happen because there wasn't anything I could offer up.

"Are you going to turn yourself in?

"What do you think?" I answered snappy like. "I'll be sent away."

Soup paused, thinking things over. "Then what are you going to do?"

"I've got to skip town."

"And go where?"

"Somewhere."

"That's pretty vague, Hub."

"Even if I knew, I wouldn't tell you."

"Why?"

"Because you'd be an accomplice."

There was a long pause. I could tell she was trying to wrap her head around all of this. Finally, she spoke.

"I know it's seems bad right now, but maybe you could lay low for a couple of days and then get dad to go in with you and explain what happened."

"Not a chance, Soup. I crossed a line. A big one. Under the best of circumstances, I'd probably get state school, and the worst, I'd be tried as an adult. I committed grand theft and stealing a cop car that had a shot gun in it makes me armed and dangerous in the eyes of the law."

"Shit, Hub! What were you thinking?"

"I wasn't."

"How will you live? What are you going to get by on?"

"I've got money stashed away. In a box, out in the tool shed. I'm going to need that. Also, grab my duffle bag and pack it up with my clothes. Anything you can fit in it and I'll come get it."

"You can't."

"Why not?"

"They're going to have a cop car parked out in front of the house. They expect you'll try to come home."

"Shit."

"Have you talked with Smitty yet?"

"I was going to call him right after I talked to you."

"What if he came over and I packed all the stuff and put it in his car?"

"Won't the cops be suspecting something?"

"No, it wouldn't be unusual for him to be here. Heck, he almost lives over here most of the time."

It wasn't a bad idea. Smitty was almost part of our family. His old man ran a funeral parlor and really didn't care what his kids did. His wife had left him about three years ago. Just left a note and took off. Didn't say anything to the kids. Packed her bags, left a note and disappeared, and the old man never quite recovered. So, the kids pretty much ran wild. Smitty liked our place because it seemed like a home. My sister, my little brother Sparky and I got along pretty good. As good as brothers and a sister could.

"It might work."

I gave my sister specific directions on where I had stashes of cash. I had to level with her because I had some unfinished business I needed to have Smitty attend to. I felt really bad because my sister was going to find out just what kind of brother I really was.

There were three places I'd stashed money. I had about $300 and that was going to be a shock to her because I wasn't working. I also needed to have Smitty deliver two sets of Porsche hubcaps to a couple of guys at school. They'd paid me for them already and I thought it best if I got them off my folk's property. The owners had probably filed a theft report and I didn't want my old man picked up for stolen goods. Maybe we could get a father/son cell and I could finally get to know who he really was.

My father was a puzzlement to me. I think a lot of it had to do with WWII. He had a scrapbook that he'd never show any of us but I knew where it was and it gave me nightmares when I looked at it. From my room down the hall from where my folks slept I'd hear him scream when he was having a bad dream. Once, I came out into the hall and he was just standing in his bathrobe and staring down the hall. He was crying and shaking his head. I asked him about it the next morning and all he said was, "It never happened."

But it did.

I made some spare change by stealing Porsche hubcaps from the Poplar Heights and Fawnbrook neighborhoods. It's where all the posh people lived. They were easy to steal. All you needed was a screw driver and a lookout. I could pop all four in less than 3 minutes. Smitty'd timed me once and those hubcaps were beautiful and they fit perfectly on Volkswagen Beetles. I got $40 for a set of four. They came off 356 Porsches and they were sweet looking. It jazzed the hell out of the VW bugs.

I'm glad I didn't have to look at my sister when I was explaining everything to her...the cash, the stolen hubcaps, the hiding places to pick up money. The tool shed was easy for the first stash of money, the root cellar behind our house was a bit creepy and my sister was terrified of spiders and cobwebs so I told her to have Sparky pick that one up. Sparky was four years younger than me and he lived and breathed for the Colts football team. His man was number 19, Johnny Unitas of the Baltimore Colts, and my brother wore a Baltimore Colts football helmet with the number 19 on it for as long as any of us could remember. More than a few times my mother had to go to school and pick him up and take him home because his elementary school teachers couldn't get him to take the helmet off. As a way to get chucked out of school, I thought it was genius.

"I don't want to go in there," my sister said. "You know how I feel about arachnids."

"Tell Sparky to dig out his helmet and go in there and get the stash."

"What about the third stash?"

"In my room, in the closest under some floor boards."

"It's an oak floor. How am I supposed to find it?"

"Take out my clothes, pack what you can and use a flashlight. Toward the back, dead center, if you walk around, the boards will squeak. Take a screwdriver from dad's toolbox and pry the boards up. They'll come up pretty easy."

"And the hubcaps?"

"Smitty knows where I keep those."

"Should I just give Smitty the money?"

"No, just stash it in the Boo Radley tree. I'll come and get it."

"Why don't I just meet you there."

"Too dangerous."

"But I'll be real careful."

"I can't take the chance."

"Okay. Hub..." my sister said and then paused, "will I see you again?" How could I answer that question? I honestly doubted it given the circumstance.

"I'll do my best to see you," I replied, knowing full well that my sister didn't believe it.

"I swear I'll call whenever I can and I'll send postcards."

"Promise?"

"Swear to God."

I really meant it. Growing up my sister and I dedicated our lives to trying to kill each other. She tells a story of me coming home from the hospital and seeing me for the first time. Even though she's barely two years older than me, she says she remembers it perfectly. My mom even verified the story. Anyway, she took one look at me all fat and pink and gurgling and cooing and turned to mom and said, "I think I want to be an only child!" My mom would laugh when she told that story and she'd swear to the high heavens that it's exactly what my sister said.

Mom and dad said Soup was born speaking full sentences from birth. And it was the honest to God truth. My sister was wicked smart and skipped from the 2nd grade to the 4th grade because the school didn't know what to do with her. She had a photographic memory and that worked out just fine for me. When I got to junior high if I happened to have the same teacher and, say, we were reading the same old boring books and were going to have an essay test, I could ask her what the questions were and she could remember them. When this happened, she'd always close her eyes and I could imagine her going through some sort of memory vaults looking for the questions. Then, all of a sudden, she'd open her eyes wide open and tell me the questions and there they would be when I got to class...exactly as she said.

It was interesting on the first day of any class when a teacher was taking roll and they came to my name. If they'd previously had my sister, they'd take pause and usually give me a nod or say, "You don't have a sister named Soup, do you?" And I'd say that I did and you could tell they were excited to have another genius in the class, one that could talk about literature the way a college professor would. The first day was always my favorite but, after that, my guess is they all wished they still had my sister in class.

I pulled some really mean shit on my sister — like the time I convinced Sparky to take mom's really good scissors and go into Soup's room and cut all the hair off of her doll collection. I could usually talk Sparky into anything because he wanted to part of my gang. It wasn't really a gang but we acted like it was and we were cool.

So, Sparky does it and my mom finds out and Soup is hysterical and crying like it was the end of the world and then my mother starts in on my brother but he won't point the finger at me because he wasn't a rat. We all knew it was me but my brother wouldn't spill his guts and my mom couldn't convict me on circumstantial evidence but she swore if she found out that I'd put Sparky up to it, she'd crucify me.

I felt like shit because when the old man came home that night from work he came into our room and took his belt to Sparky and made me stand there and watch my brother get an ass whipping. Just before he started, my father looked directly at me and said, "Hubert, is there anything you want to tell me about what happened today?"

"No, sir."

"Are you sure?" he said, looking me straight in the eyes.

"Yes, sir."

And then he commenced to whipping on my brother. It was a serious whipping and my brother started howling. I have a hard time even thinking about it now because it came from someplace very deep inside him. He cried so hard he couldn't catch his breath and when my dad stopped I was crying too. My dad looked at me and said, "There is a consequence for every action, Hub," and dropped the belt on the floor and walked out of the room.

I grabbed my brother and hugged him while he cried. He tried to speak over his sobs but it was all just gibberish and I just held him tight and apologized promising that I'd never ever put him in such a circumstance again. And I didn't.

About an hour later, my sister walked into the room without knocking. Those were the rules but she just walked in anyway. I was lying in bed reading comics and she pulled up a chair and sat real close to me. Sparky was in the top bunk sleeping. I started to say something about following the rules and knocking but didn't get a chance. She just got into my face and whisper talked.

"What you did today to me, and especially to Sparky, was downright mean."

I started to protest, but she plowed on. "He looks up to you and he'd do anything you told him to do without thinking twice so you've got to do the thinking for him."

All of this crossed my mind right now while I was talking to Soup on the phone. How I wanted to see them all and talk with them before hitting the road but I couldn't. My plan, or what it was of a plan, was well under way. The longer I hung around, the odds of getting caught got higher. I wondered if I would see any of my family again. And that troubled me deeply.

Chapter 7

I was getting nervous hanging around Mel's Market. It wasn't on a main street or anything like that but enough people took an interest in me being on the phone that I thought it was a good idea to head back toward town and use a different pay phone. Perhaps it was a bit of paranoia setting in, but who knows what had been on the nightly news. I certainly didn't, and I couldn't take that chance. For all I knew, the cops could have a photograph of me taken from our house or the school yearbook and were putting it up on all the stations with a caption something like *If you see this person, don't try to apprehend him. He is armed and dangerous!*

It started to rain so I pulled the collar up on my Levi jacket, tucked my head down and stayed away from the overhead streetlights. A half-dozen blocks later I stopped at the Lazy 13 Club and used the phone inside the door. It was a real sleazy dive and sometimes on a Friday night Smitty and I would go down there and drink beer and shoot pool. The owner, a big beefy guy by the name of Al Keffler knew we weren't 21 yet but he'd called us over to the bar and asked to see our phony drivers' licenses. Before we could even go into how they weren't fakes he said, "Look, don't bullshit a bullshitter." When he took our licenses, he nodded his head in approval. "These are pretty good fakes, boys. You can drink here if you stay toward the back of the bar by the pool tables. Any trouble and you're out the side door. Understood?" He paused and said, "Besides, I could use the extra money." We both agreed and the Lazy 13 became our hangout.

I dropped a dime and called Smitty. The minute he picked up the phone I knew he knew.

"Jesus, Hub, you're all over the news. I can't believe what they said is true! Is it?"

"Yes and no."

"What the hell does that mean?"

"After you guys peeled out of Jake's Gas-o-Rama, I had to come up with..."

"Hey, Hub, we were scared. We saw a guy pull out a sawed-off and we panicked...man we..."

"I would have done the same thing."

"We waited a while and then did a drive round and when we came back there was a cop car..."

"And the cop was going to take me home to my folks but I'd given him a false address...you know the game?"

"I'd have done the same thing."

"I ended up at the station and he called the phony number and got nothing. I was going to fess up and then some drunks came in and some hookers and shit got crazy."

"How'd you get out of there?"

"The cops were busy and then I recognized one of the hookers..."

"Who?"

"It was Warren's girlfriend from the parking lot."

"Not Rhonda?"

"Yeah, and it made me sad seeing her that way."

"She's had a tough life."

"Coming from that family I'm not surprised, but you know what?"

"What?"

"She was probably one of the smartest people in that graduating class."

"Rhonda?"

"Yes. It was the last week of school and we're sitting in Mr. Case's class and he's done with the year and so are the rest of us and he starts asking us what our dreams are and where did we see ourselves in ten years.."

"And? What'd she say?"

"She said she wanted to be an architect." I paused to let it register. "And it shocked the shit out of everybody, particularly Mr. Case. So, he asks her who her favorite architects were…kind of challenging, like she wouldn't know and Rhonda didn't bat an eye and she rattled off like five major architects and Case's jaw just dropped. The entire class was silenced and it was beautiful…it really was. And I remembered thinking, *I hope she gets a chance to do just that!*"

"Maybe she will. Maybe one day."

I think we both knew that dream probably wasn't going to happen. But it made me think about all of us and the big dreams we carry. How many people like Rhonda don't stand a chance because of the cards they get dealt?

I explained my plan to Smitty because he'd be involved in it. He didn't hesitate, he agreed to it. I was very specific to let him know that he'd be an accomplice if something went wrong."

"Where are you staying tonight?"

"The bus station."

"It's the first place the cops will look."

"I might have to just keep moving around and sleep in snatches when I get a chance."

"Hub, you can't stay at my house. My pop would turn you in the minute he saw you."

"I understand."

"But you could sleep at the parlor tonight. Nobody in there will rat you out. It'll be dead silent."

It made me laugh for the first time that day. It was such a corny joke and I'd heard it a thousand times. Smitty's dad owned the funeral parlor and it was attached to their house. Growing up, when I first met Smitty, I'd never go over to his house to play. In fact, I can't think of anybody who ever did. It just creeped me out with dead bodies stacked on top of each other and ghosts flying around all night long. But I remember going over for the first time. I was in the 4th or 5th grade and we had a science project that we partnered up on. Smitty said his old man had all the stuff we needed to make a volcano but we'd have to make it at the parlor so I agreed to go to his place. What surprised me was how beautiful the place was once you went inside. It was real quiet and spotless with deep, rich paneled walls, shiny marble floors, and a painting framed in gold with a picture of Smitty's grandfather over a fireplace and another one alongside it of Smitty's father next to it. I've got to say his old man looked a lot better in the painting than he did in real life.

It felt like a mansion inside, like something out of a movie, and I could almost imagine living there and having big lavish parties with champagne and caviar and beautiful women and a piano player and a hot band and waiters walking around with really nice food like Vienna sausages on a toothpick with an olive and a piece of cheese and slices of gooey pizza on toothpicks too. But the smell would get to me. It wasn't the kind of smell I expected, like a dead body smell (not that I'd ever smelled a dead body), but it was more like a sort of stale smell, not mildew like but a mixture of incense and too much flower plus stale.

"Thanks, Smitty."

"Anything for a fugitive," he replied, laughing because he searched for the humor in my circumstance. "I'll see you in 15 minutes."

We agreed to meet at the Copperfield Baseball Park. It was a grand name for a park that hadn't been used in years. When the copper mine closed up and people moved looking for work, the only thing left behind was a huge gash in the mountainside where copper had been extracted and a baseball field that was overrun in weeds and garbage. Nobody went there except on the weekends when we'd all sit in the dugout and drink and smoke.

It had started raining. Hard. The ball park would be a good place to get out of the rain. We were having one of those springs that would be t-shirt weather one minute and the next it was snowing. Between the two extremes the weather was like this...rain/sleet and I was getting colder by the minute.

Fifteen minutes turned into an hour and still no Smitty. I was shaking and my teeth were chattering. I was afraid that I'd get whatever that disease was where you got so cold you'd forget who you were and where you were going and you'd die if you didn't get help. Your body temperature starts to drop dramatically and every hunting season there were always a couple of articles about some hunters who'd get lost and then get found wandering around completely disoriented and babbling like lunatics. Sometimes they'd take their clothes off and do all sorts of crazy shit. Then they'd die.

My sister was the one that told me about it but I can't remember what they called it but I was cold enough that I needed to find someplace warm or I'd be in serious trouble. I decided to head back to the phone booth and call Smitty to see what was going on. Maybe he was afraid to pick me up and get involved and I wouldn't blame him.

Chapter 8

I was having a hard time walking and keeping my concentration. I was drenched to the bone and I was walking like I was ripped. My brain wasn't getting the signals to my feet and I was shaking like a sewing machine. I staggered out into the street and a car shone its bright lights, slammed its brakes and laid on the horn. Then a guy jumped out and started swearing at me. I couldn't see anything because the brights were blinding me. This guy was pissed off and if he decided to kick my ass I wouldn't have been able to do anything except curl up in a ball and hope he didn't kick my head in. I heard the car trunk open and shut and a form came running at me. Maybe he'd grabbed a baseball bat. I really didn't care.

"Hub," it yelled. "You almost got run over. What the hell were you thinking?" He quickly wrapped a wool blanket around me.

"Hypothermia," I said and again, "Hypothermia."

"What the hell are you talking about?"

"I couldn't remember the word before."

"You're shaking like a dog shittin' razorblades," he said, helping me into the passenger side of the Ford. He cranked up the heater and slipped his Fairlane into gear and drove off. It felt good to get out of the storm.

"Open up the glove box," he ordered. "There's a pint of Black Velvet in there. Stole it from the old man. Take a good swig and pass it over."

The Black Velvet burned going down my throat and I started coughing but it felt good. I just sat there letting the booze do its work. I took another glug and finally asked Smitty, "What took you so long? I thought you were going to ditch me."

Smitty slugged me in the arm. "Seriously? You think I'd ever do that?" He punched me again this time a little harder. "It's your fault I was late, Hub."

"How's that?"

"I was getting ready to leave the house when this cop rolled up in a black and white."

I got the shivers because I already knew who it was. Broadhead.

"The cop didn't waste any time. Gave me the third degree. You know, asked if I'd seen you. Told him no. Asked me if you'd tried to contact me and I told him no. Asked me if I knew where you'd go. Said no and then he started to turn up the heat."

"How so?"

"Asked me again if I'd seen you. I told him I hadn't seen you. Then he goes on to tell me if I was hiding anything and I'd seen or talked to you and he found out I'd be an accomplice in a felony case."

Broadhead was like a bloodhound and he was on my trail in a serious way.

"Then he wanted to know where I was heading. Told him I was going to the library to study."

"And he bought that?"

"I don't think so. Wanted to know where my books were and I told them they were in the back of the car."

"If he'd looked. Actually looked, my books would have been there." I looked into the backseat and sure enough Smitty's books were there slung out all over the backseat and the floor. "I wouldn't have thought of that but it's a stroke of genius."

Smitty started laughing and reached for the bottle. I handed it to him and he took a long pull. "Been there since the beginning of school. Never used them."

I laughed. It was true. No lie. Smitty and I both missed a lot of school. We'd go to our first period class so the teacher could take roll then we'd pretty much ditch school.

First period I had English with Mrs. Nelson and then a drama class and Smitty had a woodshop and then automotive class. Those were the only classes we liked. I liked Mrs. Nelson's class because we read great books and I've always loved to read. There was something about the way she helped us unlock the secrets of literature.

I think she saw something in me that I didn't see in myself and she used to give me extra books to take home to read and I'd almost always read them in a couple of days. She'll never know how much she helped me. I suppose if I end up doing time, she'd probably send me books in the pen. She was also the sort of teacher that would write a note to me like *Maybe while you're there you should form a bookclub.* The thought of it made me laugh.

I think we both liked our first couple of classes because those teachers made no judgments about us.

"You doing okay, Hub?" Smitty asked. "You're kind of mumbling to yourself."

He passed me over a cigarette. I don't know if he'd asked me if I wanted one or not but he lit me one anyway. When I took the smoke, I looked down at my hands and they were shaking.

"Thanks," I said taking a drag, "Is there any way to turn the heater up?"

"It's on as high as it'll go. I'll get you into some dry clothes. You're shaking pretty bad."

"I've never been this cold before."

"We'll be at the parlor soon."

"Did you pick up the duffel and stuff from my sister?"

"No. As soon as I get you into some dry clothes I'll head over there."

"I thought you'd already been there," I said, trying to figure out what had taken him so long to get to me. I wasn't processing anything clearly.

"I couldn't rush the cop," he replied, tossing his cigarette butt out the window, "I didn't think he'd ever leave. I waited about ten minutes and then drove a route where I'd be able to spot them if they were following me."

By the time we got to the funeral parlor I was having a hard time keeping my eyes open. It was like I was crashing from all the adrenalin I'd used up earlier in the day.

Smitty turned off his lights as we pulled into the back-parking lot of the funeral parlor.

"Wait here while I go in and turn the lights on and make sure the old man isn't playing around with one of the bodies."

I must have had a horrified look on my face because Smitty smiled and said, "I was just kidding Hub. Really."

When Smitty finally turned on the outside light at the side door and signaled me to come in, I got out of the car and made my way over to him. My balance was off and I almost fell.

He noticed.

"Are you okay? Did those cops do anything to you at the station?"

"No," I replied, surprised by his question.

We waddled into the prep room. Smitty handed me a towel and a blanket. "Get dry and I'll go grab some dry clothes for you."

It was eerily quiet. The room was all white tile and there were two large stainless steel tables where they put the bodies and probably drained the fluid out of them and then made them look good for the bereaved. It reminded me of a hospital. I mean you'd think there would be a bunch of chemicals and embalming fluid and bottles of weird colored liquid and bubbling pots but it was pretty clean and organized.

Smitty returned and handed me some sweat pants and a sweatshirt along with some dry socks and his slippers.

"Give me your clothes and I'll throw them in the dryer."

While he took my pile of wet clothes off to dry, I slid into his sweats and started feeling better immediately.

"Look," he said almost apologetically, "Like I said, I can't let you sleep in the house. The old man finds out and he'd turn you in sure as hell."

"I get it. I just need a place to crash tonight and I'll be out of here tomorrow."

"We'll talk about that in the morning, Hub."

"I really owe you, Smitty."

"Don't be stupid," he snapped. "I owe you."

"For what?"

"For the camping trip when I almost killed the old man with an axe."

"That doesn't count."

"It does to me."

We both kind of felt awkward and then Smitty said, "I'm going to put you in the showroom where we've got all the coffins on display. You can sleep in one of those tonight."

"In a coffin?"

"It's the best I can do under the circumstances."

"Right. Of course. No. Thanks."

"They're actually pretty comfortable."

At that point, I would have slept anywhere and I could think of worse places to sleep on a rainy night. I climbed up onto one of the coffins and tucked myself in and before I could think of how creepy it was, I was out. The last thing I remember is thinking how comfortable it was and then I slept like the dead. And I don't mean to be funny.

Chapter 9

That night I dreamt hard. It was one of those dreams that was absolutely real. It wasn't like a dream that seemed real up until the point where something unreal shows up and then you know it's just a dream.

It was about the camping trip we went on with our fathers and Smitty's twin brother, Leon. Just the five of us. Smitty, his brother, his old man and me and my old man.

My parents had Smitty's old man over for a barbecue because he'd recently gotten divorced and such and they thought it would be a nice gesture. The idea for a camping trip together just sort of came out of the blue and next thing I knew we were all pouring over a bunch of maps and getting serious about it.

I remember feeling excited and really close to my old man that night. Sparky, my younger brother, wanted to go but he was really too young to join us so he pouted for the rest of the night until my mom let him eat his dessert first and then dinner so he got distracted.

It turned out both our fathers were really into maps. Probably because of WWII. My dad had us bring out the sawhorses and put a sheet of plywood on top where they could spread out the topographic maps.

It was interesting watching them talk bent over the maps, cigarettes in hand, and sweat ring stains of ice-water from the beer bottles dampening the paper. They made planning the camping trip seem like they were planning for the invasion of Normandy.

The plan was to hike up a rugged stretch of mountain outside of the small town of Oakley. We'd take our station wagon as far as we could go, then hike up into Rhodes and Anchor Lakes and fish for a couple of days. We'd pack everything in our backpacks and we had to be prepared for foul weather because it was the beginning of fall and it could be sunny one minute and then things could change in the blink of an eye.

My father said it was pretty rugged terrain, but both men felt like we were old enough to handle ourselves in the backcountry. I remember feeling proud with this benediction, like we were becoming men in our father's eyes. Like this was the test. Like the aboriginal *walk about* where boys like us were turned loose and left to wander around with nothing but their wits to keep them alive. My dad said it in such a way that all three of us felt like we were making a change in that moment and that perhaps, on this trip, the secrets of becoming young men would be passed onto us. I took this seriously and packed my gear until my kit was streamlined and comfortable.

We left early, making a final stop at Keith's Café to pick up some sweet rolls and fill our thermoses with coffee. Smitty and I got coffee and loaded it up with sugar and cream to kill the bitter taste of it. Smitty's brother preferred hot chocolate and we kidded him about not being manly enough.

From Parley's Canyon, up toward Kamas, we watched as the sun burned the early frost off the fertile farmland spread out in front of us. The leaves were already turning color; the aspen leaves spinning golden on their branches reminded me of pinwheels. Smitty's father would spot game and call its location to us in the backseat.

"Deer at three o'clock," he'd say and we'd stretch our eyes to find it. When we hit Kamas, we headed toward Oakley and then cut due east toward Lars Johansen's old sheep camp. We followed an old wagon road along switchbacks toward Rhodes Lake. The station wagon spewed rocks off the edge of the road and sometimes my dad would stop the car while we boys would pile out to move a boulder or some fallen aspens out of the way. Finally, when the washed-out ruts made the road impossible for us to navigate, dad pulled the station wagon into a small clearing of pines and we unloaded our packs.

Smitty's father unfurled a topographic map over the hood of the car, marked the spot where we were leaving our car and then pulled out a compass. He called the three of us over to watch what he was doing. Out of the corner of my eye, I saw my father loading up a couple of bottles of Jack Daniels into his backpack. Maybe we'd all get to have a drink around the campfire that night. I'd never drank with my old man before so this would be cool.

"Up here," he said, pointing with a pencil, "is Rhodes Lake and here we are. These lines here are called contour lines. The closer they are, the steeper the terrain. So, we want to set our compass on true north and take a reading on where the lake is. Do you understand what I'm saying?" And the three of us answered, almost in unison, "Yes, sir!"

We watched as he traced out our course to Rhodes. He scratched out the coordinates on the map and, after consulting with Smitty's dad, we began the hike. If all went well, we'd be at Rhodes in between three and four hours depending on how many breaks we took and that would still give us plenty of time to catch some fat brook trout for dinner.

For the first leg of the hike, Smitty's old man took the lead with the three of us boys behind him with my father taking up the rear. Smitty's brother whined for a bit but when neither of us responded to him, he shut right up and fit right in. The terrain was steep and we broke a sweat almost immediately.

To our left, we could hear the rushing of water but couldn't see the stream on account of the foliage. Once, coming out onto to a flat open space we scared up a herd of elk. They'd bedded down in an open field and the minute they saw us they took off running. We froze in our tracks. A great bull bugled and snorted a warning at us. After perceiving we were no threat he casually loped off into the protection of the pines.

It was a good place to take a break so we did and lunched on spam sandwiches, hard boiled eggs, elk sausage, apples and some of mom's apricot juice. I can't ever remember a lunch tasting better in my life. Smitty's dad gave us the map and told us to figure out exactly where we were, while both men smoked. The three of us went off by ourselves, sat down and studied the map. The open meadow was the key to our location. The steep contour lines smoothed out onto flat land and then they were bunched together in a steep ascent almost immediately. It had to be where we were and when we took the map back to our dads and pinpointed our location, the men complimented us. They both smelled a bit of whiskey. The truth was that it was actually fairly easy to find our location but the three of us sort of swelled with pride. Compliments from our fathers were very few and far between.

Above the timberline our pace slowed a bit and our stops became more frequent. We consulted the map more closely. There's a hell of a lot of lakes in the High Uinta mountains and they're tucked away in small glacial basins so they're sometimes hard to find with the naked eye. The map and a compass was insurance.

We continued the climb and late in the afternoon Smitty and I got to lead us up through a pitch of granite boulders. At the crest, Smitty cried out, "Rhodes Lake...dead ahead!" When I caught up to him we could see Rhodes with its deep emerald blue water and flat grassy banks. It was absolutely breathtaking. The others caught up to us and we made the half-mile to the lake in little time. We found a great camping spot with a granite wall to our backs, a big fallen dead pine that would cut the wind and give shelter to the tents and even a fire pit somebody else had used for a cooking area.

Smitty and I dropped our packs and began gathering firewood. Our dads started chopping what we brought back and making a neat woodpile to burn through the night. When we'd collected enough wood, we rolled out our pup tents. My dad came over to see how we were doing.

"You boys planning on catching dinner tonight?" he asked.

"As soon as we get the camp set up," I said, not looking up from what I was doing.

"Why don't you leave that to us," he said, "We might be getting some bad weather and this is a perfect time to wet a line."

That was all it took. We pulled out our rods and reels plus an assortment of lures, stinky cheese bait and salmon eggs. I emptied my backpack onto the ground and we stuffed it with all the stuff we'd need. Then I threw on my poncho, stocking cap and sweater and grabbed a fish stringer, a canteen of water and a flashlight. We let our dads know we were hiking up to Anchor Lake and we'd be back before dark. Leon didn't want to go at first but, when Smitty promised he could fish with his new Garcia reel and we threw in our Babe Ruth candy bars, a deal was struck.

It took longer than we thought getting up to Anchor Lake. By the time we got there, clouds were gathering in the north and daylight was getting short. While Smitty and I assembled the rods and attached the reels, Leon skipped rocks out onto the lake. I remember thinking, for being twins, Leon was nothing like his brother. Leon was on the honor roll in school, a member of the audio/visual club and the Latin club and couldn't throw a ball or catch one if his life depended on it. He was everything that Smitty wasn't and Smitty once said that the two of us should have been brothers instead.

"Leon, come here," Smitty said, holding up the rod out for him to take. "You get to go first."

"No," Leon deferred, "Go ahead, I'm not really big on fishing."

"Get your ass over here," Smitty replied, shoving the rod into his hands when he got near enough. "Daylight's burning."

Leon's first attempt at casting ended up in a clump of line about two feet in front of him.

"Jesus, Leon," Smitty screamed, "just hold down the lock and release it when you cast."

"I told you I wasn't good at this," Leon fired back. "You do it."

"Leon," I said, trying to break up the potential explosion, "Come over here and try mine while he untangles the line."

Smitty and Leon really were about as different as night and day. Smitty was an athlete, a brawler, and everybody loved being around him. He was unpredictable and funny in a sarcastic way. And Leon...well, Leon wasn't. He was the complete opposite.

I stood behind Leon and put my hand over the reel showing him how to hold it. We reared back and cast, letting go of the lock perfectly. The bobber and salmon eggs shot out into the lake in a perfect arching line.

"Here," I said, handing over the pole over to him. "Let the bobber set for a moment. Keep your eyes on it. When it twitches, yank the pole up in the air. That sets the hook in the trout's mouth." Before I could complete my next sentence, the bobber jerked and Leon yanked the pole up perfectly.

"I got one Smitty!" he yelled. "I got a goddamn trout on the line!"

"No shit, Sherlock," Smitty yelled back. "Hub," he screamed into my ear, "Leon's got dinner on the line."

We all started laughing.

"Here," Leon said trying to hand Smitty the line, "you bring him in."

"It's your trout, fair and square. You've got to land him. Bad luck if you don't."

"I'll grab the net and stringer," I yelled.

"Don't try to horse him in Leon!" Smitty barked. "Give him some line to run if he needs to."

The trout burst from the air and cart wheeled trying to shake off the hook but it was sunk deep.

"Keep the tip of the pole up Leon," offered Smitty. He'd settled down and was really trying to help him land the trout without messing it up. You could tell he was proud of his brother.

"I got the net," I said. "Can you work him over to the shallows. I can net him there."

The trout took a run and Leon handled it perfectly, not panicking but carefully getting him back on the drag. The trout made a second run and tried to wrap around a flat rock that jutted out into the lake. I tossed the net to Smitty because he had a better vantage point and Leon turned the fish while Smitty climbed on the rock crouching low so his silhouette wouldn't spook the trout. Leon got the trout close to Smitty and he made a desperate swipe with the net and missed. In the process, he slipped and ended up ankle deep in goo and muck. "Son of a bitch," he cried. "Sorry Leon. Can you get him back and I'll net him this time? I swear!"

The final burst and the trout simply tired out. Leon guided the trout into the net.

"Holy, shit..." exclaimed Leon, "it's a monster."

"Good job," Smitty said patting him on the back. "Seriously, that was pretty cool, wasn't it?"

Leon nodded his head. "It really was." And then he thanked us both.

I picked up a rock and smashed its head in and Leon pretended to put his boot on the head and let out a Tarzan yell. Then Leon looked really serious and said, "You know, after a battle like that I could really use a smoke and a piece of ass." Smitty and I busted up something fierce because we'd never seen Leon smoke and we were both pretty sure he had no interest in girls. Smitty lit cigarettes for all three of us and we studied the trout. It was a native brook trout with rich dark purple spots and weighed at least a pound, maybe a pound and a half. That was a monster for high country lakes. "Too bad we didn't bring dad's camera with us," Leon said.

"He doesn't even let us touch it," Smitty said to me. "Got it in Germany during the war and nobody touches it. Ever."

I gutted the fish and put it on the stringer while Smitty and Leon went back to fishing. We fished hard for the next hour. A light drizzle began to fall and then gave way to heavy drops. It was magical fishing and we couldn't seem to miss. We turned the small trout back and kept only the larger ones. None of them equaled the size of Leon's first catch. It was beginning to get dark and our hike back to the base camp at Rhodes wouldn't have the benefit of moonlight because of the clouds. With seven decent sized trout, we were pretty proud of ourselves.

By the time we hit the trail it was snowing lightly and it was near dark. We stayed close to each other and followed the beam from Smitty's flashlight. We kept ourselves occupied by coming up with various ways we could spring these lunkers on our fathers. At first, we thought about telling them we didn't catch a single fish and then we'd pull out the stringer of trout all gutted and ready for the frying pan and say," except for these pigs!" Oh, how they would cheer us on.

Going down was slow work. The snow hadn't yet stuck to the granite and we had to take care not to slip and twist an ankle under the conditions. It was wet snow, not the sort of powder we often got, and our ponchos turned out not to be so waterproof. I was starting to feel a little damp around the shoulders and I'm sure Smitty and Leon were too, but I didn't say anything.

"Shouldn't we be there by now?" Leon asked.

"It's hard to tell," Smitty said, wiping the end of his nose with his jacket sleeve. "This damn snow doesn't help any."

"Where do you think we should go from here?" I asked.

"It's just that the darkness and snow changes how everything looks," Smitty replied.

"We haven't even hit the place where the elk were," Leon said, his voice full of concern.

"No shit Sherlock," Smitty replied sarcastically. "I think we all could figure that out."

"I was just pointing out that..." began Leon but Smitty cut him off abruptly.

"We get it Leon! Give it a rest."

"I think we should go down that way," Smitty finally said, pointing the beam down into darkness.

After about ten minutes we came to an outcropping of rock and the path started back up the mountain again.

"Son of a bitch!" He spat on the ground. "I think we're fucking lost!" He sounded scared for the first time, and I could tell Leon was terrified but knew better than to say a thing. "Hub, you got any ideas?"

"I don't know, but I think we're more over that way," I said quietly, pulling out my own flashlight and pointing it down the canyon into a blanket of snow.

"Shit, Hub, I just don't think we're that far over," he said to me quietly, but he agreed to give my way a try.

"Look," I said confidently, "if we don't find camp in a half hour we could build a fire and bundle up for the night and wait it out."

"Do you think we'll freeze to death?" Leon asked and before Smitty could rip his head off, I replied. "Not a chance. We've got matches, flashlights, trout and water." It was good enough for Leon and it kept Smitty from beating the snot out of him.

We plowed on slowly and carefully. Smitty asked me to tell him one of my stories so I told them the Jack London one where a guy is stuck in the middle of a snowstorm with his husky and he cracks through the ice and falls into a creek. I worked the story pretty good and then I got to the part where the guy is nearly freezing to death when he remembers that he has matches and he can build a fire.

"And he gets out?" Leon asked.

"Of course he does, stupid," Smitty barked back at Leon.

"He gets a fire going," I said, keeping up the suspense. "It's really starting to heat up, but the man has built it under some high up pine branches that are loaded with snow. The fire heats up the branches and the snow falls onto the fire and puts it out."

"So, the guy builds another fire and this time he doesn't build it under a branch covered in snow?" Leon asked.

"No," I said realizing that this might not be the best story to tell under these circumstances.

"So, what happens?" asked Smitty.

"He'd used his last match and he realizes if he doesn't somehow get warm he's going to freeze to death."

The boys said nothing.

"And then," I said cautiously, "he calls his dog over to him because he figures maybe they can huddle up together and stay warm."

"That's some good thinking," Smitty added. "So, he eventually makes it."

"Except the dog senses something's wrong," I added.

"Dogs know that kind of shit, don't they?" Leon muttered.

I should have changed the ending of London's story but I just couldn't. It wouldn't be right so I plowed on. "Every time the man moved toward the dog, the dog would move out of his reach and no matter how hard he tried to coax him to get near, the dog stayed out of his reach."

"So," Smitty asked, "what the hell happened?"

I changed the subject. "I actually think we might be headed the right way."

"What the fuck happened to the man, Hub?"

"He got really tired," I answered, and then finally told them how it ended, "and he started to feel drowsy and fell asleep."

"And then somebody found him the next day?" Leon asked, hoping that would be the punch line.

"He just went to sleep and died peacefully with his dog about a hundred feet away from him."

"Great fucking story, Hub," Smitty said angrily. "The perfect story for our situation. Got any others you want to tell us?"

"No."

"But we've got a bunch of matches," Leon offered, trying to bail me out.

"And nothing but wet wood all around us," snapped Smitty.

Chapter 10

The story was a mistake. That was clear enough. We kept trudging along and the only sound you could hear was our hiking boots scuffling along in the snow. There was no light banter between the three of us and even Smitty didn't pick on his brother. We kept our heads down and plodded step by step.

"Stop," Leon yelled jolting us all. "Stop!" he cried.

"What?" Smitty barked. "WHAT?"

"Smoke," Leon whispered. "I smell smoke."

We stood silent, sniffing the air like hunting dogs.

"I can smell it too," Smitty said cautiously.

"Me too," I added. "It's coming from over that way," I said, pointing my flashlight toward what we could barely make out to be a canyon wall.

"The camp must be around that mountain," Smitty said.

Leon began shining his flashlight slowly and methodically down the mountain and then up above us when he stopped. "There's a game trail that looks like it leads down the mountain."

We climbed back up the direction we'd already come and began making our way south along the trail. The rocks got steeper and on either side of the game trail and there was nothing by sharp chunks of razor sharp granite below us trailing off into darkness. A slip at this point would have been disastrous.

Once we got off the trail the path broadened out and the smell of burning pine intensified and deepened. I could feel our spirits lifting. And then, almost in unison we cried, "There it is!" We could see a faint glow in the dark. We closed the distance quickly and soon we could see the outline of both dads sitting together on a large pine stump by the fire.

Even after our harrowing experience we thought it might be fun to sneak up on our fathers. They were probably worried to death about where we were and why we were so late getting back. Smitty stopped us.

"It doesn't look like they set up camp," he whispered coldly. "The old man's drunk."

"You'd think...just for one day, up here...we could just have a normal day with dad," Leon added disappointedly.

"Damnit, this is bullshit. We're going to have to set the tent up in the snow."

"It's still exactly where we dropped it, covered in snow," I added.

"They haven't moved their asses since we left."

"And probably didn't even know we were lost."

When we got close enough to hear them, Smitty's old man was drunk talking.

"So, the bitch just up and left the three of us," he slurred. My father passed him the bottle and he pulled on it hard. "The whore ran off with the manager of a damn bowling alley. A fucking bowling alley! Can you believe that shit?" A large string of drool fell out the side of his mouth and he wiped it off with his sleeve. My dad started to say something but he never got the chance. Smitty let out a cry like nothing I ever heard before and charge towards his dad.

"You sonofabitch," he cried, scaring both men, and when Smitty's old man tried to get up Smitty head-butted him in the chest knocking both of them into the snow. Smitty was up in a flash. He was hysterical and crying.

"Don't you ever call our mother a WHORE you bastard!" He was crying. "You hypocritical son of a bitch! What about the waitress in Battle Mountain that YOU fucked and mom found out about?"

Smitty's dad was up on his feet, crouched low like he was ready to charge Smitty. He was moving toward him. "You watch that mouth son or I'm likely to whip your ass."

"You don't think we heard you and mom fighting about that? We did. We both did! We've got ears."

Smitty's father dove at Smitty, catching him around the legs and dropping him to the ground. He pinned his arms down with his knees, grabbed a rock and hauled his arm back like he was going to crush his skull when I grabbed a large a chunk of firewood.

"You move an inch and I'll knock your fuckin' head off your shoulders!" I bellowed. He was stunned and stared at me.

"Go ahead and hit me," taunted Smitty. "Show us what a big man you are!" His dad cocked his fist back and I swung the log at him passing inches by his face. The tip of the log sprayed sparks all over him.

He turned on me, "You want a piece of this too you son of a bitch?"

The next thing I knew my father was off the log and behind Smitty's dad putting a choke hold on him and pulling him off Smitty. My dad held tight while Smitty's dad tried to pull loose. Smitty scrambled to his feet, grabbed the axe and charged at his father. And in a blur, it was all ass and elbows. I knocked Smitty to the ground and Leon helped me pin him down.

"I'll kill you!" Smitty screamed, "if it's the last thing I ever do." He was crying hard. It was a wounded deep cry. It was such an ugly mess.

I looked over at my father. He'd loosened the choke hold and Smitty's dad just sort of slumped over in a pile.

"Did you kill him?" Leon asked.

"No," my father said. "But he'll be out for the rest of the night."

"You should've killed him, Mr. Walker," sobbed Smitty.

Then my father turned swiftly on Smitty and said, in a way I'd never heard him talk before, "Don't ever say anything like that again, young man." It was so unusual for my father to ever butt in but this came from someplace else in him. "Killing is never a fucking answer." Then he got Leon to help drag his father into the tent.

I'd never heard my father use the "f" word before and I'd never seen him respond the way he did with Smitty's father or Smitty. My dad was swift and strong but it's not how I saw him in our world. I think at that moment I realized, in one way or the other, my father had directly or indirectly killed people in the war so he knew about death, about killing. When Smitty's old man swore at me, my dad took him out. More so, I think, not because things had escalated to a point of no return, but because he'd insulted me which meant he'd insulted my mother too.

My father came out of the tent and over to where we were huddled on a log. If he was drunk, which I knew he was, he seemed very sober now.

"Are you boys okay?" he asked. We shook our heads to the affirmative.

"I'm sorry about all of this," he said, looking around at the campsite. "Let me help you put up the tents."

"One of them is completely full of water." Leon said. "He was going to put these up for us so we could go fishing."

"I'll put this one up for you. The three of you can fit in it." We nodded our heads in agreement. "Throw some dry clothes on."

Smitty just sat there on the log while Leon and I got the sleeping bags unrolled and stuffed into the tent. We put Smitty's between us. Leon handed him some dry clothes but he didn't take them at first.

"Smitty," I said quietly, "just put them on. Please."

He took off his poncho, sweater and shirt and changed into a flannel shirt. He pulled off his boots, removed his Levis and slipped into a pair of long-johns. We did the same and then climbed into our sleeping bags.

We were all shaking when we got into the bags. Partly because we'd never dried off from our adventure but probably more from the fight. Leon and I kept quiet while Smitty mumbled about his father, but soon he dozed off. We weren't far behind.

Chapter 11

"Hey, Hub. Wake up. It's time to get moving."

Somebody was shaking me. It was unclear. "Let me get my pack and we gotta take the trout with us."

"What are you talking about?"

"Smitty?"

"Hub, you've gotta get up. The cops came by earlier this morning."

I shot up in the coffin.

Smitty handed me a cup of coffee and threw me some of the clothes he pulled from my duffel bag. I blew on the coffee and took a careful sip, set the cup on the bottom of the coffin and climbed out and started to get dressed.

"Here," he said, handing me a kit.

I unzipped the bag and found an electric haircut kit with a number of different comb attachments.

"You want me to give you a haircut?" I asked jokingly.

Smitty didn't smile. "Hub, this is serious shit. You've got to change your look. These cops won't be happy until they catch you."

I sat on the side of the coffin, pulled up my jeans and didn't say a thing. Smitty was right. The smart thing to do was quit while I was ahead, still alive — turn myself in, try to explain what really happened and take my lumps. But the truth was that I couldn't see myself locked up in juvie for four or five years. Because that's the only thing I could see happening now.

"You can't stay here any longer, Hub. They'll catch you."

"I know."

"And," he said, getting really quiet, "I can't let you stay here. It's too risky for my father." He bent his head and whispered, "I'm sorry, Hub."

I shook my head. He was right. Everybody who'd have contact with me would become an accomplice. I'd made myself a leper.

"There's no need to apologize. Really."

We looked into each other's eyes. His eyes were a bit teary and I could feel myself losing control too so I spoke before getting too emotional. "Where should I cut my hair?" The question gave us a way out.

"The embalming room," he replied. "I'll go back into the house and pull together some food for you while and then we'll figure things out. Okay?"

"What about your dad?"

"Gone. Had to go to County General to pick up a couple of bodies. Head on collision. Pretty messy. He'll be gone a couple of hours at least."

"Okay."

"When you're done, come into the house and I'll have some eggs ready."

I headed down the hallway to the embalming room. I'd been there before with Smitty. It might have been in the 8th grade when he dared me to go in with him, and because I didn't want to look like a chicken shit, I agreed. The funny thing was that it didn't scare me at all. In fact, it was peaceful and quiet and clean.

I went over to the mirror, unpacked the kit, plugged in the razor, selected a comb that seemed like it might be the right depth and hesitated. I really didn't want to cut my hair but I knew Smitty was right. I studied my face in the mirror. Even though I'd slept hard and dreamed crazy, I looked and felt tired. I knew that if I stood any chance of getting out of town, I'd have to be somebody the cops weren't looking for. They had my high school yearbook picture and I looked like a greaser in it so they wouldn't look for a guy with a crewcut. I switched on the razor. It made a deep humming sound. Then I took a deep breath and made the first pass from the front of my head to the back. My hair floated to the ground in clumps.

Chapter 12

"My God, Hub. I seriously almost didn't recognize you!" Smitty rubbed his hands over my crew cut. "You know what this makes me think of?"

I did and it brought a smile to my face. "When we kept the money our moms gave us for a haircut and cut our own."

"You mean butchered our hair."

"Is it that bad?"

"Not at all. Passable, very passable."

Smitty and I had a big breakfast of pancakes, bacon and eggs, hash browns and a pot of coffee. He wasn't a bad cook and I was starved. When we were done, he asked me what my thoughts were about hanging around. I mopped up the last bit of eggs with my toast.

"I'm going to head west," I said, with no real plan in mind.

"And do what?"

"It can't be a job where I'd have to use my real name and social security number. I've got to work illegally. Under the table."

"That makes good sense. Here," he said, shoving an envelope across the table at me. "This is for you."

I opened up the envelope and there was a bunch of money folded up neatly inside of it.

"I can't take this Smitty. It's your stash."

"I'm not using it right now. You can send me a Western Union money gram when you get rich."

"I can't."

"You'd do it for me if the situation were reversed, wouldn't you?"

"In a heartbeat," I replied and I meant it.

"Then that's done."

We cleared the dishes, rinsing them off and stacking them in a neat pile on the counter.

"There should be enough to get you a bus ticket out of town."

"I'm sure they'll have pictures of me at the train station and bus station."

"Probably so."

"I was thinking about hopping a train. Pick one up at the end of the station."

"Want me to drop you off at the station."

"Not yet. I've got to do a couple of things first."

"I've got to go to school today," Smitty said. "I've got to act normal at least until you get out of town. I miss today and the cops will be looking for me because they'll think I'm with you."

"Hell, Smitty, if you show up for a full-day of school the cops will know something's wrong."

He started laughing. I had a couple of things I needed to do before leaving town. I had to go by the Boo Radley tree and see if my sister left me some money, and I needed to see if I could meet with Lindsey before I left town. I had to try and square up with her. The thought of leaving town without saying anything to her just didn't sit right. Going anywhere near school would be suicide but I had an idea and it involved Smitty.

"I've got a favor to ask, and it's a big one."

"You just have to ask," Smitty said, "and I'll do it."

"I've got to see Lindsey before I leave. At least try to see her."

"Not a good idea Hub." Smitty said, shaking his head. "You show up anywhere near school and you'll be caught."

"I know."

"And you sure as hell can't go to her house. Her dad would probably shoot you and he'd more than likely get away with it."

"I know."

"So?"

"I'm going to give you a note to give to her in school. She takes first lunch so you can just pass it to her then. Don't talk to her, just give her the note and walk away."

"And where is she supposed to meet you?"

"Downtown library. I'm going to head there as soon as we're done here."

"You can't leave with a duffel and just go walking down the street and into the library. They'd call the cops on you. You'd look like one of those homeless guys that go in and sleep on the couches and wash themselves off in the bathroom."

"Could I get some paper and a pen?"

"You sure this is a good idea?'

"She might not come but at least I'll have tried."

"Fifty/fifty."

Smitty took off and returned moments later with some beautiful stationery and an ink pen from his dad's office. The only problem was that the funeral parlor name and address along the heading. So, I asked him if he wouldn't mind bringing me some scissors so I could cut the top off.

"That would make sense," he replied disappearing again.

I walked out into the front hall of the funeral parlor and into the annex where they kept flowers to make arrangements. I snatched a red rose from a big vase full of all sorts of beautifully colored flowers. Smitty returned with a scissor. He saw the red rose.

"You're not going to want me to give her a rose too?"

"If you don't mind."

"So, I'm going to just walk into the lunch room with a note and a rose for Lindsey and not attract any attention."

"Hopefully," I replied smiling.

"How about this," he said. "What if I drop you off at the library?"

"I've got something else I've got to do."

"I'll keep your stuff in my car and meet you later on at the funeral parlor and take you wherever you want to go."

"I'll have something figured out by the time I see you," I promised.

"Stay out by the tool shed if you get there before me. I don't want the old man to see you."

"Right."

"Write your note. I'm going to send you off with my sleeping bag. I forgot to get yours from your sister and I won't be needing one any time soon."

"Thanks."

I cut the letterhead off so it was just a really nice piece of stationery and sat down to write my note. It was going to have to be good.

Dear Lindsey,

I don't know how to begin this letter but I think it should begin with an apology. I'm so very sorry for messing things up with us. I know I seemed upset when you told me you'd accepted a date to the prom with Bullet. I had no right to be upset. He asked you and I didn't. And, it's not like you didn't offer me enough hints that you'd like to go with me. I was just trying to be cool. Call it "pride" or "stupidity" but I truly regret it.

Regarding everything you've heard in the news I can only say this, it's not as bad as it sounds. I know it sounds really bad but I am not armed and dangerous. I did take the cop car but I didn't know what else to do. Honestly, I panicked. I was afraid they were going to lock me up. I'd like to explain if you'd let me but I wouldn't blame you if you didn't.

I know you'd want to try and talk me out of running away and encourage me to turn myself in but I can't. I'm going to head up to Alaska and see if I can get a job on a fishing boat. It's really dangerous work but they make good money. Maybe when things settle down, I'll come back and do the right thing. Until then, I'm going to be on the run.

If you decide to meet me, I'll be in the downtown library. Just go into the reading room. The one with the cool oak tables and the great antique reading lamps and I'll find you.

Love.....Hub

I read the letter carefully, checking it for misspelled words and I worried whether I should tell her that I loved her or not. At this point what did I have to lose? I folded the letter carefully and handed it to Smitty.

There was the slightest chance, I thought, that Lindsey might read the letter and be so scared that she'd turn the letter into the principal. I knew the cops had been to her house. I also knew that her father would have berated her for going out with me and would remind her in no uncertain terms that he'd known I was no good the minute he met me. Bullet would be acting the part of the sympathetic friend and the administration of the school would have probably already yanked her into the office to remind her she had an obligation, as a good student of Pershing High and as a law-abiding citizen, to help the cops find me. But the worst part for her was that she was probably being ostracized by her girlfriends for dating me.

Smitty made me change into some of Leon's clothes and stuffed my boots and Levis into my duffel. I put on a madras shirt and a pair of khaki pants with a pair of white converse tennis shoes. Everything fit perfectly and when I looked in the mirror, I almost didn't recognize myself. I looked so clean cut that I could easily pass for one of the Beach Boys. Hell, I probably could walk through Pershing and nobody would even notice me, but I couldn't take that risk.

On the way to the Boo Radley tree I was just day dreaming about what I'd actually say to Lindsey if she showed up and I didn't notice a police cruiser coming down the same side of the street. It slowed when it got alongside me and then kept the same speed as me walking. I thought of running away but they'd catch me in a heartbeat or worse than that, they might shoot me. I tried to stay cool and looked over at them and smiled. The cop sitting in the window held up a picture, looked at it and then at me and rolled down his window.

"Aren't you supposed to be in school, young man?"

"Yes, sir," I said calmly, "I'm on the student body council and we're meeting at the City and County Building today. We get to meet some of the commissioners."

He smiled a bit and then said, "See if you can get those clowns to give us a raise."

"I'll do my very best," I said laughing.

"Have a good day, young man," he said and then sped off down the street.

I didn't immediately go to the tree but instead climbed on top of a hill that overlooked the city and surveyed the lay of the land. If by chance the police had been trailing my sister when she went to the tree I figured they'd be easy to spot. I sat down and lit up a smoke.

I'd always loved this spot. I'd often come up here when the old man and old lady fought just to clear my head out. Out across the park a young couple was trying to interest their kid in flying a kite but he seemed more interested in picking dandelions. It reminded me of my brother Sparky when he was little. We'd take him to the park and there could be three living dinosaurs fighting, shredding each other with claws and talons and slashing long tails with pointed fins and a dragon spewing fire, but, if he'd found a potato bug, he'd never look up. He'd pick them up and when they drew their shell around themselves for safety and tucked into a protective ball, he'd just wait until they unwrapped themselves and do it all over again. And he'd do it over and over again.

I thought of those rare occasions when my family and the neighbors would meet for a summer barbecue and we kids would chase fireflies and catch them and drop them into a mason jar and pretend like they were power sources to our own superhero lives. We'd play stickball and Red Rover and Kick the Can way into the night and, finally, when we all went home, we'd be exhausted and covered in that summer salt sweat and usually wake up in the exact same position we'd hit the bed in. Half the time we'd wake up in our shorts and t-shirts. Those were my favorite memories, and I'd carry them with me wherever I ended up.

When I felt the coast was clear and there were no cops around I walked down the hill to the Boo Radley tree. There, tucked inside a canvas bag was a stash of money my sister'd left for me. I slid the bag into my pants and covered it with my shirt. It was heavier than I expected and I realized my sister had added some other things to the package. Since it was too risky to open under the circumstance I decided to wait until I got to the library. The suspense was killing me.

I've always loved libraries. There is something about the quiet and the sense of the sacred that appeals to me. I remember a field trip to the downtown library when the head librarian took us on a tour. It was amazing because there was so much more to the library than books. We went to the special collection reading room where they kept these really old books that anybody could read but you had to put on special white gloves to touch the pages and then we went to a room that was filled with boxes of old photography all carefully labeled and copies of the local newspapers that went back a million years. My favorite room was the print room where you could take classes on how to set type like they did in the old days. Our teacher asked for two volunteers who could set a short sentence or two and then a member of the printing staff would print off a copy for each of us. Our teacher picked Angela Espinoza and Renzo Caputo to set the type. Angela was a good pick but nobody in their right mind would have picked Renzo. He was way too unpredictable and we knew it.

Angela set the following sentence. *Oakwood Middle is the best!* She even had the exclamation point.

Renzo, on the other hand set the following type: *School sucks big time.* He didn't have an exclamation point because he really didn't need one.

Our teacher, Mrs. Foster was pretty heated up after the library printed off the 24 copies and, when she read it, she couldn't apologize fast enough. She had everybody pass the papers forward and then she threw them in the trash. But what she didn't notice was a bunch of students folded theirs up and jammed them into their pockets. It was classic Renzo.

I went to a secluded section of the library upstairs on the second floor where I could be alone and pulled out Soup's package.

The first thing I pulled out was a brand-new journal which I opened up. It was one of her unused journals because she'd been journaling stuff her whole life. At least from about the 4th grade on. I knew it because I'd often sneak into her room when she wasn't around and read some of her writing. She wrote poetry and short stories but what I found most interesting were her entries about our family. They were brutally honest and written without anger and I found that interesting. It was as though she had a movie camera held up to her face and she just recorded what she saw. Where she might witness the same explosion my father would have after he'd been drinking I would write, *I hate the old man and wished he'd die,* she would write something like, *I don't know what demons dad wrestles with but I only hope, for the sake of all of us, that it doesn't destroy him.* It was not only thoughtful but offered hope.

Inside, on the cover was written my full name and below it was the following. *If found please return to Soup Walker* with our home address and enough stamps in an envelope to return the journal to our home. She also wrote a note to me. *Travel well dear brother. Write the story and I'll always be here if you need me. Love...Soup*

That damn near killed me. My money was there in the same manila envelope and I knew it was all there because I always licked and sealed it with my name signed across the back of the envelope. It was really just added security in case my brother tried to open the envelope. There was a back-up switchblade and a little leather bag, almost like the sort of bag that you'd keep your marbles in when you were a little kid. It was my sister's and I knew what it contained. It was all the money she had in the world and she'd given it to me. I couldn't let that happen. She had this dream of going to France in her senior year to be a student and live with a family. I can't remember the name of the program but she certainly had all the grades and she'd skipped a couple of grades plus she spoke fluent French. Honestly, she'd be a real dream to have live in your house if you were the French family smart enough to pick her. The thought was overwhelming when I got down to it. I had a sister who would give up her dream to help out a brother who didn't have one. I couldn't let that happen so I'd have to give it to Smitty to return.

The next gift was a Parker fountain pen (probably from my dad's office) that she must have swiped and six indigo ink cartridges. Then, and this was the strangest thing of all, she'd stuck in my mom's favorite cigarette lighter, a Johnny Unitas football card and a lucky rabbit's foot key chain I'd bought her at the county fair. In a way, these artifacts represented a piece of everyone in my family.

My sister was big into the idea of being an archeologist or an anthropologist. We used to play a game where my brother and I would bury a bunch of random stuff from the house and garage outside in the dirt and my sister would spend an entire afternoon mapping out the backyard, stringing out the quadrants of the dig out and then she'd dig and label everything with little pieces of paper. Take, like, a spoon. She'd write something like: *Spoon* with a number corresponding to the dig site. Then she'd make notes like: *Tool. Purpose: object to deliver sustenance to the mouth; probably circa 1950-68, manufactured by Homo Sapiens, 20th century* and on and on. For months she called everything artifacts. In a way, I was carrying a little bit of every member of my family with me. That struck me in the chest. Hard.

Chapter 13

I had a couple of hours to kill before Lindsey would get out of school and there was no guarantee that she'd even show up so I went over to where the library kept newspapers from all over the country. I took a stack of the papers to a safe corner of the library where I could actually see if Lindsay came in and I started thumbing through the *Help Wanted* section. I started with our own local newspapers. There were a couple of jobs for *baggers* at the grocery store, an ad from a bike shop looking for a *Mechanically talented young man willing to learn the bike repair industry* and a job that offered big financial rewards selling pots and pans door to door. Of course it was pure folly, because I wouldn't be working here, but I wanted to see what was available just because.

In the *Helena Record,* there were jobs advertised for ranch-hands, big truck mechanics, loggers, construction workers and bartenders. All the jobs required experience but it was hopeful. Somehow, I'd get a job.

The state of Washington had about twenty papers and there were jobs almost every place I looked — working the ferry boat system, boiler room jobs, gate keepers, logging, fishing boats and fruit farms. I was getting optimistic about finding something away from here.

And then Alaska. There were only a couple of newspapers but there were a ton of jobs from gold mining, logging, fishing boats and tug operators, to dishwashers and forest service and the list went on.

Truthfully, I'd never have thought of just sitting down in the library and looking through a stack of newspapers. There was work if you wanted it and

I wanted it, but it couldn't be a job where I'd need to really show my driver's license or my social security card and that left jobs like picking fruit, washing dishes, and maybe ranch work, but most of those other jobs would require some sort of identification. I was nervous about having to do that. There was no telling how long Broadhead's reach really was and I didn't aim to find out.

I was just about ready to give up, pick any state and head that direction and hustle a job when I picked up a Wyoming paper. It wasn't that thick. Once you got through the national headlines there wasn't much other than farm and cattle reports, sports, wedding announcements, obituaries and the want ads. Then I saw the following ad:

Drivers wanted: No experience necessary. Adventure. Travel. $20.00 a day. Apply in person. Driver's License required. Wacko's City of Fun Carnival. Apply at Evanston fairground. Criminals need not apply.

This was good fortune and I almost missed it. Evanston was only about 2 hours north of where we lived. Easily within reach by hitchhiking although I worried about being on the open road with the Highway Patrol cruising around. And the job itself, hell, I was pretty sure it was a cash job and it was great pay. Twenty bucks a day. Almost $600 a month and there couldn't be that much expense. I'd be banking money. I tore the ad out of the paper and pushed it into my pocket and then I waited to see if Lindsey showed up.

Time didn't fly by. I stared at the clock on the wall and the minutes played out like they did in a really boring class. You'd sit there staring at the teacher and it would be like 1:20 p.m. and the class got out at 1:30 p.m. So, you'd day dream, check out the girls, start to nod off and that would go on for about an hour and then you'd look back at the clock and it would read 1:22 p.m. Waiting for Lindsey felt just like that except for the added fact I wasn't certain she'd come.

I waited.

Nervously.

Impatiently.

I went to the bathroom, came back and started writing in my journal and that helped a bit. Then, when it was past the time I thought it should take Lindsey to get to the library, I started pacing around the upper balcony. I'd do stupid things like try to hold my breath and see if I could walk from one corner of the balcony to the next, then I'd try to guess how many steps it would take to go completely around the balcony. I was pretty much going to throw in the towel when I saw her walk into the study area. She looked beautiful in a plaid Tartan skirt, white tailored button down shirt and saddle oxfords. She looked like she was right out of one of those teen magazines. I almost called out to her but thought better of it.

I circled around the balcony looking for any cops. It was a horrible thought and I was embarrassed the moment I thought of it but I couldn't be too careful. Finally, when I determined the coast was clear I headed down the staircase and walked up close to where she was sitting. She was actually studying, so I sat a couple of seats across from her. I wanted to see her expression when she looked up.

When she finally looked up, she kind of looked past me and then did a quick double-take.

"Hub?" she asked, breaking into a curious smile, "I almost didn't recognize you."

"It's quite a change, isn't it?"

"Oh, my God," she got up from the table and came over and threw her arms around me and held me tight.

In that moment, it felt like the world had righted itself. Lindsey smelled wonderful and felt even better held tight to my chest. Then, just for a second, I think I felt her shiver. The kind of shiver you get when you've done something you shouldn't do and you realize it. I pulled away and looked into her hazel eyes.

"How are you doing, Lindsey?"

"I haven't been able to get you out of my mind, Hub. I've been so worried about you."

"Me too. I've missed you so much."

"Everybody keeps asking me about you. They're making you sound like you're some sort of dangerous criminal. What happened? Was it my fault because I agreed to go to the dance with Bullet?"

"No, Lindsey," I said, leading her over to a couple of chairs facing each other and sitting down. "It had nothing to do with you. I made a really stupid series of mistakes and when you lump them all together it is much worse sounding than it was."

Lindsey reached into her purse and pulled out a small package and handed it to me. "Here, I made you some cookies. I thought you just might want something sweet in your life."

"I already have that. I've got you Lindsey." It was so corny sounding but I really meant it. "Thanks for coming. I wasn't sure you were going to show up," I said pausing for a minute before continuing. "I wouldn't have blamed you if you thought better of coming. I've put everybody who cares about me at risk."

"So, what are you going to do, Hub?" she asked taking the package of cookies from me and opening them up.

"Oatmeal raisin and chocolate chips," I said offering her one, "my favorites."

"Are you going to go back and explain what happened?"

"I can't Lindsey. The place is too hot right now. I'm hitting the road tomorrow."

"Where are you going?"

"Away. Far from here. Just until things cool down."

"But where?"

"It's better if I don't tell you. For your sake. Really."

"But how will I be able to stay in touch with you?"

"I'll send you post-cards from the road and try to call every once in a while."

"You're really leaving?"

"I am," I replied hesitating before I spoke again. "Look, if they haven't already been to your house, the cops will probably show up and ask you about me."

"They already have," she said, pausing before she spoke again trying to figure a way to a way to delicately cover for her father. "I told them what a good person you were and how you always looked out and stood up for the underdog."

"Thank you."

"And my mom did the same, but my dad... well, he didn't speak on your behalf..."

"You don't need to say anything. I think I know how your father feels about me and I certainly lived up to his expectations, didn't I?"

She started to say something but I just pulled her close to me and then I kissed her and whispered, "It's okay. He just worries about you. He does what fathers are supposed to do."

Then we just held each other without saying a word. Then, reluctantly I pulled away. If the truth be known, I could have spent the rest of my life in her arms but every second I held her put her at risk. What if somebody accidentally saw her in the library with me.

"Lindsey," I whispered, "I've got to go."

She began to protest but I just put my finger up to her lips. "I really do. The longer I stay with you the riskier it is for you. For me."

Her eyes got teary and I hugged her one more time. She handed me an envelope. I started to open it but she said, "Wait until I go, please." Her eyes were watery. I shoved the letter into my pocket. She packed up her books and gave me one last hug and then turned and headed toward the door. I didn't say anything as she started walking away. I couldn't. When she got to the door, she turned around and smiled at me and gave a little wave. Then she stepped into afternoon light and disappeared. I wondered if I'd ever see her again.

Chapter 14

I stood outside near the tool shed by the funeral parlor. Smitty's car was in the garage and his father's was gone. I knew where they kept a key so I went over to the ceramic goose and tilted it, picked up the key, unlocked the back door and replaced the key.

I could hear Chuck Berry's *Johnny Be Good* blasting from the record player in his room. I slipped out of my shoes, picked them up and tip-toed up the stairs. His door was opened slightly. He was standing with his back toward me playing an invisible guitar. I kicked the door open and shouted, "Freeze, don't move."

You should have seen the look on his face. I'd completely caught him by surprise and scared the shit out of him.

"Jesus, Hub!" he said angrily. "That's not funny!"

I couldn't help but laugh and pretty soon he started laughing. "You sounded just like one of those cops on TV."

"How'd you get in?" he asked, still a little shaken. I mean, I'd really caught him off guard.

"The key."

"Of course."

I motioned to the floor, "You forgot something," I said pointing to where he'd been wailing away.

"What?"

"The guitar. You don't want to leave it on the floor where you'll step on it."

"Very funny," he said leaning over to pick up the invisible guitar and placing it in an imaginary holder. "What'd you think?"

"Sounded just like Chuck Berry," I replied as I sat on the edge of his bed.

"How'd it go? Did she show up?"

"She did. At first I didn't think she would but she did, Smitty. I can't tell you how good it felt."

"What she'd say?" he asked and then added, "Did you guys go off to a dark corner of the library and do *it?*"

"Knock it off," I said angrily. "That's not funny."

"Just joking," he assured me. "Seriously, no harm meant."

"None taken."

"So, what happened?"

"We talked. About a lot of things," I answered and recounted the entire time I was with Lindsey. When I finished, he sat shaking his head.

"What?" I asked.

"Nothing."

"You were shaking your head. What is that's supposed to mean?"

"It's sad, Hub," he said thoughtfully. "All of this happened because you were too pigheaded to ask her to the 10th grade dance."

"Well," I said, knowing he was right, "You didn't ask anybody either."

"What does that have to do with anything? Seriously," he said digging in, "I don't have a girlfriend like you do, Hub. I don't have a Lindsey in my life and I doubt if I ever will."

"Don't. You're just saying that," I said. But the truth was that Smitty didn't have a main squeeze. As he'd often say, he was *damaged goods*. After his brother died mysteriously, just died in his sleep, Smitty didn't know what to do. Even if it seemed on the outside like they didn't get along together, they were best friends. Everything Leon was, Smitty wasn't, and it just seemed to work.

Leon was really bright and he could have probably gotten into any college he wanted to. He was just that smart. He loved school. He loved being a student. He joined every after school club he could possibly find. You name it and he belonged to it. He debated on the debate team and acted with the drama club. He was the president of the Latin Club and the assistant editor of the school newspaper. He wasn't half as popular as Smitty and that never seemed to matter to him.

"His head," Smitty'd say, "belonged to a different world."

It might have sounded crazy to most of the people we knew, but I understood exactly what he meant. My sister Soup was like that and in so many ways I envied her. She just understood things and could see how they connected together in a much bigger way than I could ever imagine. One time Smitty and I discussed the possibility of lining the two of them up for a blind date and then we almost died laughing because the idea sounded so crazy.

Smitty was the athlete and played football, basketball and ran for the track team. The girls were crazy about him and the teachers loved him. But when Leon died that all changed. He went someplace really dark and destructive. He started showing up to school drunk and got in fights almost every day. It got so bad that I didn't want to hang around him anymore and I was telling my sister about it when she just looked at me and said, "This is when he needs you most, Hub. You've got to try." Don't think for a minute that I haven't thought about this in the last couple of days.

We continued hanging out together but he just seemed to get drunk more frequently and pick fights at the drop of a hat. Then one day, I came unglued and called him a *selfish, self-indulgent piece of shit* and that was all it took. It wasn't a second before he was all over me...punching and swearing and I was doing the same to him. We were good fighters and it wasn't pretty. I broke his nose and he was bleeding all over the place and he got a solid punch to my face and my eye began to swell shut. It ended when I was on the ground and he grabbed a baseball bat and was going to swing at me. He raised it up over his head and I just froze, kind of squinting to try to see out of my good eye. If he'd swung, he would have split my skull in half. And in that split-second, him holding the bat and me waiting to be killed, he yelled out his brother's name, "LEEEEEEOOOONNNN!" in an unholy cry like a wounded animal backed into a corner. He dropped the bat and started sobbing. I had never heard anything like that — so painful and so unearthly. I couldn't quite get up, so he reached out and helped me to my feet and just fell into me crying. Two minutes earlier we were trying to kill each other and now we were clinging to each other for dear life.

Everything in his room was destroyed. Literally. When we composed ourselves, we headed down to the kitchen. I grabbed a bag of frozen peas from the freezer and Smitty took a handful of rags and some ice-cubes and we went into Leon's room and just sat there for a minute not saying anything. It felt uncomfortable being there, like I expected him to walk in at any minute. There were pictures on the wall of the two brothers, arm in arm, one at the county pool and they both were missing their front teeth. There was laughter in their eyes. And photos of Leon getting awards for this and that and a number of plaques and trophies around the room from debate tournaments and what not. It felt like a shrine. Smitty was really calm.

"I come in here a lot," he said quietly. "I come in here to talk to him. To tell him how much I miss him and what an asshole I was for not being a better brother."

"Smitty..."

"I do," he said, cutting me off. "I come in here because it's where I try to make sense of it all. My brother's dead and I lie to him. I tell him that mom actually came to the funeral when she didn't. Didn't even call or send a card to us. What kind of mother would not go to her own son's funeral?"

How could there be an answer for a question like that? I didn't even try. I just listened.

"I didn't even know he was dead. I took off for school because I had an early swim practice and when I got to my first period class I was called down to the principal's office. The principal told me my dad had gone to the hospital with my brother's body. The principal took me there and I found my dad sitting outside of the morgue just staring at his hands. When he saw me he stood up and hugged me. I think it's the last time we ever hugged each other and we both started crying."

Smitty wiped his eyes with one of the damp towels and continued telling his story.

"I felt so bad for him. He kept saying, *No parent should ever have to bury their child* over and over again. Then, when the hospital told dad they'd have to do an autopsy on Leon, he went nuts. Caught me off guard because we're in that business and my old man knew the drill."

"But it was his son, your brother, Smitty."

"Mom leaving was tough on all of us but having to bury Leon was the breaking point. We've never been the same."

"I can't imagine," I said quietly.

"People always wondered if my dad did the embalming and stuff on Leon. You know since we're in the business, right?"

To be perfectly honest, I'd wondered the same thing. It's like who cuts a barber's hair or how does a dentist fill his own cavities?

"And then the pricks started saying some really horrible sick shit about..." and he didn't finish the sentence. He just quietly shook his head like just bringing up what was said was too horrible to even to tell me.

"We did, Hub. We did take care of Leon's body and it was really beautiful the way my father took care of him. And I helped. I bathed him with my father and then I took the hair dryer and mussed his hair just like he did. At first, when I saw him, when I saw what the coroner had done, a straight cut down the sternum where they opened him up and stitched him back, I threw up all over myself. My father cleaned me off, gave me a bottle of soda water and told me I didn't have to help but I wanted to, Hub…I wanted to honor my brother. So, I never left my father's side."

And now, I thought, a few years later I was on the verge of leaving Smitty. We'd been like brothers after that fight and I felt like I was betraying him

"Smitty, you'll meet somebody like Lindsey. I just know it."

"Not here," Smitty said, "too much hurt at this school."

And then, as if being slapped back into the world, he asked me if I'd figured anything out yet.

I pulled out the ad and handed it to him. He read it over carefully and then said, "This makes a lot of sense, Hub, and Evanston isn't that far. A couple of hours. I'll blow off school tomorrow and drive you up.

"You sure?"

"How long do you think you'd last hitchhiking with every cop in the world looking for you?"

"Good point."

"Let me put it another way, would you do it for me?"

"Of course."

"Done then."

We got a pizza from Happy Days pizza and a six pack of beer and went over to the cement plant and ate our pizza and drank the beer. I told Smitty he had to try and get back into school, get involved and start being the guy he used to be.

He just shrugged his shoulders and mumbled that it was too late. I told him the last 48 hours gave me a different lens to look through and if I could relive everything, I'd do it in a heartbeat. He was listening. I could tell.

"Face it," I said, "I'm serious about this. There is nothing cool about what I did and I have no idea what the price will be. If you don't think I'd do anything just to get in a time machine…"

"I'd get in with you," he said, "I'd go back and be much better to my brother."

"You were a great brother Smitty. You've got to stop beating yourself up about that." I paused because it was getting uncomfortable, "And you have the power to change things from here on out." He nodded his head and I think it sunk in.

Normally, we would have driven around, dragged up and down State Street but because of the circumstance we thought it would be safest to head back to the funeral parlor and get a good nights sleep before taking off in the morning.

"It's late enough that my old man will be sloshed and he'll be asleep in front of the TV or passed out in the study, so I'll just let you in."

It was good to be back in the parlor. When I asked him where he'd hidden the duffel he suggested I follow him. "Right this way, please," he said very sincere like. "We have a wide array of caskets and can easily meet any requirements you and the deceased might have discussed."

"I'm not dead yet."

"Now, this one here," he said all dramatic, "...is one of our big sellers. It's the Copper Executive model. A third stronger than stainless steel, durable and unique to our collection."

The casket was beautiful but it made no sense to me to plunk a dead body in a really expensive casket and then dump them into the ground to rot.

"And here's one of my favorite features," he said, lifting up the lower section of the casket so a body could be fully viewed by the mourners. "The life after death survivors kit. Packed with everything you'd need to be on the run from the law." My duffel had been pushed down to the bottom of the casket completely hidden. I could only imagine what would happen if his father had opened up the entire casket to show it to a client and discovered my ratty old duffel.

"I'll take it," I said jokingly. "How about if I put it on a layaway plan?"

"Not in this business," Smitty said. "Too many deadbeats."

"Okay, I give," I said, "You've got too many one-liners. I'm throwing you softballs."

For the second night in a row, I climbed into the casket and drifted off to sleep.

Chapter 15

We didn't talk a great deal on the way to Evanston and the City of Fun Carnival site and that sort of surprised me. What I think I understood was that my disappearance, my trying to become invisible and avoid whatever my reality would be if I got caught, was going to be life changing. I was beginning to realize how my stupidity affected so many lives. You just don't think about those things. My mom and dad, my brother and sister, Smitty, Lindsey...they'd be left with an uncertainty as to what happened to me. I would be gone. And I couldn't let them know where I was. The only person who knew what I was up to was Smitty and after today, whether I got the job with the carnival or not, even then, he wouldn't know. If I got the job, we'd probably work in Evanston for a few days, fold up and head to the next town on their stop. Or, and I hadn't mentioned this to Smitty for the exact reasons that I didn't tell my sister where I was going...if I didn't get the job I'd hitch-hike to Alaska and try to get a job on a fishing boat. In either case, I'd not be turning around and going home with my tail between my legs.

"Penny for your thoughts," Smitty said breaking the silence.

"I been thinking about a lot of things."

"Me too." He thought for a minute and said very quietly, as if he was spilling out a big secret, "I'm going to really miss you."

I was thinking the exact same thing but the difference was that he said it and I just thought it. And that was a first because honestly, guys our age, or, hell, probably at any age, don't really know how to share our feelings. We say that sort of personal shit when we're drunk and then never talk about it afterwards, but Smitty was stone-cold sober and I knew how difficult it was for him to say that. It meant a lot to me.

"I'm going to miss you too," I finally replied. I really was but I felt stupid not saying it first because I sounded like I was just saying it because he said it to me first. "Smitty," I said thoughtfully, "you really don't know how much you mean to me." I took a pause because all of this stuff was piling on top of me. "Not because we've been best friends forever but you have no idea how much I appreciate you helping me. I've put you at great risk and I'm sorry. I'm truly sorry."

"Ten miles," he said, marking the distance to Evanston and taking pressure off the difficulty of what we were trying to say to each other. "When we get there, how do you want to play this out?"

I'd thought about this on the drive up. "When we see the carnival just drop me off and I'll figure stuff out."

"What if you don't get the job?"

"I'll figure something else out."

"You'll be stuck in the middle of nowhere."

"I know," I replied. We both understood the reality of the situation. When we got to the Evanston exit Smitty pulled into a convenience store.

"What are you doing?"

"I thought you ought to load up on a carton of smokes before you got there," he said sort of feeble like. "You know, like in prison, if you got smokes you can trade them for things."

"What are you talking about?" I replied like he'd just spoken Martian to me or something. "I'm just trying to get a job at a carnival. I'm not on my way to prison," and then added, "yet." He laughed.

"You never know," he said, and got out of the car.

"You never know," I repeated.

Inside the store, Smitty picked up a bunch of junk food — Twinkies, Ding Dongs, peanut butter and crackers...the regular crap — and took it up to the counter. A kid about our age was behind the counter and, when Smitty asked him to throw in two cartons of Marlboros, the kid asked Smitty for his identification. I didn't get anything.

"I don't show my id to kids that are younger than me," he replied and threw a twenty onto the counter.

"I'm sorry sir, but I can't sell cigarettes to somebody under the age..."

I cut him off before it could get out of hand. "Will mine do?" I pulled out my phony id and showed it to him. I don't think he believed it but he nodded his head and said it was fine. I could tell he was nervous and didn't want any trouble. He gave me the change back instead of Smitty and Smitty blew up at him.

"Asshole, who gave you the money?"

The kid fumbled with the change on the counter trying to shove it back over to Smitty.

"It's okay," I said, picking up the change and handing it over Smitty. I tipped the kid a couple of bucks. "Sorry for the misunderstanding."

"What you'd do that for?" Smitty asked.

"I don't need any trouble Smitty and you know it."

Smitty was quiet and then nodded in agreement.

"You hungry all of a sudden?" I asked, shifting the tension.

"I got all this stuff for you. You might need it."

"I'm going to be okay."

"You never know."

"That's the truth," I replied quietly.

"I'll ask one more time, Hub. Are you sure about this?"

"I am."

"Okay, then. That's that."

He pulled back onto the road and we followed the signs to the fairground. When we got where we could see the rodeo grounds, Smitty pulled off to the side of the road and turned off the car.

"You ready to do this?"

"Yes."

We got out and Smitty grabbed my duffel bag and dropped it next to me. He reached into his pocket and pulled out a pack of smokes and tucked them into my Levi jacket pocket and then threw his arms around me. We held each other tightly.

"Hub, you are my real brother." Then he pulled away. "Be careful. Don't get yourself killed. It'll piss me off."

"I won't." We kind of stood around awkwardly until I finally said, "You probably ought to go."

We hugged each other one more time and then he got in his car and drove off. When his car disappeared over the hill, I turned and headed down the road of the unknown. I was nervous.

Chapter 16

I followed a dusty footpath down toward the City of Fun Carnival that splayed out below me like an old-time wagon train. Circling the interior of rides were trailers, pickups, and flat-bed trucks I assumed they used to transport the rides and gear. Some of the trucks had campers on the top where I assumed the performers and workers slept, and there were a couple nice looking trailers. Raggedy looking canvas tents filled in the gaps and most likely served to house the other carnies. I realized that I had nothing other than a sleeping bag with me and, unless I got assigned a space in one of those tents, I'd be sleeping out under the stars. I could smell coffee wafting into the morning and bacon cooking from some of the rigs. It was a little disheartening because I assumed it would look like the Ringling Brothers and Barnum & Bailey Circus but it didn't. It was pretty shabby. But at this point, a job was a job, and as long as they were taking me away from Officer Broadhead and the trouble I left behind, I'd be happy to throw in with this outfit.

Another group of trailers and campers sat on the outskirts of a small rodeo stadium. There was a pen with a number of wild horses in it and big bulls separated into small fenced off spaces. Inside the rodeo arena there were bleacher seats, food venues and livestock with a big announcer's box dead center above the crowd. Banners touting the rodeo and the fair flapped in the morning air. Cowboys and cowgirls were starting to wander around, saddles thrown over their shoulders, with halters and such, getting ready for the day's events.

I approached the entrance of the City of Fun carnival and was stopped by one of the biggest men I'd ever seen in my life. He was wearing grease covered overalls and was missing fingers on both hands. A jagged scar ran from above his right eye down to his cheekbone.

"We ain't open yet, kid," he said, pulling a bandana from his back pocket and wiping grease from his hands.

"I'm here looking for a job," I replied trying to sound confident. I pulled the clipping from the newspaper and held it out to him.

He spit a wad of tobacco on the ground and didn't reach out to take a look at it. "I can't read," he said matter-of-factly. "Don't need to."

"Who can I talk to?" I asked politely.

"Anybody you damn well want to. It's a free country."

I didn't quite know what to say so I just sort of nodded my head like *I get it* and started to walk away when he burst out laughing.

"Just messing with you kid. Name's Big Heavy."

"Hub...Hub Walker."

"Hub Walker you'll be needing to talk with Wacko. He's the Bossman."

"Okay."

"In the double-wide behind the Ferris Wheel."

"If he ain't there his woman, Angel, will know where he is."

"Thanks," I said and hoisted the duffel over my shoulder and started heading over to the double-wide.

"A word of advice kid. Don't let him catch you eye-balling Angel. He's jealous and meaner than a junkyard dog."

"Okay."

"And he'd as soon cut your nuts off as look at you."

"Thanks for the advice."

I took a deep breath before knocking on the screen door. Some country music was playing on the radio — Patsy Cline's *I Fall to Pieces* — and whoever was inside was singing along with it. And she had a beautiful voice. I knocked on the door.

"Door's open," a man's voice said. The singing stopped and I set my duffel bag on the ground and stepped inside.

The man was sitting at a small, built-in breakfast table smoking a cigarette and ashing in a coffee can. He was pouring over some maps and didn't look up. I cleared my voice and said, "Are you Bossman?"

"Who wants to know?" he asked without so much as giving me a glance. I could smell perfume in the air but didn't see the woman I'd heard singing.

"I'm here to see about a job."

"I already got my crew," he replied and I could feel my stomach tighten.

Then the lady walked in and I didn't have to guess who she was. She smiled at me and walked over to the stove and picked up the coffee pot and filled Bossman's cup. She was wearing red high heels, a halter-top and white shorts. Her legs went on forever. She reminded me of Marilyn Monroe and it was hard not to look at her.

"Pardon my manners," she said reaching into the pantry and taking out another cup. "Can I pour you some coffee?"

I almost said *Yes* but then the man finally looked up at me and said to her, "He don't need any. He was just leaving."

"I need the work, sir, and I'm a hard worker."

He studied me carefully. "Are you runnin' away from somethin' or are you runnin' to somethin'?"

"I guess a little of both," I replied not wanting to say the wrong thing or inviting too much prying on his end.

"Don't need anybody."

I guess I'd just assumed that there would be a job when I arrived or it wouldn't have been advertised in the paper. Talk about putting all your eggs in one basket. I was about to thank him and leave when the lady spoke.

"Give him a chance, Wacko. He looks like a good kid to me."

Bossman was tough looking, wiry with well-defined muscles and forearms like Popeye. He had a ruddy complexion and his eyes were the most deep-green I'd ever seen. His hair was jet black and out of control. He was a handsome man in a dangerous way and the sort of person you'd want on your side in a fight.

He lit another cigarette off the one he was finishing up and studied me for the longest time.

"Okay kid," he said looking me straight in the eyes, "I'll give you a try."

The woman gave me a slight smile and a nod.

"Thank you, sir."

"It's Wacko or Bossman."

"Yes sir."

He looked at me like I was deaf.

"I mean Bossman. You won't regret it."

"I better not," he said lighting up another unfiltered Camel. "Twenty dollars a day. I pay twice a month. You fuck up and I'll shit can you on the spot. No drinkin' on the job. After we close for the night I don't care what you do. Any questions?"

"None."

"Good. Go find Frenchy. He'll be out by the Tilt-a-Whirl or the Ferris Wheel. Tell him I just hired you and he'll put you to work."

"Thank you, sir."

"Last time I'm going to say this. It's Bossman or Wacko. Bossman because I am the boss. Wacko on account that some people think I'm crazy. And this is Angel."

And she was an angel. If all the angels in heaven looked like her, I could easily mend my ways.

Chapter 17

Frenchy was a piece of work. I found him bent over a generator working on the ferris wheel. He was hurling a single string of curse words into the universe the likes of which I'd never heard in such a combination of physical impossibilities in my life. His voice was gruff. Guttural and mixed with some French and some other languages.

His pants buckled underneath a large beer belly and his shirt was so tight that you could see his chest hair sprouted out through the space between his buttons and shirt. Nothing about his name made any sense. I mean he didn't look French. A pint of cheap whiskey sat next to his toolbox and it was already half gone. It seemed like a bad time to interrupt him but I didn't have much choice. I needed to earn my keep.

"Are you Frenchy?"

"Who the fuck wants to know?"

"Wacko sent me over to find you."

He didn't turn around. He was trying to tighten something when a wrench slipped and he let out another barrage of colorful language.

"Sonofabitch," he bellowed, "what do you want?" With some effort, he managed to straighten himself to an upright position and sized me up immediately. I felt small standing in front of him.

"Wacko sent me over here to see you."

"You've done that."

He turned around and went back to work.

"Wants you to show me the ropes."

"Ropes, huh?"

"That's what he told me," I said, pausing for a moment, waiting for him to say something. When he didn't I added, "I'm supposed to work with you."

He looked me up and down, sizing me up. I felt uncomfortable being eyeballed like this, like I was an annoyance in his routine or something.

"You even old enough to have hair on your balls?" he asked. "Jesus Christ, we're taking 'em in younger and younger," he said, talking to the universe.

I should have kept my mouth shut but that's not one of my strong suits. Here I was, ten minutes into gainful employment, a perfect job for me to be working if I wanted to disappear and I've got a gorilla of a man standing in front of me holding a pipe wrench in his hands asking me if I was old enough to have hair on my balls.

"I've got as much hair on my balls as you have on your ass crack."

"Is that so?" he replied, dropping the wrench on the ground and reaching into his back pocket and pulling out a red bandana. "Really?"

He wiped the grease off of his hands and then roared in laughter and then held his hand out for me to shake.

"You're going to be just fine kid. I'm Frenchy. Half Cajun, quarter Indian and quarter junk yard dog."

"I'm Hub. Hub Walker."

His hands reminded me of a catcher's mitt and mine disappeared into his.

"Here's the deal. We work hard here. It's like a well-oiled machine. Everybody learns what they're supposed to do and if somebody falls behind we help them. We're a family of misfits. Nobody gives a damn where you are from or what your problems are but here is where people can start over."

"Okay."

"You'll start at the bottom and learn the ropes so, if anybody falls behind or gets injured, you can step in and help out. Wacko's dead serious about this."

"Okay," I replied feeling like this might just work out for me.

"And a couple of things we don't do. 1. We don't fraternize with the cowboys. They don't like us on account of we're carnies and we don't like them because they're *shit kickers.* So, don't go wandering over there or you'll more than likely get your ass kicked and 2. Don't mess with the bossman's girl and that ain't up for negotiation. You do, and you'll disappear or worse. Get it?"

"Yes, sir, I do."

"And drop the *sir* shit. Any questions?"

"Where do I bunk and how do the meals work out?"

"Holy mother of god!" he said, starring at me like I'd spoken to him in a foreign language. "This ain't a fucking summer camp we've got here. This is a carnival and everybody fends for themselves."

"Okay."

Actually, it wasn't okay. I had a sleeping bag and I could sleep out under the stars but I didn't have any food or anyway to cook it even if I did. I'd have the rest of the day to figure something out and mentioning this to Frenchy didn't seem like the best thing to do at the moment. I had some figuring out to do because I wasn't going to last long without food.

"Just dump the stuff in your rig and I'll send you over to work with Jesus on the Baby Octopus."

"I don't have a rig, Frenchy."

"Figure it out kid. We're up and running in less than three hours. Three days here and then we break and we're on the road again. That's how it works. Go find Jesus and you'll work the Baby with him. Tell him I sent you."

I picked up my duffel bag and headed off looking for the Baby Octopus and Jesus." I made my way through the carnival. Tents were going up. There was a concession tent and a couple of guys were hanging up a sign advertising what was available. Hot dogs, hamburgers, fries, onion rings, corn dogs, cotton candy, popcorn and a host of other City of Fun Carnival delicacies. My stomach grumbled. I took some comfort knowing I wouldn't starve. I had the stash my sister stuffed in my bags so I could at least buy something to eat. But I was going to have to find something else.

Go find Jesus I thought as I walked by the rides and checked the layout of the carnival. The line made me think of Officer Broadhead and what he'd told me on the way to the police station. He'd said, *maybe if I found Jesus, my life would change.* I was about to meet Jesus and I was counting on the fact things were going to change. I'll bet Broadhead never expected me to meet Jesus before he did.

Chapter 18

Nope. Hell, no. I do not believe Officer Broadhead could have ever imagined the Jesus I was about to meet. It wasn't Broadhead's Jesus, all reflective and suffering like on account of carrying all the sins of the world on his shoulders. This was Jesus Ortega Fernandez Lopez in the flesh and he was about 135 lbs. of ripped muscle and tattoos. He was shirtless and carrying a stack of ride seats. I couldn't take my eyes off of his tattoos and I just studied him before introducing myself.

His back was fully tattooed from top to bottom and his arms looked like sleeves from a jacket like he'd just slipped into a snake skin or something. The top half of his back depicted a beautiful devil woman — really beautiful with these hypnotic eyes and snakes and serpents coming out of her hair like the Greek goddess Medusa but without the ugly face. The snakes slithered down both arms in and out of skulls and at the bottom of his right arm a snake had unhinged its jaw and was swallowing a small child whole. Separating the top of his back from the bottom was the skyline of an empire of some sort like with domes and castle walls but they were all on fire burning like the end of the world. And then below this, but upside down was a beautiful woman at total peace with herself. It was religious. The Black Madonna or the Black Virgin and I knew this because of my sister, of course. She was fascinated by all sorts of religious things from the medieval time period and earlier and she'd show me these really interesting pictures in the *Encyclopedia Britannica* about martyred saints. I was pretty damn certain this tattoo was of the Black

Madonna.

"Looking at them, aren't you?"

"Yes." I couldn't lie because they were mesmerizing and he knew I was looking. They were truly beautiful.

He turned to face me and the front of his body was a continuation of the back and it was a story of some sort. Not random tattoo stuff but a novel of sorts. A skin story. It wasn't the jailhouse ink I'd seen on some of the guys at the bar or the tattoos of anchors, or big busty ladies and all the standard crap you'd expect, but this was genuinely good stuff.

I was enthralled because the front was a story of hell. Jesus, the biblical one, was inked directly over Jesus' heart with a crown of thorns and his eyes turned down in great sadness. And the rest of Jesus' tattoo was like the layers of Dante's levels of hell. This wasn't done by accident. Either Jesus or the artist or somebody else convinced him that if he was going to use his body as a canvas, it had to count and mean something or else he was just another tattooed nobody.

I thought of another book I'd read in Mrs. Nelson's class by Ray Bradbury called *The Illustrated Man*. It's about this drifter guy during the depression when work is hard to get. Anyway, he's drifting across the country looking for any kind of a job and he happens on a guy sitting around a fire. This stranger invites the drifter to share his food. It's a hot night...really hot and he tells the guy to feel free to take his shirt off and he can camp at his site. The drifter doesn't want to because of his *skin illustrations*. The stranger tells him he's seen a lot of tattoos and his can't be that different and the drifter says they were done by somebody from another world and they are alive. I got to tell you when I got to that part it really messed my head up. What imagination, right? And he tells the stranger that he's roaming the earth in hopes of finding the woman that did this and that he's going to kill her. I'm fearful for the stranger because this drifter is completely off his rocker. Then the drifter takes his shirt off and the stranger can't believe what he's seeing. They are alive and they are moving across his body. The stranger says it's the most amazing collection of tattoos he's ever seen and the drifter corrects him by saying something like, *These are not tattoos, they are skin illustrations.* He says it in such a way that the stranger gets that he shouldn't make that mistake again. But this is the killer. The stranger asks the, yep, you got it, the illustrated man about an empty spot on his back. And the illustrated man tells him not to look at it because it will show him the way he's going to die. Just thinking about this gave me goose pimples.

All this went through my head in seconds but it must have seemed like hours because Jesus asked me what I was doing hanging around the grounds before the carnival opened up.

"Right," I replied awkwardly, "Frenchy sent me over to work with you."

"No shit." He genuinely seemed surprised. "Frenchy must have had some sort of stroke." Then he said, "You were looking at them weren't you?"

I couldn't lie because I was mesmerized by the art on his body. "They're beautiful tattoos."

"Skin illustrations," he corrected me. "They're skin illustrations."

"*The Illustrated Man*?" I said, realizing if he'd coined the term from Bradbury, I was at least in the company of perhaps the only person who read in the carnival.

"Yes," he replied, smiling broadly at me. "I read. I read a lot."

"Me too."

He stuck out his hand and introduced himself to me and then I dropped my duffel by the generator and got to work helping Jesus build the Baby Octopus up from the dirt.

It was hard and dirty work and I soon broke into a healthy sweat. It reminded me of playing with erector sets with my younger brother. It really wasn't that different except that the pieces were huge. Once we'd gotten the arms hooked onto the octopus, and the seats mounted in place, we erected the metal fence around the ride so people couldn't sneak on when it stopped and also to keep, as Jesus said, *The cowpoke trash from stepping in front of the octopus and getting the shit knocked out of them.* When all of the octopus was erected, Jesus had me set up the ticket booth and he brought over a cash box, a roll of tickets and a little hand punch to click each ride. I was exhausted and the carnival hadn't even opened yet. I'd be earning the $20 a day.

"Go drop off your gear and get cleaned up and then we'll fire up the octopus and I'll let you ride it to see if it works."

"I actually don't have a rig," I said, feeling like I was starting to sound like a broken record and added, "I hitch hiked here."

Jesus regarded me like I must have been joking and when he stopped smiling he said, "Seriously?"

"Yeah. I thought they'd have places for the workers to stay."

He roared with laughter. "Here at the City of Fun Carnival?"

Jesus was doubled over in laughter, "Oh my God, that's too much! You must have been thinking that this was the Big Top or Barnum and Bailey or something. Hell, we consider it a miracle if we get paid at all. This is a no-frills operation, Hub."

I simply nodded my head. I couldn't think of anything else to do. After a moment, he said, "Listen, I got a pickup truck. It's got a big toolbox on the back that I built myself. It's got all my gear in there. It's got room for your duffel and you can sleep in back of the truck if you want. I sleep in the cab or with one of the rodeo buckle bunnies if I'm lucky. If it rains, you ain't coming inside the cab with me but you can crawl under the truck. How's that sound?"

"I'm much obliged, Jesus. Really. Thanks."

"Anything else?"

"One more question."

"Shoot."

"Where do I clean up and bathe?"

"Holy shit, you really are a rube, Hub. You sink wash whenever you get a chance. Over in the public restrooms by the rodeo."

"Okay."

"For now, just go to the men's pisser but be careful."

"Meaning?"

"Watch out for the cowboys. They don't like us and we don't like them."

"Why's that?"

"They think we're the lowest form of life in the world."

"I'll be careful."

"Do you carry a blade?"

"Yep."

"Good. Keep it on you at all times and if you have to use it, make sure it counts."

"Thanks. I will."

We hadn't even opened up the carnival yet and already I'd had warnings about looking at Angel, keeping my distance from the cowboys and being prepared to use my switch blade if I had to. I couldn't help but wonder what else I needed to know in order to survive. Lindsey already seemed like a lifetime ago and the innocence and comfort of my own life, as screwed up as it seemed at times, had dissolved in this lopsided carnival where I was without food and real shelter and the possibility that at any time I could be jumped by a bunch of goat ropers.

I headed off to where Jesus told me I could find his truck, threw my duffel into the bed, climbed up, and opened it. I slid my switch blade into my front pocket, grabbed my toilet kit, some clean clothes and a towel and headed off to the rest room to clean up. I surveyed the outside of the bathroom to see if any cowboys were headed into the crapper. When nobody went in or came out after a few minutes, I entered.

The mirrors over the sink were broken and the place smelled like shit. I mean really, but I guess I shouldn't have been surprised because it was, after all, a shitter. I turned on the tap and the water was rusty at first and then cleared up and the hot water was actually hot. I took my face cloth and washed my face and it felt great to get the salty sweat off me. Then I took my shirt off and did a quick body wash. I was putting on a white t-shirt when they walked in. Two cowboys maybe in their 20's with big rodeo buckles, cowboy boots with spurs and cowboy hats large enough to sleep under. I tensed up.

"Well, well, well," the bigger one said nudging his buddy with his elbow. "What have we got here?"

I didn't say anything because I already had this feeling. A feeling that whatever I said to them would be wrong. So, I picked up my clothes and toilet kit while I quietly slid my hand into the front pocket of my Levis and palmed my switch blade. I was going to have to pass them to get out and there wasn't much room.

"You one of the carnies?" the smaller one asked suspiciously.

I closed the gap between us. I had to keep going because if I stopped or engaged in some sort of bullshit with them it wasn't going to be pretty.

"Nope," I replied, watching them both carefully, "just a guy cleaning up and passing through."

"Bullshit," the bigger guy sneered. "You smell like a carnie to me. You smell like shit."

"It could be the stuff you got on the bottom of your boots," I said straight faced and staring at his eyes. "They're covered in horse shit."

I learned a long time ago to watch a guy's eyes in a tense situation. It's the first thing just before a fight breaks out and his eyes looked uncertain, confused, like he didn't know if I was insulting him or if I'd just made a quick retort. My thumb was on the switch but if I pushed it the blade would flip out and they'd see it and there would be no turning back. I waited to see which way this was going to go because it would go down quick and I'd be the first to make a move. Two against one and I planned to be the one walking out of the crapper.

"Whoopee, we got us a comedian," the big one laughed. "Pretty good kid. Pretty quick."

They made room for me to pass by them but I never took my hand off the switch just in case.

When I got back to the baby octopus, Jesus had already fired it up and it was running smoothly. I walked over to his truck and dropped my stuff off in the duffel and headed back. He turned around as I got close to him.

"Any problems."

"None," I replied. "Everything was fine except the crapper smelled like shit."

"Cowboys," he said nodding his head. "This place will be crawling with them in a while so get ready."

He slowed down the Octopus and shut it down. He opened the entrance gate to the ride, walked over to one of the seats, lifted the safety bar and beckoned for me to come over.

"As promised," he said bowing and ushered for me to sit down. "A promise made is a debt unpaid," and then added, "besides we got to test this out before the rubes get here to make sure they don't go flying out of the chair."

I couldn't tell if he was serious or not and then he winked at me, walked over and fired up the Octopus and off I went. *Robert Service*, I thought. *A promise made, is a debt unpaid* was a line from one of his poems, "The Cremation of Sam McGee." It's the only poem I'd almost memorized in Mrs. Nelson's class for extra credit. And here I was, working for Wacko's City of Fun Carnival with a guy by the name of Jesus Ortega Fernandez Lopez who read novels and poetry. It made me think how funny life was and I broke into a broad smile.

Chapter 19

From the moment we opened the ride until midnight, we were busting ass.
Jesus taught me how to run the Octopus, take tickets, help kids and parents
get on and off the ride and, in some cases, while parents rode with their older
kids, I even ended up holding little kids that were too small to get on the ride.
For the most part, it was pretty cool holding little kids. I'd never really done
that before — they loved running their hands over my buzz cut. I had one little
kid push his finger up my nose and I almost dropped him. He was, at most, a
year and a half. I was going to have to remember that move in case I got into a
close-up fight. It took about five minutes before my eyes stopped watering.

At first I was a bit shy with the people and then I got pretty chatty. I
charmed the old ladies who brought their grandchildren to the carnival. When
I'd put a little smart ass kid on the ride, one who was mouthing off or such,
I'd wish them *good luck* and when I latched them in I'd quietly whisper that *I
hoped they didn't get thrown off like some of the kids at our last stop.* Some of the
kids started to cry so I stopped doing it.

Midway through the evening, Wacko and Angel came by to see how I was
doing, which I thought was pretty cool. I talked briefly with them. Wacko
wasn't much of a talker but Angel couldn't have been nicer. To be honest, I
couldn't tell you what she said to me, I was all nervous and such and then
when she turned to Wacko and said she wanted to ride the Octopus I almost
died because that meant I'd have to latch the safety bar across her lap.

I unloaded everybody off the ride and closed the exit and then went back to let the next batch of riders in. I mumbled something to Angel like, *Right this way, please*. Or, and I hoped I didn't say this, *I just want to tell you how beautiful you are*. That would be stupid because it would be the end of my short life. I have this habit of thinking something and saying something completely different. This would not have been the time nor the place for a moment like that.

Instead, I walked her over to one of the chairs and, when she got comfortable, I reached across her and snapped the safety bar into place. My arm brushed across her lap and I thought I was going to die. When she smiled and thanked me all I could say was, "You smell nice."

She giggled the kind of giggle you'd get from your almost girlfriend in middle-school or something and said, "Aren't you about the sweetest person alive."

When the sun started to go down, the carnival took on a different look. It was a kaleidoscope of whirling colors and blaring music. Most of the people seemed excited we were in town. I only saw Wacko one other time that night and was disappointed when Angel wasn't with him.

By the time we wrapped everything up with the Octopus, covered the generator, closed up the ticket booth and dropped off the cash box with Frenchy, it was almost midnight. I decided I'd make a call home and try to talk with my sister.

I placed a collect call home. I was pretty sure my parents wouldn't pick up the phone because they were usually dead drunk at that time of night. My brother picked up the phone and while the operator was saying it was a collect call, I shouted over her voice and told him to accept the charge because I was certain he wouldn't know what to do. It was great to hear his voice and I didn't realize how much I missed him. He started telling me about Johnny Unitas and the Colts when I asked him if Soup was around and then told him to go get her. He dropped the phone on the counter and I could hear him running up the stairs to get my sister..

"Soup...hey Soup, Hub's on the phone!"

I don't know what I expected but the volume that came out of his little voice would certainly alert my parents and I didn't particularly want to talk with them. Finally, after what seemed like a long time, I heard somebody pick up the phone. If it were either parent, I'd just hang up.

"Hub?"

"Soup?"

"My God, you're still alive!"

We spoke for about half an hour and I brought her up to speed and let her know I was in Wyoming with a traveling carnival. She thought that was pretty cool and wanted to know what the name of the carnival was, but I didn't tell her on account that I was worried she might spill the beans. When I told her to tell mom and dad that I was doing *okay* she got quiet.

"They've been worried sick," she said. "They told me that if you ever called to tell you that they loved you and wished you'd come home."

That got me. It was nice to hear and I'd actually been thinking of what I'd do if I were a parent and my kid disappeared.

"Just tell them that everything is fine but don't let them know what I'm doing. Okay?"

"Okay."

"I've got to get back to work but I'll call again from the next town. Okay?"

"Okay."

I felt much better after talking with my sister. She's always been my anchor, the person I'd confide in if things got tough.

I decided to walk back past Wacko's trailer just for the hell of it. The light was on in the trailer and I pulled up near a giant cottonwood tree where I was partially hidden and lit up a smoke. Nothing seemed to be happening, or at least it didn't appear that way until I saw Angel walk into the kitchen area. I tensed. I got the same feeling when I'd gone hunting deer with Smitty and his dad. Angel turned on the faucet and got a glass of water. I wondered if it was possible that somebody could feel themselves being watched. She turned off the light and the trailer went dark. I was just about to leave when a light turned on in the back of the trailer. I could see Angel's silhouette through the curtain. She was taking off her clothes. She pulled her blouse up over her head. I ground out my cigarette on the heel of my boot and moved closer. I double-checked to see if anybody was around. This was sheer madness and I knew it but I couldn't help myself. Then she reached back and unfastened her bra.

I tried to imagine what her breasts looked like. I moved closer and accidentally kicked over some beer cans that had been tossed into a pile and froze. Angel stood still. Angel reached down for a towel or a blouse to cover herself and then moved to the window to see what the noise was about. That's when I took off running.

I knew what I was doing was wrong and suicidal but I couldn't help myself. When I got away from Wacko's trailer I slowed down and walked over to Jesus' truck. He'd just brushed his teeth and was getting ready to turn in for the night when he saw me.

"You disappeared. I was looking for you earlier."

"Had to make a phone call to my family."

"Kind of late for that, isn't it?"

"My sister would be up. She never sleeps."

"Thought you might have headed over to the rodeo to pick up some leftover buckle-bunny."

"Nope. I'm so drag-ass tired I wouldn't know what to do if I met one." Jesus laughed and we each had a smoke and then turned in. I was beat. I remember spreading out my sleeping bag in the back of the pickup, getting down to my shorts, climbing into the bag and staring up at the stars, and then it was lights out.

Chapter 20

I was up early, even before Jesus, so I slipped out of my bag trying not to bounce the bed of the truck too much. I dug into my duffel and pulled out my Levi jacket and threw on my clothes and then slipped into my jacket. It was surprisingly chilly. I pulled up my collar and thought how beautiful it was the way the light woke up the morning. You'd never guess how noisy it was the night before with the rodeo and carnival going full blast and now, six hours later, it was a peaceful landscape of farmland, with the smell of mowed alfalfa, the sst-sst-sst of big impact sprinklers spraying over a hay field and a chorus of chirping and whistling birds.

I sat on the bumper thinking how little I noticed such things back home. Everything seemed so busy and rushed. I could smell coffee and bacon wafting in the air and it made me hungry. I realized I'd have to figure out the food situation before too long or I'd probably starve to death. Since we didn't open until the afternoon I figured I could maybe hitchhike into town and pick up some supplies. My hands had some pretty nasty blisters on them so I'd need pick up some gloves, band aids and maybe some disinfectant like hydrogen peroxide or iodine to keep them clean.

I walked over by the Ferris Wheel and Frenchy was sitting down on a log having himself a smoke and a cup of coffee. He nodded his head.

"Morning, kid," he said. "You're at it pretty early."

"Guess so," I answered. I pulled out a smoke and lit up.

"Had any coffee yet?"

"No."

"Help yourself," Frenchy offered, nodding toward the diesel engine where a battered Stanley thermos sat on the ground in the shade.

"Thanks."

"Just black. No cream and sugar."

"Black's perfect. Thanks, Frenchy."

He got up, walked over to the Ferris Wheel, made a couple of adjustments on the guide wires and then came back with a log for me to sit on.

"How long you been working on the Ferris?" I asked him fishing for something to say.

"Seems like most of my life." He took a drag and replied, "Me and Big Heavy trade off. For a carnival like this, the Ferris *is* the ride."

We sat in silence enjoying the moment and then all philosophic like he said, "She reminds me of a woman, the Ferris Wheel."

I nodded my head.

"With the lights glittering like jewelry, she's irresistible."

"Never thought of it that way."

"And dangerous like a woman can be," he said. "One false move and it's all over. I should know." He waved his finger stubs in the air. "And hypnotizing... and sometimes you know you should stay away, but you can't. So, be careful kid, you could get hurt."

"I'll be careful around the Ferris, Frenchy," I replied.

"Around women," he said looking me straight in the eyes.

Confused the hell out of me. I wondered if he'd seen me spying on Angel but he didn't say it. For a moment, I thought about bringing it up and then thought better of it. I was playing with fire, I knew that.

Frenchy ground out his cigarette with his boot and then asked, "You got anything on your mind, kid?"

"Not really," I replied, lying through my teeth.

"Got a girl back home?"

"I do."

"Then that's what I'd keep my mind on. Get my drift?"

"I do."

"Good."

I thanked him for the coffee and turned to walk away when he added, "And you better get some gloves for those hands. They don't look good."

"I will. Thanks again for the coffee."

"No problem, kid."

Walking back to Jesus' pick-up I thought about what he'd said and he was right. I'd run away from trouble and it seemed I was drawn to it again. And her name was Angel.

Jesus was up and about when I got back to the truck.

"Morning, Hub. How'd you sleep?"

"Can't remember sleeping that good in a long time."

"Want some coffee?"

"Had some with Frenchy a few minutes ago."

"Frenchy?" he asked in the form of a question. Like that was some sort of unusual thing.

I showed him my hands and he whistled. "Don't you have gloves?"

"Forgot to pack them."

"There's a hardware and grocery store in town. Want to take my rig and drive in and get some?"

"That's okay? I'll just hitch a ride."

Truthfully, I'd love to take his rig but I didn't want to take the slightest chance of being stopped by the cops.

"We don't open til noon. It shouldn't take you long."

"How far away?"

"Two, maybe three miles."

"Maybe I'll just walk. Hitchhike. Somebody'll probably give me a lift."

"You sure? I don't mind."

"Yep. Need anything while I'm in town?"

"Maybe a couple of packs of Lucky Strikes."

Jesus reached into his back pocket to grab his wallet.

"Don't worry," I said, "I've got you covered."

"Thanks, I'll get you back."

"Seriously, no problem."

"Hub, you got any food?"

"Not really. Thought I'd pick some stuff up in town."

"We should double-up. Split costs," he said. "I've got an Eskimo cooler and we can keep the cold stuff in there. Replace the ice when we need to...and, you know, split the price of food."

"Sounds good to me."

We made up a list that included beans, ham, bread, eggs, onions, potatoes and peppers. I appreciated Jesus' generous offer. I had some money stashed away and I insisted on buying the groceries. It was the least I could do.

"Take my backpack. It's in the cab."

"Okay." I grabbed the pack, slung it over my shoulder and took off for town. I walked back up the hill and out onto the highway. It seemed funny that I'd only been with the carnival for a day and I actually felt comfortable around these guys.

I heard a car truck coming down the road so I stuck out my thumb and was surprised when a beat-up Ford truck slowed down and pulled right up to me. A sheep dog sat in the back sniffing the air. The driver was a kid about my age.

"Where you going?"

"Into town."

"Hop in. Goin' that way myself. The feed store."

"Want I should get in the back?"

"No need. Plenty of room up here."

"Thanks."

I climbed in. We got to talking and when I told him I worked with the carnival, he thought that was something else. Said he'd like to do something like that but he couldn't on account of a family farm. I told him that I thought farming must be a pretty satisfying way to make a living. Watching stuff growing and feeling like your family was responsible for putting food on people's tables. He laughed and looked at me like I was touched in the head. I offered him a smoke and he took one. He coughed when he lit up.

"I don't smoke much," he said smiling. "My family is Mormon. I'd like to but the old man would kick my ass."

"So would mine," I replied and added, "and he's not even Mormon."

He seemed like a good kid. He told me where the café was and even dropped me off there. I thanked him and told him to come by the Ferris Wheel and I'd give him some free passes for him and his girlfriend.

I was starved so decided to grab some breakfast before going to the grocery and hardware store. It was a seat yourself little mom and pop café so I took a small table by the window where I could see things going on. I was staring out the window watching a little mutt with a long tail going around in a circle trying to bite its own tail when the waitress startled me.

"Hi," she said, flipping over a coffee cup and filling it up without me even asking. "My name's Lacey. We've got waffles and fried chicken on special."

"I'm Hub," I said like an idiot, sticking my hand out for her to shake. She giggled and shook my hand.

"You're not from around here," she said.

"No, I'm not. How'd you know?"

"Because everybody knows everybody in a small town like this. And besides," she offered, "nobody ever introduces themselves to a waitress with a handshake."

"Right. I'll try the special, please."

"Any juice?"

"Coffee's fine."

"What are you doing in town? We're kinda off the beaten path."

"Just passing through with the carnival."

"Really? Sounds exciting. I've never met anybody from the carnival before."

"Well, now you have."

Lacey was a beautiful young girl, and I was chatting like a damn fool.

"Been over to the rodeo yet?"

"No, ma'am. In fact, I've never been to a rodeo in my entire life."

"You're kidding?" She seemed surprised. "Maybe you ought to go. I'm one of the Rodeo Queens and we're riding into the ring tonight just before the Star-Spangled Banner."

"Sounds like an invitation to me," I said bold like. I didn't know what was getting into me. First Angel and now Lacey. This world seemed to be crawling with good looking women. There weren't any games with Lacey like there was with the girls at Pershing. She was easy to talk with and I didn't feel shy at all.

"We open the rodeo every night. It's the Rodeo Queen and her attendants, the little mutton busters, 4-H, bronc riders, ropers and then the clowns. When that gets done, then I get ready to compete in my event."

"Broncs?" I asked. I had no idea.

"Barrel racing," she answered.

"How much of a head start do the barrels get?" I asked and that got her laughing. Then, her boss called up an order. She turned to walk away and then looked over her shoulder and asked. "Waffles and fried chicken?

"Sounds perfect," I replied.

She delivered the order to a couple of farmers and then went over and sat down with a couple of girls her own age. They looked over in my direction and I smiled and nodded to them. They returned the smile and giggled a bit.

Waffles and fried chicken was a strange delight. Nothing I'd ever had before and I thought how much my brother would like this dish. Her boss didn't seem to be upset about her talking with me. I added on a piece of homemade banana cream pie just because it was homemade and Lacey threw a couple of scoops of vanilla ice cream on the side. I had a couple more cups of coffee and then, when Lacey closed me out at the register and I walked back over to the table and left her a big tip. She was busy taking an order when I left.

I hadn't gone very far when she came running out of the café.

"Hey, Hub," she called, "the Felts, the folks who own the Feed Store always have a barbecue and dance during the rodeo. The big one's tonight and some good fiddle playing and country western dancing."

"I love fiddle playing," I said, lying through my teeth.

"You could come see me ride tonight and then come to the barbecue," Lacey said smiling broadly.

"We don't close down 'til midnight."

"Oh," she seemed disappointed.

"But, if you want to swing by the Baby Octopus after your event and bring your boyfriend I'll give you some free tickets."

"I don't have a boyfriend. We broke up a month ago."

"Sorry."

"No need to be."

"Well, come by anyway and I'll give you some tickets."

"I might just do that."

"I hope so," I said pausing. "It'd be nice to see you again."

At the general store, I grabbed a basket and started picking up the supplies from our list. I found the section where they kept the bandages and picked up some gauze, hydrogen peroxide, and merthiolate as well as bandages. I picked out a pair of good leather gloves and asked for a couple of packs of Lucky Strikes and Marlboros. The kid checking me out said he couldn't sell them to me on account of my age. I pulled out my phony id and showed it to him and he raised his eyebrows, charged me for the smokes and then apologized for making me show my id. I packed up everything into the backpack and headed back to the carnival.

My luck hitchhiking back wasn't as good as it was heading in. A postal truck passed me up and so did a truck loaded with bales of hay. On the other side of the road, a Ford pickup slowed down when they passed me. I could see a couple of young guys in cowboy hats talking back a forth with each other and looking pretty carefully at me. I gave them a nod and then stuck my thumb out when they passed me.

Then they flipped around and came up slow on me. When they pulled the truck off the side of the road started to get out of the truck, I got that gut feeling that things were about to change. I recognized them almost immediately. The guys who'd hastled me earlier.

My perfect morning of meeting Lacey and feeling like the world was going right was about to change. I slid my hand into my pocket and pulled out my switch blade and flipped the blade open. I kept it palmed in my hand.

"Well, I'll be dipped in shit," the taller one said. "Ain't this the little shit-bag we ran into in the crapper."

"The one who said he didn't work for the carnival, right?"

"He's a carnie and a liar, ain't he?"

"Yes and no," I said, catching them by surprise. "Yes, to being a carnie and no to being a liar."

They looked at each other confused like.

"See, the deal was like this," I explained, letting the tip of my blade show. "I hadn't gotten a job with the carnival yet. But I did get one. So, no lie. No harm. No foul."

The tall one reached into the back of the truck and pulled out an axe handle and the smaller guy started moving around to my side. I let the switch completely slide down to my hand. When they saw the blade, they held up a bit.

"What do you think you're going to do with that?"

"Cut your eyes out," I answered and then looked at the short guy and added, "and cut your balls off."

I slowly let the backpack slide off my shoulder so I could bring it up to my chest to ward off a blow from the handle if things got that far. Something was going to happen. I knew that. As much as I wanted to avoid any of this because it would bring in the local police and that wouldn't bode well for me, it's just one of those things. I didn't know these guys and they didn't know me but they hated me because I wasn't like them. When I pulled the blade out they must've figured me out as a carnie.

Hate is a powerful thing. It can ignite in a flash and it goes from zero to 100 mph and there isn't any way around it. We were close to ignition.

I was surprisingly calm under the circumstance. I tried to break down how things might go. The big guy swings. I block it with the backpack. It breaks the impact of the blow or it shatters my forearm but I have to stab him somewhere. Lose. Lose.

The little guy tries to punch me or take me down. Backpack block. Punch or stab. Big guy swings...maybe hits the little guy. A total cluster. Maybe I just turn around and try to walk away. Big guy splits my head open and they drive off laughing.

Other thoughts: maybe we try to sit down and talk things over...tell each other our most intimate feelings...maybe how our parents don't understand us and all that psycho bullshit. Or maybe I just break it down. Straight up about what's going to happen because if nobody is talking or insulting each other we are only seconds away from a big hurt. Perhaps an introduction is in order. Just crazy enough. Might work.

"What's your name?"

"None of your business," the big guy says.

"It's an interesting name. Bit long."

"Huh?"

"And you?" I ask the little guy.

"None of your business," he snarled back.

"Two guys with the same name. What are the odds of that?" I asked. *Sometimes you're just to clever for your own good, Hub.* I'd heard that more than a few times in my life and this was one of them. The humor escaped them and I got ready for the inevitable. I crouched down, backpack up and blade ready and then the three of us see it coming down the highway. Another pickup truck. Slowing down in the opposite lane like they might offer up assistance if there's a problem. Flat tire. Busted axle. Broken bones.

The big guy goes to wave the truck off like, *we've got this one covered...no need to stop.* But the guy gets out and he is bigger than all of us put together and he doesn't look happy because he knows danger and he smells cowards and bullies. He reaches into the back of his pickup and pulls out a pipe wrench and walks over and asks me if I'm okay and I say that I am.

The short guy goes to say something but he doesn't get very far, before the guy, the guy with the pipe wrench, says, "If I were you, I would just shut my pie-hole." And he does.

Then the big cowboy, because neither of them seemed too bright goes to say something and manages to get the following out before he's stopped. "That guy right there stopped us and was trying to give us a bunch of crap so we were going to..."

"Let me stop you for a second," Jesus, my Jesus, said, "just so I can get a complete picture of this. You two," and he pointed to them, pipe wrench punctuating the air, "were just driving along when all of a sudden you saw this kid, walking along, minding his own business, carrying a backpack of groceries trying to hitch a ride and you're telling me that somehow this young man managed to stop you...made you get out of the car and threatened you?"

He paused and waited for one or the other of the cowboys to say something.

"So, here's what's going to happen," Jesus said slowly so these guys didn't miss a single word. "You're going to climb back into your rig and get the hell out here."

"Or what?" the little guy said.

Jesus punched him in the face and he fell to the ground. The big guy moved in but I pulled up my knife and dropped the backpack on the ground.

"Don't even think about it," I said, crouching down ready to get on him. Jesus had his arm cocked to the side ready to wreck some havoc on the guy with a pipe wrench.

"Okay," the big guy said, throwing the axe handle into the back of the pick-up. "We're getting out of here." The short guy was having difficulty sitting up and the big guy was trying to help him stand up so he could get him into the front seat. "But this ain't over, assholes."

"It better be," Jesus said flatly.

We stepped back and watched the big guy lump his buddy into the seat, get into the pickup and roar off onto the highway spraying gravel and dust all over.

"Thanks," I said. "I'm glad you showed up when you did."

"Lucky guess."

"Seriously?"

"Nope. Had to pick up a couple of parts at the hardware store for Frenchy."

"Thanks anyway."

"Don't mention it," and he smiled broadly.

I pulled out my cigarettes, lit one for Jesus and passed it over to him. My hands were shaking and he noticed.

"First fight?"

"Nope," I answered. I started to tell him that I couldn't have gotten into a fight even if I wanted to because the cops were after me, but I decided against it. "I'm glad that's over."

"It's not, Hub. It's just beginning," Jesus said nodding for me to get into the truck, "And this shit can get pretty ugly in a hurry."

When we got to town, Jesus went to pick up some parts and took me back to the grocery store to pick up a block of ice for our cooler. I kept my eyes open for the cowboys just in case they doubled back into town. I didn't want to run into them under any circumstance. Once we got back into the truck and left town, Jesus asked, "Would you have used your knife on those clowns?"

"If I had to," I replied.

"Good to know, Hub. Good to know."

Chapter 21

After we got the parts to Frenchy and got set up for the afternoon, I had a bit of free time so I walked around the grounds. Already I was beginning to understand the rhythm of the carnival; how it worked, how the pieces moved together and connected with each other. I was tempted to wander over to the rodeo fairground but I was still a bit unsettled about our earlier experience with the two cowboys so I just putzed about.

As I told Jesus later, I stepped into the men's room and threw some water on my face and freshened up a bit before getting ready to open the gates. Coming out of the bathroom, I almost crashed into Angel.

"I'm sorry," she said, embarrassed like.

And quick as a wink, I said, "I'm not. You looked pretty last night."

She blushed, or I'm pretty sure she did.

"Thank you, Hub," she said, "I'm glad somebody around here still takes notice."

That's when I decided I had to say something to Jesus because what I said to Angel was certainly a way to get myself disappeared.

Jesus listened intently and when I finished telling him what I'd done he was silent for the longest time. "Okay," he said, "Tell me the story again and this time tell me how she sounded and how you sounded when you talked to her."

"I told you everything," I answered defensively.

"The way you said it?"

So, I went over the story again trying to explain how I sounded and how Angel sounded. Every once in a while, he'd interrupt me and ask a question.

"When she said, after she nearly bumped into you, *I'm sorry,* and you said, *I'm not. You looked pretty last night,* you weren't flirting with her were you?"

I didn't reply because I *was* flirting and Jesus knew it.

"Listen, Hub," he said striking up a smoke and offering me one from the pack. "I'm going to try and help you understand something and try to make it very clear. "Okay."

"I know Frenchy and Big Heavy told you this, but Angel, in every which-fucking-way, is off limits to everybody."

Jesus was serious.

"Do you understand what I AM saying?"

"Yes."

"Because if you don't, Hub. Wacko will kill you."

"Got it, Jesus."

But I didn't.

What I didn't tell him was that my conversation was actually a bit longer. And it wasn't that I was coming out of the bathroom. I'd actually gone over to the pay phone to make a call to Smitty and let him know that I was fine and that I'd found work and that is when I really bumped into Angel.

"Hello, Hub. Seems like we're destined to keep running into each other." She took off a scarf from around her head and wiped the back of her neck. "I enjoy talking with you."

"Me too," I said, feeling really uncomfortable.

"Oh," she laughed, "You enjoy talking to yourself?"

I blushed. "No, ma'am...I meant to say I enjoy talking with you too. That's all."

"God, it's going to be a scorcher this season. I wish our trailer had a little swamp cooler on the top. A fan just isn't cutting it."

"I know what you mean," I replied. I didn't know what else to say.

"I sleep naked at night. I wet down a sheet, wring it out and cover myself with it. It makes the heat bearable."

I was starting to feel real uncomfortable and didn't want to be in this conversation at all. The thought of Angel, her long legs curled under some damp sheets, or maybe pulled back so her breasts were exposed was too much for me.

"Well, I guess I'd better be getting," I said.

"Sure," Angel said, "I'll see you around."

"Yes, ma'am."

"Bye, Hub."

We were packed when the fair opened up. Today seemed bigger and busier than the previous night. When I asked Jesus, he told me that tonight was the biggest night at the rodeo which meant that it would be crazy busy until the rodeo started, slow down a bit and then, after the rodeo let out, it'd be crazy again.

"Tomorrow will be average and then we pack up and hit the road. Next town. Next rodeo. It's kind of like a bad dream you get stuck in over and over again."

About half way through the night I noticed the young kid that gave me a ride into town. He was all dressed up in his western clothes, pressed white shirt with a red bandana tied around his neck, cowboy boots, Wrangler jeans with a big rodeo belt buckle. Along with him were a couple of cute girls about the same age.

When he got to the gate, I nodded to Jesus and told him these three rides were on me.

He smiled when he saw me. I went over and chatted with him for a bit and he introduced me to the two girls he was with. The cutest one, said, "Aren't you the one that Lacey fancies?"

"I don't think so," I replied honestly. Hell, I'd only chatted with her at breakfast and then she ran outside after I left her a big tip and told me to come watch her ride. Other than that, I didn't know what her friend was talking about.

"You're the guy," she said with certainty. "Lacey said she invited you to the barbecue and dance after the rodeo."

"That's true," I answered but didn't have much else to add.

"Well, she's been talking about her new boyfriend and I guess that would be you."

"She's very kind."

"She rides tonight. Mid-way through the rodeo."

"Barrel racing. She told me."

"You going?"

"I'm going to try and get there but I work late."

"She'll be disappointed."

"Not as much as I will."

"That's sweet," she said and her friend nodded her head in agreement.

"I can't wait to tell her I met you. She'll be jealous."

"Wish her the best of luck for me if I can't get there."

"She doesn't need luck. She's leading in the scores and if she places first or second she'll have enough points to travel on the circuit."

"Meaning?"

She looked at me like I was dumb.

"She'll travel the west. Probably following the same route you all take."

"Come on!" somebody in the line yelled. "Get this ride going."

"Okay folks," I said, "follow me," and I took them over and buckled them into their seats. Jesus flipped the switch and they started giggling. I stood back and watched them swirl around and every time they passed by the booth they waved to me. I nodded back.

Fortunes can change on a dime. That was an expression my gram would always say and I never knew exactly what it meant. She had a number of those expressions and when she'd drop one into a conversation it was always at the end of a sentence as though that was that. Thinking about it now, I felt like this was the appropriate phrase for what might or might not happen with Lacey. The thought of her traveling the same circuit was exciting and yet, at the same time, I couldn't help feeling that I was betraying Lindsey by just thinking about Lacey and Angel.

In all honesty, when I saw Lindsey in the library I realized we could never be a couple. Because of who I was. Not that both of us didn't feel deeply for each other, but I was carrying a lot of baggage with me and I had no idea how things would turn out. Her parents hated me and thought she could do much better. I guess I agreed with them.

Besides, if I ever returned home there would be a major shit storm. At minimum, State School for Juveniles or, because of what I'd be accused of, I could see them throwing me into an adult prison. With Angel, it was a pretty one-sided equation. I had a super hot'n horny crush on her. Like my gram would say, *It's a one-way street.* And, in this case, Wacko would be standing at the end of the street with a shotgun in his hands. No thanks.

Around 9 p.m. it started to slow down. I must have seemed particularly restless because Jesus ask me what was going on.

"Nothing," I said.

"It's the cowgirl, isn't it?"

"Sort of. Other things too."

"Tell you what, I can handle this tonight. Why don't you clean up and go to the rodeo. Watch her do whatever she does."

"Barrel race. She barrel races."

"Never quite understood any of that."

"Me neither."

"You know, in all the years I've been with Wacko, I've never been to the rodeo."

"Seriously?"

"It's not safe for a guy like me. Just asking for trouble."

I didn't say anything. I knew what he meant. He was Mexican. Came across the border with his family when he was four years old. He told me he wasn't legal and could get deported at any minute. His family worked the California picking circuit. Fruit, vegetables, anything. Wherever farmers needed cheap labor, his family was there. What was most interesting to me was when Jesus told me about this part of his life, he spoke, not with anger, but with a softness that surprised me.

"To be honest," he'd said, "Growing up I never ever felt like we were poor. We were dirt farmers. Only we did it for other people. We'd meet the same pickers and families from year to year. It was a community. Like a family. We'd eat together, work together, play in the irrigation ditches and marry each other. I started picking when I was five years old."

"How long did you do it?"

"Until my father was killed in a farming accident. Run over by a combine."

"I'm sorry."

"It was tough. Really tough. My mom tried to keep us all together but we ended up splitting the family. I hit the road when I was 14. And the worst part is that I've lost touch with my entire family. Like they've just disappeared."

There wasn't much I could say really. The night before when we were talking Jesus opened up a very small window into his life and let me look in. It made me think of my own family and how I'd really just abandoned them. Deserted them was probably more accurate.

Jesus lived a life where he was always on the run. It wasn't his fault. It's just that he was born in another country and his family wanted a better life for themselves and came here. They did what they had to do to try to find a better life. It's not a story I could tell. I was on the run because I'd screwed things up so badly at home. I'd made some bad choices and could only blame myself. There was so much I wanted to talk with Jesus about, like how did he manage to stay invisible for all those years and not get caught? For him and his family being invisible was a matter of safety, of survival.

"Hub," he said breaking the silence.

"Sorry, I was somewhere else."

"And that *somewhere else* should be heading over to see Miss Rodeo."

"Right. And thanks."

"It's not without a price," he said, smiling. "I'm going to need the same favor in the next town we play."

"Fair enough."

"I've got a lady there I like to see." He paused, as though he was going to tell me a bit more about her and then finally said, "Get out of here. Be careful."

I did.

Chapter 22

By the time I got a ticket and found a place in the bleachers, they'd already completed the competition for tie-down roping, team roping, saddle bronc riding and were just beginning the bareback bronc riding.

I looked around nervously to see if I could spot the two cowboys I'd had a run-in with but didn't see them anywhere. At least not close to where I was sitting, but I kept it in the back of my mind. I tried to figure out where all these folks came from because there must have been 1,000 people in the crowd and if there were 200 people in this little town I'd be surprised. I started to ask the cowboy next to me about this when the announcer introduced the first rider. He gave some stats about the cowboy's ranking in the rodeo circuit and then spent as much time about the bronc the rider had drawn.

The bronc was named *Sidewinder* and had a pretty ugly reputation for tossing cowboys in the first few seconds. I don't know how much of this was true or just hype to get the crowd amped up but when the cowboy next to me looked over and said, *This is going to be over quickly,* I just nodded my head like I knew and replied, *Tough draw.*

When the pen opened, the bronc exploded up and out into the arena, completely airborne, and the cowboy's hat went flying off his head. I've never seen such raw power unleashed and it was mesmerizing. Hell, I'd never been to a rodeo before but I instantly got it. Right there. The flesh and blood of it. The danger of what I was watching.

When the bronc landed on the ground it immediately spun about 90 degrees to the left, kind of like the fury a dog gets when it chases its own tail, and the cowboy was almost parallel to the ground. Then *Sidewinder* bucked over toward the corral fence and the crowd let out a collective gasp and jumped to their feet, myself included. It was intentional. *Sidewinder* was trying to ram this poor cowboy into the fence. Next thing you could hear was a clashing on the metal rails and this rider was being smashed up against the chute. A louder gasp from the crowd and then three rodeo clowns went after the bronc waiving red silk bandanas in *Sidewinder's* face and another clown grabbed *Sidewinder's* tail and gave it a sharp yank. *Sidewinder* immediately went after the first clown who quickly jumped the fence into safety and then turned on the other. Holy hell, I couldn't believe what I was watching. I looked over and the rider was clumped up in the fetal position. He looked like he'd been knocked out. He wasn't moving.

"Get them pickups in there!" the cowboy next to me yelled. "Now! Damnit!"

Pickups? What the hell was he screaming about. It seemed like that was the last thing they needed was some pickups in the arena.

Two riders were galloping across the arena at full speed and headed right toward *Sidewinder* as a distraction. Meanwhile a couple of medics, or whatever, were helping the cowboy get to his feet. He was unsteady, and it reminded me of trying to help a drunk walk. I should know. I'd had more than enough of that sort of experience in my own family. When the rider eventually and feebly waived his hand to the crowd like he was *okay* the announcer came over the speaker.

"Cowboys and cowgirls please give Ronnie Lockhart a round of applause."

And the crowd did just that, me clapping as hard as anybody else.

"A tough ride of only four seconds that must have seemed like a lifetime for Ronnie but he's a bronc rider and he will be back."

Again, the crowd went crazy.

"He never got a chance to mark *Sidewinder* out," the cowboy said.

"I didn't think so," I answered.

"He's going to be one sore cowpoke come morning."

I was riveted by this sport and couldn't figure out why anybody would intentionally climb onto the back of a crazy bronc that weighed nearly a ton. What would make anybody in their right mind do something like that?

Rider after rider I watched cowboys launched into the air in every conceivable way and land in the most remarkably painful looking positions; on their backs and shoulders and faces and asses. Only a few lasted long enough for the pickups to ride alongside the broncs so the rider could grab onto the pickup's back and slide on or off to the ground in safety. There was nothing safe or sensible about this. The bronc riders were crazy, no questions asked, the pickups, those riders who put themselves directly in harm's way to guard bucked riders, clearly had a death wish and as far as the clowns went, there was no explanation for being that unhinged. You think clowns, you think funny, right? The Big Top, Barnum & Bailey? Clowns tripping and falling, throwing fake buckets of water that turn out to be confetti into the front row, bopping each other with fake hammers, and styrofoam planks and such. It's pure entertainment, a break from the animal acts and trapeze artists and poodles riding on the back of horses and really smart horses that run around in a circle and do cool moves like all of them standing up and walking on their back legs. Circus clowns are those sorts of clowns but these rodeo clowns are in a different league all of their own. They have a death wish. How else can you explain it?

After the last bronc rider was catapulted end over end and the scores were tallied, the announcer reminded the audience that there was plenty more excitement to come. He invited them to get beverages and all the crap you'd expect to find at any event like this and then return to see *them little darlin' barrel racers* and then the rodeo would close with final big-ticket item, bull riding and fireworks.

I was pretty excited because I hadn't missed Lacey's event. I'd surprise her because I was pretty sure she wouldn't expect me to be there. I quickly grabbed a soft-drink, and went over to the staging area to see if I could find her and wish her good luck.

Over by the bull pens, cowboys were loosening up, stretching in the most contorted ways. Some were going through a crazy-looking pantomime, spinning left and right, their right hand above their head, trying, I suspected, to envision and invoke a body-memory of riding every bull they'd ever ridden.

And, then I saw her. And him. The little short guy who'd gotten whacked by Jesus when he and his buddy tried to jump me. He had on chaps, a pressed white cowboy shirt and the number 18 pinned to the front of his shirt. The little punk was a bull rider and it explained why he was dumber than a brick. He'd had his brains stomped from riding bulls.

Lacey was all dressed in her riding outfit and she looked beautiful. She wore a turquoise western shirt with white pearl buttons, a white silk scarf tied around her neck, tight Wrangler jeans and a cowgirl belt with a large rodeo belt buckle.

She didn't see me and I wasn't about to walk up to her while she was within spitting distance of the punk. Then she did something that changed everything for me. Lacey walked up to the punk and began talking to him. I wanted to shout out a warning but they seemed to know each other. Finally, and this killed me, she gave him a hug and a kiss on the cheek. The punk tipped his cowboy hat to her and walked over to the bull chutes, and I headed back to the bleachers with my soft drink.

Before I'd gotten 20 steps, I heard her call out my name.

"Hub," she cried. "Hey, Hub, over here."

I pretended not to hear her and just kept my gaze toward the bleachers.

"Hub!" she called and then let loose with a piercing whistle that stopped me in my tracks.

I turned toward her and she came running up.

"You came!" she exclaimed, all excited.

"I did," I said, sounding a little stupid.

"Thank you! Oh, my god. That's so sweet of you."

"My partner let me slide out early tonight."

"So, you'll stay for my race and then maybe go to the barbecue and dance afterwards?"

Lacey was a good actress and I didn't know what to say exactly. Here she was, moments ago, kissing her boyfriend and now really excited about seeing me. It didn't add up.

"I think I'll have to pass on the invitation, Lacey," I said, trying to avoid her eyes.

"Do you have to go back to the carnival?"

"It's not that," I began and she cut me off.

"What is it? Don't you want to go with me?"

"No, it's not that, Lacey, it's just that I…"

"You what?"

"I don't want to get between you and your boyfriend."

"What boyfriend?" She looked perplexed. "I told you I didn't have a boyfriend. What makes you say that?"

"I saw you kiss that cowboy. The bull rider."

"Oh, my god, aren't you the sweetest," she said, smiling broadly. "He's not my boyfriend. He's my brother and I was wishing him good-luck."

"Your brother?" I said, stunned by the coincidence, by the circumstance.

"If we both ride well tonight, we can qualify to go on the road together. So, keep your fingers crossed."

"Okay," I said weakly and with a forced smile. "I'll do just that."

"I'll meet you back here after the race. I can't wait to introduce you to my brother. He's going to love you!"

"I wouldn't bet on it."

"Why would you say that?" she asked, looking a bit hurt by the question,

That was a stupid thing to say, but I couldn't help myself, and now I was scrambling for an answer.

"It's just that, you know," I punted, "brothers and sisters...we're always suspicious of their dates, right?"

"You have a sister?"

"Yeah and I never meet anybody without giving them the once-over."

"Well," she replied, "you two will hit it off, trust me."

Lacey got part of that right. The hit part. Hit was the operative word. She came over and gave me a kiss on the cheek. It caught me by surprise and it would probably be the only kiss I'd get from her.

"Meet me here after I race and we'll go to the barbecue together."

"And your brother?"

"He won't be with us. You'll have to meet him later. He and some of the other bull riders always go out and get drunk after their event."

That was fine with me. Just perfect.

Chapter 23

I had a difficult time trying to understand and make sense out of bull riding but when I saw the first rider come out of the chute on one ton of wild muscular animal that spun in circles, bucking with such ferocity, it made me wonder what would possess anybody in their right mind do such a thing. Mrs. Nelson my English teacher, would have asked us *What was the conflict? Was it man vs man, man vs nature, or man vs himself?* but the literary folks who came up with those categories clearly had never ever been to a rodeo before. I can, *darn tootin'* guarantee that as a fact. They'd have to make a brand-new category called *man vs hell plus Satan.* And that was being kind.

As much as I wanted to hate Lacey's brother, I had to give him credit though. It took a heap of guts mixed with equal part brain damage to strap yourself onto a raging bull. This is the part that is inexplicable, but the bull riders actually slip one hand into some sort of gizmo and then strap their hand in real tight. They actually cinch this leather strap with their teeth. Pull it tight.

One cowboy pulled a whirlwind of a bull that would spin left and then, mid-air, change directions the minute it came out of orbit and crashed onto the arena. He was thrown on the second jump but he couldn't get his hand loose and the bull was thrashing him all about like a rag doll. His ride was three seconds and if it hadn't been for those clowns, that bull would have killed him. Plain and simple. He had to be carried out of the arena.

It was a relief when the bull riding was over and I was really looking forward to watching Lacey in the barrel racing. That seemed like more my speed but again, I was completely blown away. Speed was the purpose. The kind of speed you'd see in westerns where the good guy was chasing the bad guy in a full-gallop.

As close as I can figure it out, barrel racing works like this: there are three barrels spread out in the arena in a triangle maybe 100 feet apart, and the riders have a starting line about 120 feet away from the barrel at the apex of the imaginary triangle. When they get the signal, they have to circle each barrel so it kind of looks like a clover leaf. They lose points if they touch the barrel or knock it over. Once they've circled all of the barrels they ride hell-bent-for leather to the finish line. The cowgirl with the fastest time wins.

Lacey was something to watch. If I'd have tried barrel racing, I'd be on my ass the second the horse took off. And if I was lucky enough to make it to the first barrel, the horse would make the cut around the first barrel and I wouldn't. I'd have gone flying toward the bleachers. She was the third rider and was in first place until the last cowgirl bested her time by two seconds.

When I got over to the gates she was brushing down her horse and didn't see me approaching. I watched while she was talking to her horse as she brushed it.

"You're such a beauty," she whispered in a quiet steady voice. "Such a good, good girl."

"So, were you, Lacey," I said.

"Hub! You startled me."

"Sorry. That barrel racing was beautiful, Lacey and you were great."

"Thanks," she answered, shyly.

"I mean it. I was mesmerized watching you...the other riders. It was," I paused, looking for the right word, "breathtaking."

"Thank you, Hub. That means a lot to me."

"But you must hear that a great deal."

"Not really. In our family it's all about bull riding. It's all about my brother."

"Yeah, but he's crazy."

"Still, it's nice to hear it. Thanks."

There was an awkward pause and neither of us knew what to say. Finally, Lacey handed me an extra grooming brush and asked if I'd brush down the other side of her horse.

"I'm afraid of horses," I said quietly.

"Seriously!"

"This is the first time I've ever been this close to one."

She started giggling. "Here," she said putting the brush in my hand. "Her name's Little Britches." Little Britches turned her head toward Lacey at the sound of her name and she rubbed her head. "Here, go ahead and rub her head and say something soft to her."

I tentatively started to reach out and then pulled my hand back. "She's not going to bite me, is she?"

"Not unless she thinks you're a sugar cube. Go ahead."

So, I rubbed her just as Lacey did. I brushed her from the bridge of her nose down to her nostrils and was surprised how soft Little Britches was. Her face was hard and bony but just above the nostrils, it was incredibly soft.

"Congratulations," Lacey said. "Now go ahead say something nice to her."

"Like what?"

"Anything. Anything at all."

"Good horse."

"That's it?"

"You're a beautiful horse Little Britches. Really beautiful. You remind me of Lacey."

"Is that a compliment?"

"Yes."

"You think I'm a *pretty horse?*" she asked, teasing me.

"No. Yes. Not that you're like a horse."

"Thanks."

"But you are beautiful."

Little Britches snorted, and I jumped back.

"This is too funny," she said, "I wish I had this on film."

Lacey slid her arm through mine and walked me around Little Britches.

"Quick lesson. Neck. Shoulder. Barrel. Thigh." Lacey patted each section on Little Britches as she pointed out the anatomy to me. "Be thorough. Brush downward with her coat and you'll be fine."

"Got it." Then she started to go back to the other side of Little Britches."

"You going to leave me here on this side on my own?"

"It's simple, Hub. And don't forget to talk to her."

"If you do a good job we'll be out of here in half the time."

"Right."

I'm sure Little Britches knew I was a beginner but she didn't try to kill me. While I brushed her I talked to her about my family. Described my parents and that got Lacey laughing. Told stories about my brother and sister. And pretty soon we were done.

"Thank God you don't barrel race elephants. You'd have heard my entire life story."

"I wouldn't mind that at all, Hub," she said. "Want to lead Little Britches back to the stable."

"I think I'll pass, if you don't mind," and added, "Congratulations for qualifying."

"How'd you know?"

"I met a couple of your girlfriends and they told me if you took first or second place you could compete for the nationals. That's a big deal, Lacey."

"I know. It hasn't quite sunk in yet."

"Will you travel the circuit?"

"I think so."

"That would be great because you're really good."

"And it means I'd get to see you," and then added, "I'd like that."

"Me too."

We took Little Britches to her stall and Lacey filled up a water bucket while I put hay and concentrates into a feed bag.

"All done," she said, rubbing Little Britches before closing the gate. "Okay, Hub, you ready to go dancing?"

"I know how to barbecue but I've never done much dancing other than school dances. The kind where you put your arms around each and slowly turn in a circle."

"We do things differently up here."

"I figured as much."

"Where are you parked?"

"I'm not," I replied, smiling broadly. "This is my transportation I'm afraid," and I stuck out my thumb and gave her my best hitchhiking pose.

"Seriously?"

"I'm afraid so.

"Well then, that's how we'll get there," she said walking out to the road.

Lacey asked me a little more about my family, about what my parents were like, and my friends and what I did for fun. I made things up that I thought she'd like to hear. I made up stories about fishing with my buddies, about hunting and hanging out, about sneaking into the drive in with a bunch of buddies.

"What about school? Shouldn't you be in school?"

Lacey wasn't giving me the third degree. I think she was just interested but it caught me off guard. Answer a question with a question, so I asked her the same question back.

"What about you? Aren't all of you supposed to be in school too?"

"That's the advantage of living in a farming community. We get out earlier than the city schools. Agricultural necessity. Farm families need their children to help during spring crops."

It bought me some extra time to think of something.

"I actually skipped a grade so I graduated a year ago."

"Get out of here, Hub. That's really cool. I've never met anybody who skipped year of school."

"It's no big deal. My sister actually skipped two."

"Are you serious?

"She's really amazing."

Lacey started laughing, "I never knew anybody who skipped a grade but I know a bunch of boys who got held back."

"So, you never have to worry about truant officers then?"

"Not so far. Can I ask you something personal?"

"Shoot."

"Do you have a girlfriend?"

"I did."

"Was it serious?"

"Yes."

"Did she breakup with you?"

"It was a number of things. Mostly my fault."

"I didn't mean to pry."

"It's not that. It's just complicated."

"Hey, a truck's coming. Let me do it. Let me stick out my thumb."

"Anybody would be happy to give you a ride."

When the truck got closer, I froze. I recognized it. It belonged to the guys who tried to beat me up. I slipped my hand into my pocket and grabbed my blade and held it to my side.

"It's Donny's truck! He'll give us a ride!"

I didn't know what was going to happen but I'd use the knife this time. The truck started slowing down and pulled up alongside us.

"Hey, Lacey," a voice called out from the inside the cab. I couldn't make out the face because of the way the sun hung down on the horizon.

"What're you doing driving your brother's truck?"

"He's getting drunk with your brother."

I took a deep breath and slipped the blade back into my pocket.

"We're going to the barbecue."

"Get in. I'll give you a lift."

Lacey got in, taking the center, and I took shotgun. She introduced me to Billy and then added that I was with the carnival.

Billy's face changed expression.

"Really? Is that so?"

"Yes. Why?" I didn't like the way he asked.

"Those carnies are nothing but trouble," he paused, and added, "They don't mix well with us."

"What do you mean, Billy?" asked Lacey.

"They're nothing but low-life scum. Felons. Rapists. Ex-cons. You name it."

"Hub's my friend."

"I wasn't talking about him," and he looked at me and added, "No offense."

"None taken."

Lacey wouldn't let it go. "That's an ignorant thing to say Billy. That isn't like you."

"I guess your brother didn't tell you?"

"About what?"

"He and Donny got jumped by a couple of carnies the other day. Ran them off the road for no reason at all."

It took everything for me not to bust out and tell him that his brother was a lying son-of-a-bitch.

"And the Spic sucker-punched your brother when he wasn't looking and the other guy had a switch blade. I'm telling the truth. Ask your brother."

"I don't like people using those words Billy. It's wrong." Lacey wasn't faking on my account. She was really pissed off. "And you know what, I will ask my brother."

Silence held heavy in the air.

"Billy, mind if I ask you a question?" I asked.

"It's a free country," he replied, annoyed by Lacey's challenge to his story.

"Does it make any sense that a couple of carnies, who know that townspeople hate them, would run a couple of cowboys off the road and try to rob them?"

"Are you calling me a liar?"

"He's not calling you a liar, Billy. He's just asking a really good question."

"I don't like the way he asked me."

"Sorry. I meant no offense."

"None taken," and he seemed to calm down a bit.

"None of us in the truck know what happened, right?" I continued.

"That's true," Lacey answered immediately.

It took Billy a few moments, like it was some sort of trick question and finally said, in a controlled voice, "No, it doesn't."

"The police will figure it out."

Billy was all over it. "That won't happen."

"Why?" Lace asked.

"Because they didn't call the cops."

"Why not?" she asked. She wasn't going to let this die.

Billy's case was falling apart in a big way.

"Because they're not snitches," Billy answered proudly, like that was the end of the story and he'd won. "Plus, Donny said they'd even things their own way."

Lacey squeezed my hand. I knew why. It was an apology of sorts for Billy's ignorance.

We turned down a gravel road that seemed to go on forever. Then we came to a big white sign painted in deep red that said:

**The Felt Family Welcomes all!
To the 14th Annual Rodeo Roundup
Barbecue, Dancing and Music by Dusty and the
Saddle Pickers.**

Billy parked his truck and left to go meet some of his buddies. Lacey grabbed my hand and led me over toward the food. The place was packed and the evening was starting to cool down. There was a slight breeze in the air and it felt welcome. There was a big dance floor, covered by a canvas tent, with lights strung out all over the place. The band was already playing and people were dancing, kids were running around playing tag and folks were milling about talking and laughing. I was probably the only one that wasn't dressed like a cowboy and felt like I stood out like a sore thumb. I had on a black t-shirt, my jeans and biker boots. If I didn't have a crewcut I would have gotten the snot kicked out of me.

"I'm sorry about the ride out," she said, "about Billy."

"Don't worry about it," I said squeezing her hand.

"This is the biggest thing that happens in Evanston," she said, "that is, the biggest thing next to the rodeo and the Christmas Nativity."

"It's a big ranch."

"It is. The Felts own pretty much everything in town. The hardware store, the lumber store, the café I work at. Just about everything."

"Good people?"

"Really good people."

There was a pretty good sized line when we got to the barbecue pits. A cashier was at the head of the line and the moment she spotted her, Lacey ran over and gave her a big hug.

"Darlin' you rode fantastic tonight."

"Thank you, Kaye. You got to see me then?"

"Just got here about an hour ago and I'm covering for Laura while she eats something. We rodeo women have got to stick together." She paused for a moment, noticing me for the first time and realizing I was with Lacey. "Well, who's this handsome young man you got here?"

"His name's Hub. Hub Walker. This is Kaye Johnston and everything I ever learned about barrel racing, I learned from her."

"How do you do, ma'am. It's a pleasure to meet you," I said as polite as I could possibly do and shook her hand.

"Don't go flattering me like that cause it ain't true," and then, confidentially, whispered to me, "Lacey's natural born to barrel racing, young man."

"She sure was something to watch," I said, smiling broadly and looking over at Lacey.

"Hub's with the carnival," Lacey offered and I could feel the temperature change.

"Is that so?" She gave me a look of disapproval like she was telling me I wasn't good enough for Lacey. Well, Lacey, I've got to get back over to the cashbox before someday steals it."

Maybe I was a little too sensitive but I could swear she meant me. Thank God that some of Lacey's girlfriends saw her and came running over to greet and congratulate her. I got lost in the mix. I had no idea how big a big deal her qualifying meant to the town. One of Evanston's own could go on to the nationals. Maybe even win.

I stood off to the side while she visited with everybody that greeted her and when she looked over I motioned that I'd get us a couple of plates of food and she mouthed back, *Thanks.*

I went over to pay for a couple of tickets. I waited my turn and while Lacey visited with her girlfriends. I was fascinated by the cook line. Ranch cooks were flipping burgers and hot dogs on a barbecue made from a 50-gallon drum. *Necessity is the mother of invention,* another one of my grandmother's favorite expressions, and I smiled thinking about her. Behind those cooks was two large smokers where barbecued ribs and chicken were being slathered with barbecue sauce. I was practically drooling when I got up to Ms. Johnston the cashier.

"Two tickets please," I said smiling at her.

"Lacey don't pay tonight, but I'll take your money. Five dollars."

I kinda thought she might acknowledge me but she didn't. I gave her a ten-dollar bill and she handed me a fiver back. When I asked if it would be possible to get five one dollar bills, she asked me what was wrong with a five-dollar bill.

"Nothing," I said, politely. "I just wanted to leave a tip."

"We don't need any tip from your kind," she said curtly and turned to the next customer.

I took the plates and started piling on food for both of us. By the time I got the meat loaded onto the plate, I had a masterpiece of architecture in front of me. I had potato salad in mounds, butter beans holding up the rolls and then finished off with a heap of ribs and chicken that counterbalanced each other.

Lacey came up and poked me in the back.

"Hey," I said, "I'm glad you got here in time. Sorry I didn't get you a plate of food."

"What's the second plate for then?"

"It's an all you can eat, and I can eat all this. You'll have to get your own."

"Seriously?"

"Just kidding." She slugged me in the arm and I handed her the plate.

"There's a quiet little table over there," she said, nodding over by some bales of hay that some older people were sitting on. "That way we can talk a little before it gets too crazy."

That sounded great and I followed her over to the table.

"Did you get any silverware?"

"No, I didn't, but I'll go grab some."

"Okay. I'll grab us something to drink. What do you want?"

"What are you going to have?"

"An ice-cold beer," she said without as much as a second's hesitation. It surprised me because she was clearly not old enough to drink beer.

"The same," and she disappeared over to the bar.

Lacey returned, handed me a cold beer, placed the napkin on her lap and lifted her beer to me.

"Cheers, Hub. How much do I owe you for the dinner?"

"Nothing, Ms. Johnston took care of it for you."

"That was sweet of her. She must have been charmed by you."

"Not at all. In fact, she acted like we hadn't met and wouldn't let me leave a tip for the cooks and staff."

"Really? That doesn't sound like her."

"She probably thought I was one of those carnie rapists or serial killers."

"That's just silly."

"I have a favor to ask."

"Ask away."

"Please don't introduce me as somebody who works for the carnival."

"Hub, I'm sorry."

"No need to apologize. Ms. Johnston was smiling until the the moment you mentioned the carnival. Then everything changed. I could see it in her face."

"And then there was the crap Billy vomited out of his mouth."

"He's just passing on the hate."

"It's unfair."

I changed the subject because I didn't want this night to change directions. It was Lacey's night. "Will you go on the road now that you're a world champion barrel racer?"

"I don't know, Hub, I don't think my parents will let me."

"Seriously? This is a big deal Lacey. I thought they'd be excited for you."

"They are, but it's just that...," she hesitated, "I'm a girl."

"Right. What's that got to do with it?"

"They're afraid of what could happen to me."

"But your brother will be on the circuit too."

"It's different."

"Not in their eyes, Hub."

"But you'll be traveling with other women riders, right? They all travel."

"You're lucky Hub. My parents aren't like yours."

"What do you mean?"

"They let you take off. Join a carnival."

"It wasn't like that. Not the way you think."

"How so?"

"I didn't tell them."

"And you did it anyway."

"Yes."

"But they know where you are now, don't they?"

"No, just my sister."

"They must be worried to death."

"My sister keeps them informed."

"But why wouldn't you just tell them?"

"Because it's complicated. They wouldn't understand."

"Understand what? What made it complicated?"

This was not the way I wanted the conversation to go. If I told Lacey about all the stupid things that brought me to this moment, she'd probably just get up and walk away from me. Not only that, but it would convince her that people like Billy were right. That carnies were nothing but a bunch of misfits and drunkards.

"Cowboys and cowgirls," the leader of Dusty and the Saddlepickers said, "we're going to slow it down a bit and let you catch your breath. Here's a Patsy Cline tune."

"Let's dance," I said.

"Oh, my god," Lacey said, smiling at me, "you willing to give it a try?"

"It's crazy but I'm willing to give it a try." I stood up and offered my hand to Lacey.

"I'd be honored, Hub."

The dance floor was crowded but we managed to find a corner spot and I put my arms around her and began with my best slow turning in a circle. Lacey giggled.

"Is it that bad?" I asked, unsure of myself.

"It actually feels good. I think I like this."

"Me, too."

They did three slow tunes and we never left the dance floor. Just when I was starting to gain some confidence in my two left feet, the fourth tune was full-country. I started to lead Lacey off the dancefloor but she didn't move.

"Now it's my turn to lead."

"I don't think so. I mean, you'd be taking your life into my own hands."

"I'll risk it," she said. "We'll start slowly. Just follow me."

"You sure?"

"I am."

The first few numbers I was glad Lacey had on cowboy boots or I probably would have broken every bone in her feet. She showed me these really cool moves where I'd spin her around and then slide into an embrace and this sort of pretzel twisty thing where we'd have our hands together and then we'd go up and spin under each other's arms. By the end of the night, led by Lacey, I felt almost competent. We finished out the night with a final slow dance and at the end she gave me a big kiss. I'm not talking about a little peck on the cheek but a full-on kiss. The kind of kiss that makes you dizzy. The kind of kiss that makes you want to confess all your sins.

It was getting pretty late and people started drifting away to the pasture to get into their trucks and head out.

"Well," I sighed, "I don't want this night to end but it's a long walk back to the carnival."

"You can't walk that, Hub, and neither can I. We'll just get a ride back with somebody. I'll be right back."

Lacey took off to find us a ride and I kinda just stood there thinking about the whole wonderful evening. I felt something deep for her and I knew it was crazy, particularly since I hadn't even known her 48 hours. But who makes up the rules? You feel what you feel and react to it in ways that surprise yourself.

There was something so grounded about Lacey. She came from the earth and lived on and off the land. I didn't live that way and neither did anybody I knew. Somebody like Lacey would have a hard time understanding the girls at Pershing. There were the stupid games they played, we played. Other people decided who you should hang out with and what you were supposed to wear and what clique to belong to. Maybe they did that at her school too. Maybe it was a universal thing and part of growing up, but maybe, with her it was just different.

"Hub," she called out. "We got a ride. Come on, hurry up."

I ran to her and she grabbed my hand and we ran off to the parking lot. There was a moment where it crossed my mind that maybe the ride back was with her brother or his assassin, Donny. But it was stupid.

"Hey, this is Hub," Lacey said to a couple of girls and the guy that I'd gotten a ride with heading into town.

"We already met, at the carnival. He gave us all free rides."

"Now, I know who spilled the beans about when I was riding," Lacey said laughing.

And the girl that had told me when Lacey was riding started laughing.

"It was a good thing wasn't it," she said to Lacey and she just nodded her head.

The young kid, and to this day, I don't think I ever got his name, asked us if we wouldn't mind riding in the back since he had a full load in the front.

"Not at all," we said in unison and then climbed up onto the truck.

It was slow getting off the ranch because we were all leaving at the same time and it gave us a little time to visit.

"When do you take off, Hub?"

"We finish up and take it all down tomorrow and then take off the next day."

"Where's the next stop?"

"Rawlins. Then Casper, and Cheyenne. Cheyenne is the big one for us."

"After that?"

"We drop down to Colorado. Fort Collins, Denver and some other places I forgot."

"Am I going to see you again. Is tonight the last night?"

"I hope not." Honestly, I really didn't know what to say to Lacey. "If your parents won't let you go, then I guess it might be."

"Maybe I'll just run away like you did," she said snuggling up to me.

"It's not a good way to leave, Lacey. Trust me."

"But my parents are pretty firm about it."

"Then you've got to make your case. Build a strong case about your talent and how this is one of most important things in your life. You've got to find out for yourself how good you are. If you don't, Lacey, you'll always regret it."

She was quiet and then said, "How did you get so smart?"

"Trust me, I'm not. I've made about every mistake one can make in their life."

Then Lacey kissed me again and we pretty much made-out until we pulled into the fairground parking lot. I felt like I'd worn my lips out and I'd be happy to do it all over again.

We walked into the stable so Lacey could see how Little Britches was doing.

"Will I see you tomorrow, Hub?"

"I don't know. It takes a full day to tear things down and then we take off."

"I don't want this to end. I love being with you."

"Me too."

"Does it mean if I want to see you again, I'll have to run away with the rodeo?"

I wanted to tell Lacey to run away. I wanted to be able to see her, to hangout with her, to be her boyfriend, but I knew the sort of pain and self-doubt that came with such an action. In her mind, I ran away because I was brave and wanted to chart my own course...to hit the open road. It was a romantic notion, the idea of making your own way in the world against the odds. But what I'd done was anything but that and I needed to tell her so. I ran away because I was afraid and desperate. I ran away because I was a coward and put my family in the spotlight in the worst way. And, I'd burned all my bridges.

"When you do something like that, you can never go home."

"Who said that?"

"My sister. It was one of the last things she said before I left."

"It doesn't make sense, Hub. Of course you can."

"It was from a book. I think I get what she meant."

"You lost me."

"Literally, we can go back home, but we're never really the same."

Lacey thought it over carefully but didn't say anything. She grabbed a horse blanket and looked over at me.

"Do you need help putting it over Little Britches."

"It's not for Little Britches," she said smiling. "It's for us. Follow me." And I did.

Chapter 24

By the time I dragged my ass back to the carnival the next morning, people were starting to mill about. Jesus was breaking down his gear and I felt pretty sheepish dragging in so late. He smiled at me and before he said anything, he offered me a smoke.

"Thanks," I said taking one from his pack and lighting it.

"Good time last night?"

"Yes," I replied, taking a drag.

"No problems with any cowboys?"

"None, really. Actually, barring a couple of smart ass comments, I had a great time. I went to the barbecue and dance."

"With the rodeo gal?"

"Yes."

"Get any?" he asked laughing.

"It's not..."

"Hub, I'm just kidding. None of my business."

Jesus broke things down for me on how the last day went. The day before we moved out, Angel and some of the other ladies in the carnival made a big breakfast for the crew. The works. Pancakes, eggs, sausage, pots of coffee and homemade biscuits. Then it was all about getting the carnival down, broken up and packed and then we'd hit the road early in the morning.

"I should have come back earlier last night. I'm sorry."

"Don't worry about it. But Wacko came looking for you and he seemed pretty upset."

"Shit."

"I'd stay clear of him if I were you."

All I could think of was Frenchy, Big Heavy and Jesus's warning about showing any interest in Angel or Wacko would kill me or worse. In that category I'd failed miserably. Wacko didn't seem like the kind of boss that would let me explain how I'd ended up bumping into her, complimenting her and then peeking in on her when she was undressing in the trailer. I needed to go over and just tell him I was quitting and head out immediately.

"I think I'll go tell him I quit," I told Jesus, straightening up and brushing some hay off my shirt.

Jesus busted up laughing. "I was just screwing with you. Wacko's gone. He's never here on the last day."

"Why's that?"

"He's a 24-hour man."

"Meaning?"

"A 24-hour man is the guy who leaves a day early and gets to the next town to make sure everything's ready for us. Permits and stuff like that."

At first I was annoyed with Jesus, but then started laughing because he'd gooned me royally.

"Let's grab some breakfast and get to work. It's going to be a long day."

"Deal."

The grub looked great and I was starved. Jesus and I grabbed our plates and loaded up. Angel was at the end of the line pouring coffee for everybody.

"Morning, Jesus. Morning, Hub."

"Morning, ma'am," I replied and Jesus actually responded to her by calling her Angel.

We found a spot at the same table with Frenchy and Big Heavy and a rather mysterious looking woman. I guessed it to be Zola, our resident fortune teller. There wasn't much conversation going on. This was the only free meal you got with the carnival so the carnies were shoving it in before things started getting cleaned up.

Between bites, Jesus talked to me about what I'd probably be doing. "We'll get the octopus broken down first. It'll take about 2-3 hours to get it done right and then we'll split up and help whoever needs it. Okay?"

"Okay."

"I'll put you with one of the more experienced carnies. Maybe Big Heavy or Frenchy. That way you won't get hurt."

I checked to see if he's was kidding me or not but he didn't seem to be.

"Okay."

"And when we're all done, you'll get baptized tonight."

"Pardon?"

"It's a ritual."

"Ritual? So, I'm going to be sacrificed to the carnie gods?"

"Worse. We drink Panther Piss, and we'll give you your handle."

"Handle?"

"Nickname."

"Right. I can't wait."

I knew he was joking. Carrying on because I'd fallen so easily for the Wacko thing and I was drag-ass tired.

We scraped off our plates although they didn't need it and headed back to break down the Octopus.

"Start with the chairs and stack them up over here. I've got to grab a flatbed over here and then, once it's broken down, we'll grab a couple of guys to help us get the heavy stuff loaded up."

"Okay."

Jesus took off to do some other stuff and I got to work. By the time he got back, I was dripping in sweat. Mid-early morning I guessed it was already over 80 degrees. He had me direct him as he backed up the flatbed until it was almost on top of the diesel engine.

Then we worked together dismantling the Octopus. Jesus was meticulous in his approach and things had to go a certain way because all of the machinery and the ticket booth and protective fencing had to fit into a space that looked impossible. I thought of a picture I once saw in *Life* magazine where a bunch of college students, maybe 20 of them, managed to squeeze into a telephone booth. It took us the better part of three hours to finish up. Both of us shined with perspiration. The salt from my sweat kept running into my eyes and, while we had a hard-boiled egg and some jerky for lunch, he went over to his pick-up and brought out a blue bandana for me that he rolled up like the ones you see Hell's Angeles wear and tied it around my forehead.

"This should help a bit," he said, chewing on some jerky while he talked to me.

"Thanks, man. I appreciate it."

"It's yours. Don't forget to drink water or you'll pass out."

"Right."

"Let's take a 10-minute break and then I'll take you over to help Frenchy. That okay with you?"

"Sure," I said acting like it was a good idea. I didn't know whether it was or wasn't a good idea. I wanted to ask Jesus if it would be okay if I just worked with him but I didn't want to be a wimp so, once we cooled off, we walked over to the Ferris wheel.

"Frenchy, we're done. Hub volunteered to give you a hand."

"I could use one. Thanks, Jesus"

"Ever seen one of these put up before or taken down?" he asked me.

"I built one with an erector set when I was little if that counts."

"It's pretty much the same thing only it's bigger and if you don't pay attention it can kill you."

Another carnie joined us.

"Nuts, this is Hub. Let's make sure he don't lose any body parts."

We shook hands and then Frenchy put us to work. For all his gruffness, Frenchy was a good teacher. While we worked, by his order, he schooled both of us on all the parts. *Towers, spokes,* the chairs which he called *gondolas, the booms, arms the elephant ears,* and *guide wires.* And you didn't just take one gondola off and then the next. Everything we did at the bottom we'd then would do at the top to keep the Ferris wheel in balance. The engineering of it all, the mechanics and physics of it, surprised me. It was slow and laborious work.

Another carnie joined us. His name was Bumpy and I'd actually met him the first day. He told me not to ask how he got his carnie name so I didn't. Pretty soon we had another couple of guys join us and Big Heavy came over to help with a couple of his guys. It was clear Big Heavy and Frenchy had done this dance forever. We'd just finished taking the last gondola off and Big Heavy had us boost them up onto the flatbed and a couple of his guys stacked them in the cage. I don't know about the other guys but my muscles were starting to strain. Every piece we disassembled felt like it weighed a ton but slowly the Ferris wheel started becoming a skeleton of itself.

"Boys," Frenchy bellowed, "doin' good. Only an hour more and we'll be done. Tonight, Panther Piss. Got an initiation tonight." He looked over at me.

It made me proud to hear I was going to be initiated. I dug deeper, pushed myself, tried to put the strain against my puny body out of mind and stayed focused.

"I've heard that before," Bumpy grumbled. "Probably more like three. The Frenchman can't tell time worth shit."

In between directions Frenchy gave us the history of the Ferris wheel. "The first Ferris was made out of wood and the one we know now first appeared in the 1893 Chicago World's Fair. Designed by none other than

George Washington Ferris himself."

"He's so full of shit," Bumpy whispered.

I don't know what his problem was with Frenchy, if they had bad blood between them, but Frenchy didn't seem to me like a guy you'd want to cross. The moment I got a chance to switch partners, I did.

I once saw a short trailer done in black and white by Kodak where they did an accelerated time release film about a circus throwing up a big top. I kind of thought it might be cool to do one on the carnival because every chance I got to look around the midway something else was coming down. The canvas for the Freak Show, that only moments earlier was untouched, had disappeared. A couple of smaller tents along the midway that housed carnival games like the Planko, Balloon & Darts, Ball and Basket, Baseball and Bottles, and Ring Toss vanished. Wacko's City of Fun Carnival was disappearing.

It took us about four hours to finish dismantling the Ferris wheel and the only thing I wanted to do was crawl into my sleeping bag and sleep for a month. Heading back to Jesus's truck I noticed the only ride not taken down was the Kiddie Boats, the spot where we'd go to dunk in the water and clean up. The flatbeds were loaded, pickup trucks hitched-up and it looked more like we were just arriving than departing early in the morning.

Jesus was putting on a clean t-shirt and Levis and nodded at me.

"How you doing?"

"Man, I'm flat-ass worn out."

"You did well today, Hub. People noticed."

"Thanks. Going to do a quick wash and take a quick nap."

"Then what?"

"Meet Lacey at the fairgrounds for a little bit before we take off."

"Not without taking some Panther Piss with everybody."

"You were serious about that?"

"Yeah, and it's part of your initiation. Have a few and then head out."

"I'm pretty set on seeing Lacey."

"Sure."

"And what's Panther Piss?"

"It's a ritual. First successful week in a new town. Everybody meets over by the caravans and we mix up a batch of Heinz 57. Whatever you've got to drink, we pour it into a big plastic garbage can, throw some ice into it, stir it up and drink it."

"It sounds horrible."

"It is. That's the point. They've been doing it ever since the carnival's been around."

"I think I might pass on it," I said, knowing that I didn't have any booze to contribute.

"You've got to. It's your first week on the job and it wouldn't look good if people thought you were too good for them."

"I don't have any booze," I added sheepishly.

"I've got you covered, Hub. Got a bottle of Everclear so there's no excuse."

After I freshened up, we headed over to the party. It was going strong and I was surprised how many people were actually part of the carnival.

"All these people work here?"

"For the most part. Let's pour the bottle into the piss and I'll introduce you to the carnies."

"Sounds good."

By the time we got to the garbage can it was already ¾ full and people were smiling and laughing. Frenchy and Big Heavy seemed to be the guardians of the Panther Piss.

"Hey, kid," Frenchy said in his thick accent, "we didn't kill you today."

"You came pretty close," I said grinning.

"The kid is a hard worker, Jesus, he done good."

Big Heavy nodded in agreement and then handed us each a paper cup full of Panther Piss. Jesus threw his down in a couple of glugs, but when I took the first glug I thought I was going to puke. It would be hard to describe the taste but it was kind of like Nehi grape soda and rocket fuel. Not that I'd ever tried rocket fuel but it really had a powerful kick to it so I kind of just sipped the first one.

Jesus introduced me to a bunch of people as they came up to get some Piss and every single one of them welcomed me with a toast. I had to fake taking a big glug because I'd get really drunk and I didn't want that to happen. I wanted to get over and see Lacey before we took off. I'd promised her.

As I kept getting introduced to some of the workers, the Panther Piss got easier to drink and went down much smoother.

The older woman I saw at breakfast came walking over to the party. She seemed somehow important. I don't know, but the carnies quieted down a bit when she appeared. It was subtle, or maybe I was just imagining things, but when she came over to the Panther Piss folks just moved aside.

Frenchy and Big Heavy were very polite as they poured her a cupful. She had long, jet-black hair pulled back to the side off her shoulder and she wore a beautiful silk scarf around her head. Instead of Levis like we all wore, she wore a billowy black skirt, a crisp white shirt with puffy sleeves, and a jacket vest plus a number of gold necklaces with foreign coins and pearls, nothing like I'd ever seen in any store I'd ever been in. The pockets of her vest were studded in copper rivets and on both wrists she wore a ton of different gold and silver bracelets. Her ears were pierced with interesting studs like a feathers, crosses, skulls, broken hearts and big gold loops and she had a number of scarves were wrapped around her waist.

I kind of knew she would be there. I'd seen her walking around the midway late at night. but I asked Jesus who she was and what she really did. He kept a close eye on her when he answered.

"That's Zola. Queen of the Future."

"I figured that out earlier but what does she actually do?"

"She reads people's palms, tarot cards and predicts the future. She's got a following. People swear by her."

"Has she read yours?"

"No."

"Why?"

"I don't believe in that sort of shit."

When he finished his sentence, Zola turned her head and looked directly at him like she'd heard him talking about her. She fixed her gaze on Jesus.

I noticed her eyes for the first time. They were two distinctly different colors. One was bright, deep aqua blue and the other was a deep emerald green. It sort of unnerved me like they came from a different world.

Mysterious.

Then she headed over to where we were standing and I could feel Jesus tighten. I couldn't have moved if I'd wanted to. Our eyes were locked on to each other.

"Jesus," she said in a curiously deep accent, "who is this young man?"

"Hub," he said nervously, "he just started working for us."

"Welcome, Hub," she said, clasping my forearm arm in hers, like I'd seen knights do in movies like, *Robin Hood and His Merry Men.* "I'm Zola."

I need to say this. I'd had a couple of full cups of Panther Piss. More than I should have but when she clasped my forearm I felt a surge of something transfer into me. Like a force. Like electricity and it was warm and safe.

"A pleasure meeting you."

"Hub. An interesting name but you are also someone else," she smiled a knowing smile, like she was keeping somebody's secret and they knew it. "Aren't you?"

"Aren't we all?" I replied not really thinking before answering.

She laughed but did not let hold of her grip. "You are a curious young

man, Hub. Very curious and we will get to know each other." Then, she let go
and I felt the energy go with her. She turned and walked off into the night.

"Hub...what the hell do you think you're doing?" Jesus asked. He sounded
angry.

"Nothing. Being polite," I answered defensively, "introducing myself.
Looking people in the eye when I'm spoken to. That's all."

"You do not want to get involved with Zola. Period."

"Why?"

"She's a gypsy. A real gypsy and she can see shit about your future."

"Okay, but it sounds sort of interesting."

"Don't be stupid. I'm not kidding, Hub."

"What's the worst thing that could happen?"

"She could put you under a spell or something."

I started to laugh, "You mean like a wicked witch or something?"

"I'm not kidding here." Jesus was getting worked up. "Some of the guys
have had her read their futures."

"And?"

"She told them things about themselves that NOBODY could have
known!"

"Okay, I'll be careful. Sorry, I didn't mean to make light of it."

"You noticed the tattooed tears under her eyes?"

"I did. Three of them. What's that all about?"

"Remember the skinny guy you first worked with?"

"The guy who works as a butcher?"

"Right. He spent time in the pen for manslaughter."

"Okay."

"I asked him about the tears. He said they were either for people she's
killed or for members of her family that might have been murdered."

"No shit."

"No shit and that's why I stay away from her. She's got black magic."

I had another Panther Piss and the night really got hopping. A couple of the guys broke out guitars and started playing. Boils, one of the older guys with the carnival, busted out his accordion and started playing some zydeco music and Frenchy who was pretty lit up on the Panther Piss, started dancing *The Bogalusa Shuffle* and I've got to admit, even with his big lumbering frame he was light on his feet. Dust was kicking up all around and then he grabbed me and Darnelle, the young girl who managed the concession stands, and a couple of other people and taught us the steps. It was kind of like a line dance and pretty soon there were about 10 or 20 of us crazy dancing and everybody was laughing up a storm.

When the dance stopped, the Zakas twins started doing a Greek dance where they held bandanas in their hands, did a step where they dropped to one knee, jumped back up and yelled, "Oooopla!" Soon a circle of people were dancing around doing the same thing and I was right there in the mix with all of them.

Then Jesus and a couple of the other Mexican carnies did this dance with some of the women carnies that was way out there. I had another cup of Panther and watched while they danced. First the men did this sort of struttin' with their hands clasped behind their backs and they'd come out and circle around the women and back off and then the women would respond to the men. You had to see it to believe it. It was like their bodies were telling a story of love or courtship or something. It was one of most spectacular nights of celebration I'd ever seen.

I was sweating like a pig, so I went back for another cup of Panther and it seemed like we hadn't made a dent in the garbage can. While I was waiting my turn, Juan Carlos offered me some tequila or something that looked like it. It had a worm at the bottom of the bottle and when I told him that he laughed and explained how they put a worm in the bottle to show people that if they drank the stuff they'd never get worms.

Jesus came over and I told him how cool the dance was and he started laughing.

"What's so funny?" I asked.

"What language are you speaking?"

"Huh?"

"You're slurring your words."

And I got to laughing because I was feeling so good. I was going to say, *'No I'm not!'* but it came out sounding like, *'Numb nut.'* Then we all got busted up and I was in tears I was laughing so hard.

Somebody suggested taking the Kiddie Boats out of the water and going for a swim and the next thing I knew, the boats were all beached and people started getting down to their underwear even the girls. Crenshaw told us to grab onto heavy metal bars that hooked onto the back of the boats and he'd give us a ride. All of us in the water grabbed a spot and sure as hell, ole Crenshaw did just that...he fired up the ride and we started off going round and round and round.

The water felt great after a long day in the sun and I couldn't believe how much I felt like I was part of this crazy family.

Every time we'd come around to the gate, somebody would shove a bottle of something or other in your hand and you had to take a drink. Jesus was standing there, his shirt off and doing a play by play commentary. Kind of like an announcer at the horse races.

"Yes, Ladies and Gentlemen, it's a fine night for the boat races at the Wacko City of Fun Carnival....." He held the tequila bottle up to his lips like a microphone. "And they are off!!!! Underwear is falling behind and Hub and Darnelle are neck and neck."

He was really funny and he was bringing down the house. Everybody started hooting and hollering at me and Darnelle so we looped around for a second pass, she looked over at me and said, "Hub, let's give them something to hoot about!" and as we came around she planted a wide-open kiss on me, tongue and all. It was completely out of the dark and I accidentally let go. Next thing I knew people were crashing into me and rolling over each other. Pretty soon it was a big mess of tumbling bodies that broke into a water fight.

I tried to get out of the Kiddie Boat ride but kind of flipped ass-over-tea-kettle onto the dirt. It looked like I'd been rolled in bread crumbs. When I tried to stand up I knew I was in trouble. My legs were acting independent of each other and I didn't have a helluvalot of control over them. I started laughing. I tilted my head back to look up at the moon then held my hands out to the side of me and starting twisting in a circle. It was like a ride on the Crack-the-Whip.

Then everything went black.

Chapter 25

"Hub. Hub. You need to wake up. It's time to go."

The voice was light and it seemed like it drifted in from some floaty place. Maybe Lacey.

"Hub, honey, it's time to leave."

I tried connecting memory to voice and then I realized I was sleeping in a bed. Somewhere. Maybe at Lacey's but my head was thumping and I was having trouble pulling myself together. The *who, what, when where of it* was completely absent. I was cognizant enough to raise my right arm up in the air, like *don't give the 10 count.*

"I'm trying," I mumbled into the pillow.

"I washed your clothes and I've got a cup of coffee you can take with you, but you have to go. Jesus and I are always the last ones to leave."

Angel! *Holy Mary, Mother of God, pray for us sinners now and at the hour of our death. Amen.* How the hell could this have....???

I shot straight up and tried to focus. Everything still seemed lop-sided and I must have been hallucinating because I was in Wacko and Angel's queen sized bed with nothing on. No! No! No! Please no!!! And I was naked. I had nothing on but a bed-sheet wrapped around me.

"Hub," Angel said quietly, knocking on the side of the door before she walked in. "The caravan took off about an hour ago. But you need to leave and go find Jesus."

"Angel, I'm so sorry. How did I get here?"

"It's a long story, but it's time to go."

I must have looked terrified because she added, "Nobody knows and I want to keep it that way."

"Me too!"

"Jesus has been waiting around for you. He wasn't going to leave until he found you."

"Has he been here looking for me?"

"He was headed over this way and I cut him off. Told him I hadn't seen you."

"What did he say?""

"'Son-of-a-bitch. The fairground!' And then he took off looking for you."

"How'd he seem?"

"Not happy. Why do you suppose he went to the fairground?"

"I have no idea," I lied.

"Get dressed. Here are four aspirin and a glass of water. You're going to need these."

"Thanks."

She left the trailer and I could hear her fire up the truck and back it up to the hitch. I quickly tried to get dressed and was climbing into my underwear when the trailer shook as the hitch engaged. I fell over with one leg in and the other partially in. *What a pitiful excuse for a human being!* How could anybody so completely screw things up? I was going to be killed by Wacko and they would never find my body parts. That wasn't fair to my parents, wondering what had happened to their miscreant son, and it would destroy my brother and sister. I started to get teary-eyed so I slapped myself in the face.

Forget the fact I woke-up in Wacko's bed, because that was instantaneous death. No trial. No plea bargain. And if Angel didn't say anything, I'd already learned that the carnies saw everything. Particularly, Frenchy and Big Heavy, not to mention Zola our fortune-teller. And who else might have seen me?

Jesus, Hub? Huh? The guy who kept you from getting beaten to death! The same guy who watched over you since you got here? A great friend you are, Hub?

Did you leave anybody out, Hub?

Lacey!

Lacey. Beautiful Lacey!

Breath taking Lacey!

In my own defense I told her I probably couldn't meet her at the barn because of work. But you knew. Deep down in your black little heart you knew she'd go there. *Sure as rain.* And that's why Jesus was headed there. To bail your ass out one more time.

And SEX!!!

What about SEX?

What If I had SEX with Angel? This was the *Wacko will kill you, or worse!!!* part of the equation. It would be a slow death. What if he brought me back to life and killed me multiple times?

I paused before opening the trailer door to see if I could see Jesus anywhere. Just as I started to open it, Angel opened it and damn near scared me to death.

"I'm so sorry about all of this. I'm am so embarrassed, and ashamed..."

"Hub, go find Jesus," she said sternly, like she didn't have enough of my blather already. "I think he's really angry at you. I'll see you at the next stop."

"Okay," I said sheepishly.

With that, Angel jerked the chalk blocks out from under the trailer tires, threw them in the back of the rig and drove off. I watched her drive off. It was so quiet that it seemed impossible that only a day ago, this place ever was alive in the way it was.

I hurried over to Jesus' truck. At least I could pack my kit together so if he gave the boot I could get back on the road and head off to the coast and then, if I couldn't find anything, up to Alaska to sign up on a fishing boat.

My gear was packed-up neatly and in the back of the truck. Jesus would be at least an hour late now because of me. I just stood there waiting for the wrath of Jesus to fall down on me. I felt lucky to be vertical and I just waited for Jesus in the hot sun. My head felt like it was splitting in half and I had such cottonmouth I couldn't spit if I wanted to. Then I saw Jesus coming over the hill.

As he got closer I braced myself for a solid blow to the face.

"Jesus," I began, "I'm so very..."

"Shut the fuck up and get into the truck. We're late."

"It's all my fault, I just wanted to say..."

"Hub, I'm serious. Keep your mouth shut. I don't want to hear it. Get in the goddamn truck!"

I walked around the back of the truck just to keep my distance from Jesus. He fired up the truck and peeled out, leaving a billowing cloud of dust. Once we got onto the highway, he goosed it and we roared out of Evanston. At this speed, I suspected we'd catch up to the other rigs in no time but we had a great deal of road ahead of us. It was going to be a long, quiet and angry drive.

I found myself having a hard time keeping my eyes open. I could feel myself start to nod off. Just as my eyes started to close my head would slump forward and Jesus would intentionally swerve the pickup so I'd jerk awake. Just enough to let me know that I wasn't going to sleep while he drove.

I could only imagine what was going through Jesus' mind. Certainly, disappointment, the burden of me and betrayal. I understood that and felt at a complete loss of what to say to put things back the way they were. That was probably a good thing because I was in bad shape and I knew whatever I said wouldn't make a helluva lot of sense. I settled for silence.

An hour passed in silence and then another and my mind wandered all over the place; to home, Soup and Sparky, Smitty, school, how I got here, my future whatever that might be and then to Angel and Lacey, to action and consequence. Then, Jesus slowed down, signaled and slowly pulled off the side of the road. He got out, slammed the door and walked to the Eskimo cooler, opened it and pulled out two ice-cold Dr. Peppers. He got back into the truck, told me to hand him the church key in the glove compartment and flipped off the bottle caps and handed me one. He pulled back onto the highway, took a big guzzle of Dr. Pepper and nodded to me to do the same.

For a moment, I studied the bottle, with its logo that read, *Dr.Pepper, 10, 2, 4* on the outside. Ice-cold beads of sweat slowly slid down the bottle and I rubbed it across my brow. I remember the first time I ever had a Dr. Pepper. It was on a trip my sister and I took with our dad through the great battle fields of the Civil War. The old man was a history buff and he dragged us along after my mom had given birth to Sparky. We'd stopped at a gas station and while the old man had a cigarette and watched the attendant fill up the tank, clean windows and check the oil he told us to go get three Dr. Peppers from the cooler. We both stared at each other before wandering over, lifting the top of an ice cooler and finding Coke, Dr. Pepper and 7-Up.

"Dad," my sister said, "they've got Coke and 7-Up too. Can we get one of those instead?"

"Nope," my father replied, grounding out his cigarette with his shoe. "It's Dr. Pepper or nothing at all. Your choice."

"You want one?" Soup whispered to me.

"You think it's safe?"

"Think dad would poison us?"

"No."

"It's cold. Let's get one," she replied.

My sister let me pop them open on the bottle opener and we kept the bottle caps as souvenirs. After paying the attendant for the gas and the Dr. Peppers, my dad had the attendant throw in some pork rinds for snacks.

"Fort Sumter, here we come," bellowed dad. "That's where it all began, kids!"

"Let him drink first."

Our father took a long swig from the Dr. Pepper and he didn't die. "Oh, my God," he exclaimed, "even better than I remember!"

He took another glug, reached down and tore open the package of pork rinds with his teeth, shook out a few into his mouth and passed the bag back to us.

"When did you drink Dr. Pepper?" my sister, always the inquisitive one asked.

"Officer training, during World War II. Right here in South Carolina." While my dad talked about his training, my sister kept interrupting him with questions. What most fascinated me was my dad's Adam's apple. While he drank his Dr. Pepper, I watched it move up and down as he swallowed.

"What does the 10, 2, 4 mean on the bottle?"

"Good question. Great question," he replied. "There's some science behind the numbers. Our blood sugar lowers during those points in the day. So, the people in advertising at Dr. Pepper built that into the brand."

"Was the guy who invented Dr. Pepper a real doctor? Is it named after him?"

"Nope," he wasn't. "His name was Charles something and he named the product after the first girl that he loved who got away."

"That's pretty romantic," Soup said taking a slug of Dr. Pepper and following it with a pork rind.

Jesus finally broke the silence and it was none too soon.

"Always wondered what the 10, 2, 4 meant on the bottle. Do you know?"

"No. Always wondered myself."

It didn't behoove me to show off right now. That's not what I wanted to say to Jesus. I wanted to talk to him. Set the record straight so we could start off clean when we hit Rawlins. It went silent again. We caught up to the caravan and followed behind Angel's trailer.

"Jesus," I said tentatively, "I'm going to talk whether you want me to or not. I need to set some things straight between us or it's going to be a long difficult summer for us."

I waited for his response. If he agreed, I'd tell him everything with the exception of waking up in Wacko's bed. What he said next absolutely blew me away.

"I'm sorry, Hub, about last night."

I didn't know how to respond. How could *he* be sorry. He had nothing to do with my stupidity. Nothing.

"I'm truly sorry." He lit a cigarette for both of us and passed one to me.

"I'm the one that screwed up, not you."

"But I should have been looking out for you. Particularly since I was the one that encouraged you to drink Panther Piss."

"I didn't have to drink it. I did it on my own. That's not on you."

"I knew better than that. We all goaded you into it."

"You guys didn't tie me down and force me to drink Panther Piss."

"In a way we did and I think I was pissed at you this morning because I was pissed at myself."

"It won't happen again."

I was dazed. Jesus was the real deal. He didn't have to say that. And having him apologize to me made me feel like shit. After a while driving in silence again, I finally told him my story.

I told him about everything. I told him about stealing the police car and the chase. I told him about my sister giving me all her money and Smitty letting me sleep in the coffin, about how I cut my hair to change my look, about Lindsey, about the warrant that was certainly posted for my arrest.

Jesus, whistled. "How much do you think you're worth if I turn you in?" His tone was just serious enough to make me wonder if this had been a mistake.

"About $50," I replied.

"Not nearly enough for a gangster like you," and he began laughing and punched me lightly on the shoulder.

When I told him about the dance and Billy's version of the fight he got a scowl on his face. I told him about the entire night including the fact that Lacey's brother was the small cowboy he'd knocked on his ass. He didn't say anything until I mentioned the tension I felt when Lacey'd introduced me as a carnie worker and how people reacted differently after that. I made it a point to let him know that Lacey had stood up to Billy when he said we were ex-cons, child molesters and everything else. And I emphasized the fact that Lacey had called Billy ignorant when he'd called Jesus a spic. Probably more than anything, I wanted him to understand that she wasn't like them...most of the townspeople. Then he said something that made me realize how different our two lives were.

"What do you think would have happened if those two clowns went to the cops with that bullshit story?"

"I think the cops would get it. I mean I had witnesses, including the kid who picked me up and took me into town who would vouch for the fact I was by myself and that those dickheads were going kick the shit out of me before you came along."

"It would be their word against yours, Hub. And they weren't witnesses."

"But they could testify those cowboys were bums."

"So you think justice would be served?"

"Yes," I answered feeling like it was a loaded question. "Plus, you have a witness, Frenchy, that would testify he'd sent you in to town to get some parts, right?

"Equal justice for all, Hub? The truth triumphs over evil? And the scales of justice are without prejudice? You're naïve, Hub. You can't help it, but you are."

"Why would you say something like that?"

"There is a built-in gullibility because you're white."

"Bullshit. Being white has nothing to do with it," I protested.

"No offense, Hub, but it has everything to do with it."

"Justice for you is the same for me."

"Hub, you mean to tell me that if we'd gone to the cops you really think that they'd believe us over the two shit-kickers?"

I was less sure when Jesus put it like that.

"I'll frame it differently. It sounds like a bad joke, but it goes like this: two local cowboys walk into the courthouse and accuse two carnies of trying to run them off the road and attempt to rob, rape, and beat them to death. So, the carnies," and Jesus paused for effect, "that would be you and me, present their case with witnesses to prove their absolute innocence. And do you know what happens?"

I shrugged my shoulders.

"The judge takes all the testimony into account. He weighs the evidence presented in the case and then pronounces his verdict. He calls the court to attention and says one word. And do you know what that word is?"

Jesus was leading the witness. He was walking me down a well-constructed maze and I didn't want to play. This is where justice and reality collided.

"Innocent?" I offered.

"Guilty!" Jesus barked. "And you know it, don't you? You've felt it, Hub."

There wasn't much I could truly say because Jesus was probably right. No, in fact, he was right.

"And here's the kicker, Hub. You'd get off on probation and do you know what would happen to me?"

"The same."

"You don't believe that. I'd get gone. I'd disappear and nobody would care."

"That's bullshit, Jesus."

"Really, Hub. Justice isn't blind. Maybe for whites it is. But not for me. Not for my family or the other forty thousand migrant workers that are taken advantage every single fucking day. And, if something happens in that world and it's clearly intentional there is no recourse. Period."

"It'll change, Jesus."

"You're dreaming. You may believe that because it's much tidier that way. But it's not the truth. Deep down you know it."

Jesus lit another cigarette but I passed this time. For a while it was quiet in the cab and I welcomed the silence. I couldn't argue with Jesus because I'd never been in his circumstance and being white offered me privilege without question. We passed a sign stating we were still about 100 miles out of Rawlins.

"I've got to get some gas at the next station, and that'll give us a chance to stretch our legs."

"How's this work? Can I chip in on the gas, Jesus."

"No need. I keep my receipts and Wacko squares up with me on payday."

"Oh."

"But I'll let you grab us some chips and something to drink, okay?"

"Okay."

"Go ahead and close your eyes for a while. I know you're hung over and I'm okay driving."

"You sure?"

"Yeah, and I won't run off the road."

"Thanks."

I nodded off in a few seconds. I don't know how much time passed before I bolted awake. I was a bit confused for a moment on where I was and I was perspiring.

"You okay?"

"Yeah, why?"

"You were mumbling in your sleep."

"I don't remember dreaming about anything."

Jesus seemed to mulling something over because I felt he wanted to say something.

"Got something bothering you?"

"Sort of and I've been weighing whether I'd tell you or not."

"You don't have to tell me if you don't want to, Jesus."

"And you shared a bunch of really personal stuff with me earlier that you didn't have to share."

"Yeah, but I did. I owed it to you."

"I feel the same way, Hub."

"Okay."

"Ever heard of a man named Cesar Chavez?"

"I don't think so," I said racking my brain.

"He's an organizer. Goes around the country, the migrant trail, and talks about forming a union to protect the pickers, get them better conditions and that sort of thing."

"I'll bet he's popular with the owners."

"Not at all. He gets run off a lot. Anyway, we were picking grapes when he came into our camp at the end of a long hot day. Everybody knew who he was. And he started talking about the working conditions, the dangers of picking when they were spraying DDT all over us and other things dealing with housing, fair pay and providing sanitary living conditions."

"Preaching to the choir."

"True, but in this case, he was one of us so we all listened. And my father, a proud man, one of the leaders in our camp spoke and told him about the deplorable conditions. My mother kept trying to get him to keep his mouth shut. But he didn't. He wasn't that kind of man."

"Like father, like son."

"I was nothing like my father. He was in a league of his own." Jesus paused for a moment before continuing. "The way it works in these camps is like this. The owner hires one of us, an overseer who's supposed to keep things under control. He makes more than the pickers, gets privileges like housing and other benefits. But his job is to keep control of the pickers. Complete control. He takes a percentage of everything we get paid. It's not much, but given the numbers of workers on payday, it adds up. If you complain, you're fired on the spot. So, nobody complains. Not even my father."

"That's all messed up."

"You know how I said my father died in an accident?"

"Yes."

"It wasn't true. Not long after his speech the day Chavez spoke, maybe a couple of weeks, he was killed. He disappeared."

"Murdered?"

"One in the same. We never found his body. He just disappeared and everybody knew who it was."

"And nobody said anything? No investigation of any sort?"

"No, but I knew. Everybody in the camp knew."

"Nobody contacted the police?"

"We don't talk to police."

"So, it's never been resolved."

"No. But it was avenged."

"How?"

"I killed him."

Hearing that sent shivers through my body. I couldn't believe it. I couldn't believe that Jesus had murdered a man.

"I was only 12 when my father died, but when I was 16, I was about the same size I am now and I was strong. I spent those four years planning it out.

One payday, I quit and thanked the boss for keeping me on but told him I was going back to Mexico to get married. And the motherfucker had the gall to thank me for my loyalty and even gave me $20 for my wedding."

I bummed a smoke and lit one for the both of us.

"I waited three months before I made my move. By then, I was forgotten. Just another migrant who moved on."

"What about your mom and brothers and sisters?"

"She was crushed. She believed I was really getting married and cursed me for not telling her. It kills me that I had to lie to her."

"You never let her know? Or, one of your brothers or sisters?"

"No. I couldn't. You did the same thing when you left."

"True."

"I knew his patterns at every single stop. I knew every whorehouse he visited and when he'd go there and I waited. I waited until he came out of the puta casa. Then I stepped out in front of him with a machete held to my side. He didn't recognize me and greeted me with this big shit eating grin and said, *Mi amigo, que pasa?* When I told him who my father was, and pulled the machete out, his face turned white. I told him I was going to kill him."

"And you did. Just killed him."

"Yes. He begged for his life, said he didn't do it, told me he'd pay my family and then when I didn't budge, he said he was sorry and that he was forced to do it and that he thought highly of my father."

"Did he say anything else? Tell you who put him up to it?"

"There wasn't anybody else. He was an absolute dictator. He made the decision and we both knew it. He tried to run but he was fat and out of shape. I caught him and killed him. Drug his body down into a ravine and left him and then became, as you said, *invisible*."

Jesus flipped on his blinker and we pulled into a Little Stinker gas station and told the attendant to fill it up and check the oil. I got out and headed off to grab some cokes and something to eat. My stomach had been gurgling all day.

"Hub," Jesus called after me. "I gotta take a piss. Make it beer instead of Coke, okay?"

It was. After two serious confessions, I wasn't sure that beer would be strong enough. After I paid for the beer and pretzels, I headed to the bathroom too. Jesus came out and handed me the key chain for the restroom and I gave him the stuff. I did my business and then splashed my face with cold water and wiped it off on a dirty hand towel. Before leaving, I stared into the mirror. Somehow, my face looked the same but I felt older.

I climbed back into the cab and Jesus had already cracked me open a beer and the bag of pretzels sat between us.

"You got any questions for me?" he asked.

"No."

"Got any reservations about traveling with me."

"None," I answered, taking a swig of beer. "Do you have any questions for me?"

"One and I want an honest answer."

"Okay, you'll get one."

"Where were you last night?'

I wasn't going to lie to Jesus again. We had enough to put each other away if we needed to.

"I slept with Angel."

Jesus had just taken a big slug of beer and when he heard that it came spraying out of his mouth and he started laughing. I thought he was going to choke to death.

"Oh, my God, Hub, that's the funniest thing I've ever heard. That is too funny!"

It was the truth and Jesus never brought it up again.

Chapter 26

By the time we arrived in Rawlins it was early evening. We pulled in and were greeted by Wacko. I'd hoped that Jesus would wave and we'd slide right by, but he slowed and stopped right next to Wacko and rolled down his window.

"Evening boss," Jesus said.

Wacko leaned up against Jesus's door and greeted us both. I'm certain I slid as close to the passenger side as I could in case Wacko came flying through the window and tried to strangle me.

"Want us to set up in the usual spot?"

"Same old, same old," he replied and then looked over at me. "Everything working out okay, kid?" he asked.

"Yes," I answered trying not to look him in the eyes. *What kind of question was that? Did he just ask for the sake of asking or did Angel confess something to him?*

"Nothing you want to tell me?"

"About?"

"Last night?"

There it was. Angel must've said something to him and he was just baiting me. I couldn't help but wonder why she'd do something like that knowing that I would be killed. The space between his question and what I was going to say seemed like hours. *Should I say anything? Deny it all? Tell him that I appreciated the job but I needed to get back home to my family because all of the members had contract the Black Plague and I was the only one who could care for them.* It was only a few seconds before Jesus rescued me again.

"You know, boss," he replied making a quick glance at me before speaking, "Hub got bit by the Panther last night and it's been a long day for him."

Wacko roared. "Well kid, you're not the only one that looked rough this morning. You probably won't die but you'll feel like it by the end of the night. Good to see you stuck it out with us."

"Thanks boss."

"It won't kill you, but there's still plenty time for that to happen."

"Jesus, when you get set up swing by the trailer with the kid. It's pay day."

"Will do," he replied and then we drove over to the spot where we'd set up the Baby Octopus.

"Well, Hub, I guess Angel didn't say anything to him."

"I guess not," I answered and then Jesus started laughing like it was the funniest thing in the world.

I grabbed my gloves from my kit and Jesus suggested we have something to eat before getting to work since we hadn't had any real food all day.

"How about you make us a couple of bologna sandwiches each and break out the last bag of chips and a couple of Dr. Peppers while I take off the cargo straps. We'll eat and then start setting things up."

I grabbed the cooler and a small wooden board we'd been using as a chopping block and spread out some Wonder bread, slathered on a thick layer of mayonnaise and mustard and slapped a couple of pieces of bologna on each and some cheese to top it off. By the time Jesus got back, I'd already wolfed one of the sandwiches down and glugged half of the Dr. Pepper without him.

"Did you say grace before sucking the sandwich down?"

"I did and I also offered a prayer to St. Anthony, the patron saint of lost things"

"Because?"

"Because I was hoping he might be able to help me find my brains."

"Hub, you don't have any. That was a wasted prayer."

"Probably," I replied, finishing up my second sandwich and shoving a handful of chips into my mouth.

Getting something in my stomach felt good. Jesus told me to start unloading the seats and spreading them around in a big circle so when it came to attaching them to the arms, we wouldn't have to continually walk back to the flat-bed.

"Go grab a couple of guys to help us take off the diesel engine."

"Where from?"

"Go over to Frenchy. He can probably free up a couple of guys."

I headed over to the Ferris wheel with the idea of avoiding Wacko and Angel when I almost crashed into a couple of midgets.

"Sorry," I mumbled to the closest one.

They started laughing.

"How's your head feeling today, Hub?" the tallest one asked.

"Like I got hit by a train," I replied, completely baffled by what they were talking about and who they were and why they were here.

"We thought we'd die when we watched you and Frenchy dancing…"

"Not to mention the Kiddie Boat races and Darnelle planting a big one on you at the end."

"Yeah," I said playing along because I didn't remember any of it. At least, not yet.

"And every time we'd help you up off the ground, you'd thank us and kept telling us that you'd never met a…what was he calling us, Stretch?"

"Lilliputians. I think that was it, Little John?"

"Yep. Hub, what the hell is a Lilliputian?"

Right, like I was going to tell them the story of *Gulliver's Travels* and the Lilliputians who were only six inches tall. They'd probably taken enough crap in their lives without me adding an insult on top of it.

"Where you headed, Hub?"

"To see if Frenchy can free up a couple of guys to help unload the diesel."

"We'll walk over with you."

When Frenchy saw me he called out to his crew, "Gentlemen, a warm round of applause for one of the greatest dancers Wacko's City of Fun Carnival has ever seen. Mr. Fred Astaire."

I cringed but the guys gave a bunch of hoots and whistles. Apparently, I'd put on quite a show.

"How you feeling today, Mr. Astaire?"

"Like I got run over by a train," I answered trying to fake like it was no big deal.

"That," he emphasized, "was some kind of show."

"Thanks, I'm glad you liked it."

"We loved it. I haven't seen anybody that drunk since," and he paused looking around the at the crew, "since Crenshaw got all lubed-up and decided he was going over to the pens and try to ride a bronc."

Crenshaw threw his arms up in the air like a prize fighter and did a little shuffle.

"What happened?" I asked.

"We didn't let him get that far," Frenchy said. "What do you need?"

"Jesus needs a couple of guys to take the diesel off the flatbed."

"Take Little John and Stretch back with you and I'll throw in Crenshaw to help out."

"Thanks, Frenchy."

Jesus had already laid out the arms and we all got together and set the diesel in place. Stretch had climbed on Little John's shoulders so they were tall enough to reach the flatbed. It might have looked funny to an outsider like me but neither Jesus nor Crenshaw blinked an eye. When we were done,

Crenshaw asked if we needed an extra hand.

"Frenchy have enough hands over there?"

"Plenty," Crenshaw replied.

"Fine. Let's get this puppy set up."

In about half the time it took us to take down the Baby Octopus, we had it put together. I set up the ticket booth with Little John and Stretch, Jesus and Crenshaw put the fence around the ride. When we were done, they headed back to the Ferris wheel and I was going to join them when Jesus said Frenchy probably had enough help.

"You know what we both need?" he asked.

"A cold beer?"

"Better than that. A shower."

"They've got showers around here?"

"No, but there are some irrigation sprinklers."

"Okay?"

"Just west of here they've got wheat fields. We'll go there."

"And it's okay?"

"As long as we don't get caught trespassing."

"Out here, they'd probably shoot us wouldn't they."

"Probably. But the one good thing about it is that we'd die a *clean* death."

"Very funny."

"Thought you'd like it."

The thought of being clean and getting into clean clothes sounded great. I was in desperate need of a shower after last night. I felt dirty in a deep way. Dirty to the bone and I felt dirty because I had ended up in Angel's bed. Worse than that, I felt horrible for not seeing if Lacey showed up at the stable for me. I would have called her when we stopped at the Little Stinker but I'd never asked for her phone number. It was a night of stupidity followed by a day of regret. I was hoping that maybe she'd show up at the rodeo and when I got showered and all, and since the carnival wouldn't open until tomorrow, I could wander over to the arena and look around the stables to see if she was there. It's the only thing I could think of that made any sense. Otherwise, I'd left Lacey in the lurch.

"This is how it works," Jesus said, "uncapping a couple of bottles of beer and handing me one. "I know a spot where we can park in the shade. Unnoticed. We'll take our clothes off down to our skivvies, walk across the road and into the field and shower. We'll be in and out in nothing flat."

"Sounds good. Thanks for the beer."

"I debated on that. I don't want you to end up with Angel again."

"Jesus," I replied angrily. "Don't bring that up again." And, then I added, "Please."

Jesus stared at me for a moment, took another sip and said, "Okay, Hub. Fair enough."

I followed behind him with my towel thrown over my shoulder and was surprised at how much water these sprinklers shot water out into the fields. Already, I could feel the mist on my skin and it gave me chills.

"Notice how they spray, Hub and then time it so you walk with them. Lather up, follow the spray, and when you're done soaping, follow it back to where we started the whole time getting rinsed off. Nothing to it."

We dropped our towels behind the arc of the spray, took our bars of soap and walked out into the spray.

"Holy hell! It's freezing, Jesus."

"But, how does it feel?"

"Like heaven."

We laughed through the sprinklers and when we were done we headed back to the pickup truck.

"Hub, I've got somebody to visit here in town. Remember me mentioning that the other day?"

"Yeah, I'm not brain-dead."

"Good to know because it looked like *touch and go* for a while. Can you cover things while I'm gone."

"I'll grab my kit and set up someplace else for the night."

"Why would you do something like that?"

"Because you'll have your truck."

"She's picking me up."

"Oh."

"You going to call your barrel racer?"

"Probably my sister. Let her know I'm okay.

"And not your cowgirl?"

"Probably not."

Jesus started prying. "So, the truth comes out. Meaning, Hub, when you told me about her, your eyes went rolling back of your skull and all of a sudden, you're not going to call her?"

"It's not like that," I protested.

"Then what?" Jesus started laughing, "Did she dump you?"

"No."

"So?"

"I never got her phone number," I answered, feeling pretty damn stupid.

"Well that makes it a little difficult, doesn't it?"

"Yes."

"Better luck next time Hub. I'm going to have to give you a few pointers about women."

"Whatever."

When we got back to the carnival, Jesus got all dressed up for the night. He slapped some cologne on and smelled like a French whore. Not that I'd ever smelled one but I didn't say anything.

"How do I look?"

"You clean up pretty good."

"We'll head over to Wacko's and pick up our pay and then I'm out of here."

Outside the trailer, the carnies were already lined up. Under the trailer a table was set up with a table and a cash box. Wacko was standing beside Angel and she was passing out pay envelopes and checking each carnie off as they picked up their packets.

"Any chance you could just pick mine up for me?"

"Not a chance, Hub. No show, no go."

Standing in line behind Jesus, I wondered what was going to happen when my turn came. Would Angel say anything to me that might tip Wacko off, or would she be all business? Little John and Stretch came up behind me and they brought along their sister with them. She was also a midget and she was beautiful. She had a shock of vermillion hair, alabaster skin, deep blue eyes and carried herself like nobility. Her name was Annabel and, when you spoke to her, she gave you her absolute attention as though nothing else in the world mattered.

While I was talking to Annabel, I noticed Zola moving toward us from her tent. She was dressed in black silk pantaloons, with gold ankle bracelets, a dramatic billowing white silk blouse, a red scarf tied around her head that flowed down one side of her arm and a necklace of blood red stones and lipstick to match. It was difficult not to notice her and I did my best not to.

"Come, little one," Zola said to Annabel and took her hand and they walked to the front of payroll. The gorillas, the muscle of carnival and carnies moved aside when she approached and both women picked up their paychecks and headed back to the tent without so much as a look back at any of us.

"What the hell was that about?" I asked Little John.

"Nothing," he replied like it was nothing out of the ordinary.

"But she grabbed your sister and they butted in the payroll line."

"She's Zola, Hub."

"I know that. But what's Annabel have to do with her?"

"They're partners."

"In what way?"

"She's Zola's shill. She finds the marks."

"What's that mean?"

"She's the person who ropes people into Zola's web. Finds the marks for her."

Jesus was up next and made small talk with Wacko and Angel and then I stepped up to pick up my pay packet.

"Evening," Angel said, smiling at me. "First payday. How does it feel?"

"Good. Very good," I answered looking for any sign of acknowledgement or regret or co-conspiracy. But nothing at all betrayed our night.

"Well," she said with a tenderness, "it's good to have you on board."

"Thank you, Angel," I replied and then looked over at Wacko. "Thanks for hiring me Wacko."

"Welcome kid," was all he said and that was plenty good for me. I walked away and opened up my pay packet and pulled out five twenty dollar bills. It felt good. It felt honest and I'd made it through my first week without being killed. Things were looking up and that's the first time I could remember that feeling in a long, long time.

Chapter 27

I walked over to the phone both by the rodeo arena. When I got there, a pretty long line of carnies were waiting to use the phone so I stood there making small talk with the guys I knew. The midgets pulled up alongside me and we started talking. I picked up where we left off and asked them to tell me more about Zola and Annabel. At first, they didn't want to say much. I guess they had their reasons, or maybe, as far as they were concerned, there really wasn't much else to say. But I pressed them.

"What do you want to know, Hub?" Stretch asked.

I started off easy, asking how they ended up with Wacko and what brought them to the carnival.

"Back when we hired on, the carnival had a freak show. It was full of weird shit, people like the Snake Lady, the Fat Man from Mars, pinheads, real freaks like the Big Headed Drooler, and then us."

"And get this, Hub," Little John interrupted, "we were billed as the Wild Pygmy Children of an African King."

"Not to be rude, but you guys don't look like you're from Africa."

"We did when the Professor brought us onto the stage and we started our routine."

Stretch jumped back into the conversation, "We were completely black-faced up and wore grass skirts with crazy wild wigs, cheap shiny necklaces and carried spears. One of the carnies who didn't show up until the third stop of the season found some of those little phony shrunken heads we wore around our necks. We'd come out, all angry like, mumbling a bunch of gibberish and running to the front of the stage menacing everybody, threatening to throw our spears at them and then when the Professor tried to calm us down, we'd attack him."

"The crowd would go crazy and we'd be pulled off by a couple gorillas from the carnie. It was really the best act the freaks had because it offered the possibility of the unknown. Of danger, maybe even death."

"People fell for it?" I asked.

"You wouldn't believe what people fall for. We're all gullible, Hub, even you. And Zola and Annabel are the masters of the hustle. They rake it in. Annabel makes twice what we make and nobody knows how much Zola has stashed away in her trailer. Probably millions."

I laughed but neither brother did.

"You think we're kidding?"

"It's not that, it's just I saw them pick up their checks like everybody else and it will be a long time before any of us are millionaires on what we get paid."

"Anything Zola makes off of things like Tarot card readings, fortune telling, three-card Monte, the Baby Guess, and what Annabel makes off of the hustle and henna tattoos, they keep after giving Wacko a cut."

"Wacko's no fool. He knows what side his bread is buttered on," Stretch said seriously. "That act is probably the most valuable piece of the carnival."

"At least it's the biggest money maker."

"Have you ever asked Annabel what they haul in?"

"Yes," Stretch replied, "and do you know what she said? Quote, unquote. It's none of your fucking business and if I ever find either one of you trying to find my stash, I'll cut your balls off."

"Annabel?"

"In the flesh."

"Holy shit," exclaimed Little John. "Look at that will you?"

Stretch and I looked over to where he was pointing. It was a brand spanking new, cream-white, Cadillac DeVille convertible with the top down driven by a woman who looked like a movie star. She was dressed in a white sleeveless dress, wore matching white sunglasses and her blonde hair was wrapped with a white scarf that drew loosely around her neck and blew in the wind behind her. And her lipstick? The color of lust.

When she honked the horn and waved toward us, everybody forgot what they were standing in line for and started waving back. A few of the carnies, hollered out yelling out stupid shit like: *I'm here, honey. I'll be right over!* And, *hey, baby, I just got my paycheck, how about night out with me?* And some pretty crude crap I'd feel stupid writing about.

Then Little John said something that got us all laughing. Not because we thought it was funny but because it was so sincere and so impossible.

"Do you think she's here to join the carnival?"

"In our wildest fucking dreams!" Stretch replied trying not to choke on his own laughter."

"I just meant," Little John said, trying to gain some ground. "that maybe she..."

"When pigs fly," one of the other carnies yelled back over his shoulder.

"Maybe it's our mother finally coming to take us home," Stretch added, embarrassed for himself and his brother.

There were four stragglers behind us waiting for the phone and because I didn't want to have anybody listening to me talk with my sister, I let them call before me.

"Not going to call anybody?" Little John asked.

"My sister, but it's kind of private."

"Nobody gives a crap, Hub. Just give her a call."

"It's just that it's her birthday and I don't want anybody hearing me sing

Happy Birthday to her."

"Suit yourself," he said, stepping up to the phone and dropping a handful of change into the pay slot.

"Hub, if you're not doing anything after your call come on over to our camp and maybe we can get a card game going?"

"I'll pass tonight. Thanks. I need to get some sleep."

"Suit yourself. If you change your mind, you know where we are."

Then, coming back the road, we all saw her again and this time she had a passenger with her.

"Is that..."one of the carnies started before he was cut off by another.

"Jesus?"

"Hell yes," his buddy replied. "That guy has ladies stashed all over the circuit."

"Lucky son-of-a-bitch!"

"What's he got that we don't have?" another voice called out.

"Ten inches."

"When it's folded in half," Crenshaw yelled, and we all fell apart.

Chapter 28

I wandered over to the stock pens to kill some time and to see if maybe Lacey was there. Perhaps she'd persuaded her folks to let her hit the circuit but I was fairly certain it would be a tough sell. If she wasn't, then I was SOL and it would be one of those opportunities that I'd missed and couldn't get back. Note to self...get a phone number stupid!

When I returned to the phone booth, everybody was gone so I picked up the phone and called my sister, Soup. She picked up on the second ring.

"Walker residence, Soup speaking."

"It's me."

"Hub?"

"None other."

"Oh, my God, Hub, you're still alive!"

"And I'm doing my best to stay alive."

"Where are you? What are you doing? Are you okay?" she asked in rapid rapid succession.

"Call me back at this number. I don't have much change on me. I gave her the number of the phone and she called back instantly.

"It's great to hear your voice, Soup."

"Yours too! So, where are you now?"

"I'm okay. If I tell you where I am, you can't tell mom or dad but you can tell them you spoke to me and I'm doing okay."

"Fair enough."

"I'm traveling with the carnival. We move all over the west."

"With the carnival? Oh, my God, Hub, isn't it dangerous?"

"Yes and no."

"Don't you work with a bunch of carnies?"

"Soup, I'm a carnie now and honestly, they get a bad rap."

"What do you do?"

"I work the Baby Octopus with a guy named Jesus."

"Seriously? Jesus? You're making that up."

"No and he's a really cool guy. He's sort of taken me under his wings. And he reads."

"Duh, everybody reads, Hub."

"Not in this group. He has a full body tattoo that is patterned after Dante's Hell and when I mentioned he had great tattoos, he corrected me and said, *skin illustrations.*"

"*The Illustrated Man.* Bradbury."

"Yep. And they're beautiful. Haunting. Hard not to stare at them but I've never seen anything like it."

"When are you coming home?"

"I don't know. I don't think any time soon. Have things quieted down?"

"No, and they have your picture up all over town. In almost all the stores. *Have you seen this fugitive? If so, contact the police department immediately. Consider him armed and dangerous.*"

"Fuck."

"Hub. Your language."

"Around here that word is used in every way possible. You'd be impressed."

"But I'm not."

"I apologize. How's Sparky?"

"He misses you fiercely. It'd break your heart."

"Tell him I miss him too and I'm doing okay. Tell mom and dad too."

Before hanging up, I told her about all the characters in the carnival from Wacko down to Zola. She was full of questions and I could hear her mind working overtime. I also told her about the Panther Piss tradition but didn't tell her how it ended up and when I mentioned we'd showered under giant agricultural sprinkler systems she thought that was the coolest thing of all."

"On the road, like Kerouac, huh?"

"To some degree but Jack never did the things I've done."

"I hope you're writing all this down, Hub."

"When I get some spare time, I jot stuff down." It was a bold-faced lie.

"You've got to. How many people do you know that have had a chance to do what you're doing?"

"None."

There was a pause in the conversation and it came from her end. I felt it.

"What's going on, Soup?"

"This's been really hard on mom and dad, Hub. They feel like it was their fault. And every time they go into a store, they see your picture and it makes it worse."

It's not like I didn't think about that every day. It's just that I couldn't see a way back home. Not when I was on posters all over the place.

"I can't come home, Soup."

"Hub, you can't run forever. Deep down you know that, don't you?"

"Better than you do, Soup," I answered with an edge. I regretted it immediately.

"Damnit, Hub, don't you dare speak to me that way! I'm serious!"

"I'm sorry, Soup. It's just I can't figure this out. I know I can't run forever but I'm afraid to come home."

"I don't know what to tell you. I can't even imagine what it feels like for you."

"You'd never put yourself in a situation like this. That's the truth."

A cowboy drew up behind me waiting to use the phone.

"I've got to go. There's somebody waiting to use the phone."

"Don't go," she begged.

"It's time. I'll call again at the next stop. I promise."

"Is there any place I can send you a care package?"

"I'm afraid not."

"Just a box of cookies for your birthday."

"Not really. Goodbye. I love you."

"Be careful, Hub, please."

"Call Smitty, let him know I'm still alive."

"Okay, but please don't keep saying *I'm still alive*. It really makes me nervous."

"I won't say it again. Promise."

It felt great to talk to Soup but it made me homesick. The kicker was that I'd completely forgotten my birthday was coming up. Go figure.

I wasn't ready to go back to the carnival just yet so I headed back over to the rodeo arena. One more check to see if, by some miracle, Lacey had shown up.

It seemed to me like the number of trailers and cowboys had doubled since I made the call to Soup. I walked around the bleachers looking for Lacey and keeping my eyes out for her brother. I pretty much was drawing a blank when I saw the tall cowboy, Billy's brother, Donny, getting out of his pickup truck. And a second person, Lacey's brother, was climbing out of the passenger side. I didn't know if a person could ride in a horse trailer but maybe Lacey was in there too, so I stayed put and waited. And hoped.

When I realized Lacey wasn't with them I headed back to the carnival. On the way back, a kid was hauling a bunch of programs over to the ticket booth. He had a pickup truck full of bundled programs so I offered to help him carry them.

"Why'd you want to do that?" he asked.

"Because it's hot and you looked like you could use some help."

He shook his head like I must be crazy and finally said, "Hell, yes."

With two of us it took only fifteen minutes and when we'd dropped the last stack off, he cut a bundle open and gave me a program

"Here, take one of these."

"Thanks, I appreciate it."

It's exactly what I'd hoped for but a smarter person would have asked for one up front. Even paid for it. I rolled the program under my arm, lit a smoke and headed back. Once I got to the truck, I popped open one of the last beers, pulled out my sleeping bag, made myself comfortable and started thumbing through the program. I immediately went to the barrel racing section and there wasn't a listing for Lacey. Since I didn't even know her last name I thumbed over to the bull riders and there he was, a picture of Lacey's brother trying to look all tough and get this, his name was Tad Dalton. Tad. Tad Dalton. What kind of name was that? I started laughing. It just wasn't the name for a cowboy. Maybe one of the rodeo clowns but not a bull rider. But now I had Lacey's last name and I could get her parent's phone number from information and give her a call.

I climbed out of the pickup bed and went over to the midgets to see if I could get some change from then.

"Hey, Hub," Stretch greeted. "Make your phone call?"

"I did."

"You here to play a few hands of cards with us? We could use a 7th at the table."

"Actually, I came by to see if I could get from change from you guys."

"What do need?"

"Couple of bucks worth of quarters."

Stretch lifted a couple of bucks worth of quarters from the pot and I gave him a couple of Washingtons and headed back to the phone booth. I got ahold of information and scribbled down the number. There was only one Dalton in Evanston so that made it pretty easy. I scribbled down the number and dialed. On the third dial, somebody picked up. It was a woman, Lacey's mother I guessed.

"Dalton residence."

"Is this Mrs. Dalton?"

"Yes, it is. Who's calling?"

"I'm a friend of your daughter. Is Lacey there by any chance?"

"I'm afraid she's not. She's down to the café. May I take your number and I'll have her give you a call when she gets home.

"That's okay. Maybe you could just tell her that Hub called."

"Hub? I don't believe I know you, do I?"

"No, ma'am, I haven't had the pleasure of meeting you."

"Well, Hub, give me your number and I'll give it to her as soon as she comes in."

"I'm actually calling from a pay phone but if you just let her know I called, I'd much appreciate it. Please tell her I'll try to call back later on."

"I most certainly will young man."

And I hung up. Oh, how the world had just shifted ever so slightly. Contact. I'd made contact. I was not so alone. I was floating off the ground thinking I might be able to talk to Lacey when I turned back onto the midway and made the mistake of walking by Zola. Normally, I would have kept my distance but I was dreamy over Lacey. When I realized where I was, I made a slight turn away from Zola.

I'd heard what the guys said about Zola so my plan was to never let her get her claws into me. Whether or not Little John and Stretch thought Annabel was crazy for partnering up with Zola, it was none of my business and I didn't hold it against her. She had to make a living like everybody else and who was I to make any sort of judgement?

My slight change of direction was so obvious Zola started to laugh. It was clear I would not have made a good spy.

"Avoiding your future, Mr. Hub?" she asked in her thick accent.

"No," I answered firmly.

"Come here, Mr. Hub."

"I'd like to, but I've got a lot to do before we open tomorrow. Plus, Jesus needs some help."

"Oh, Mr. Hub, I'm disappointed in you. I did not figure you for a liar."

"I'm not lying, Zola, really." I should not have said a single word.

"The Baby Octopus is ready to open," she stated, without any emotion, "and as for Jesus, he is in his own paradise. This is not his first rodeo."

"I apologize," I offered, hoping that would be enough to let her excuse me.

But here's the deal. I was already in her web and I knew it. Honestly, it made no sense. How hard would it be to just turn around and walk away? But, for some reason, I couldn't.

"Mr. Hub, come sit," Zola said, offering me a chair in front of where she was sitting.

"Thank you," I said politely, "but I'd prefer not to."

"As you please, Mr. Hub. Zola forces nobody."

"Thank you."

I started to walk away when she said, "You'll see her again."

"What? Who?"

"The cowgirl."

There was absolutely no way she could have known that. Known that I'd tried to call Lacey. Known about Lacey. And because of those two words, I sat down in front of her.

"How much is this going to cost me?" I asked.

"You are not like them," she said. "Zola does this for you. For free."

"Thank you, Zola," I said, and I sat down across the table from her.

She reached out and took my hand, delicately turned it over and studied my palm. Her own hand was surprisingly warm and soft. For the longest time she didn't say a word, but traced the lines lightly with her fingertips. It was as though her fingers were searching for the story, the narrative of my future. I watched her carefully, realizing I had never paid such attention to my own hands before.

She asked no questions of me, my date of birth, the time I was born, where I was born or any of that, and it came as a surprise. I was a skeptic when it came to these things, the seeing into the future routine, the communing with the dead, and the channeling crapola. Seriously, you had to be pretty damn gullible to believe in any of it and yet, here I was, sitting in front of Zola with my hand opened up to her.

"Here, Mr. Hub, look," she said, tracing the life line that ran from the fleshing part of my hand beneath my thumb up to the base of my index finger, "this is good and long. You will live longer than you expect and you will be surprised."

It meant nothing to me. It sounded pretty good but you could say that to anybody and there was no way to check it out, right?

"You are running away from something very serious, Mr. Hub. You are in serious trouble."

Duh, really? What a surprise. Almost everybody in the carnival was running away from something or someone. Not much enlightenment here. It would be like saying to anybody, *Sometimes you have bad days and sometimes you have good days,* and the suckers would nod their heads, like *God, isn't she something.* I wasn't buying it.

Then she said, "Your parents are worried about you, but it is your sister and brother that are hurting the most."

The only person in the carnival that knew anything about my family was Jesus and judging by how much he distrusted or disliked Zola, I couldn't imagine him walking over to her and mumbling that I had a brother and sister. That was pointed and specific. I started paying attention.

"You will be married two times." She showed me the marriage lines on my palm. The first one was short and the second one was long and branched off to two shorter lines.

"What do those mean?"

"The first marriage will not work, Mr. Hub. The second marriage line is long. You will be married for a long time to the one you were always meant to marry."

"And these two lines?"

"They will be your children. A girl and a boy."

The idea was preposterous to me. I couldn't even figure out how I'd survive my current predicament, let alone comprehend the idea of being married twice and being the father of two children.

"You find this hard to believe, Mr. Hub?"

"I do."

"Mr. Hub, I tell you what I see. You are not required to believe."

"Okay."

"Mr. Hub, do you want me to stop?"

This was my way out. I could thank her, get up and leave, but I was curious. "No, please continue."

"It will be the dark part. Are you okay with this? Some people do not want to know."

Before I answered, I gave it some careful thought. I had been warned about Zola's readings but since she'd told me I'd have a long life, what harm could come of it?

"Yes, Zola, please go on."

"You are in great danger here and you will be hurt badly."

This was a dangerous job but my immediate thought was Wacko. Would Angel tell Wacko I'd slept with her? Somehow, I didn't feel that would be the case. Maybe something with heavy equipment, diesel engines, power lines, or steel arms from the Ferris wheel or Baby Octopus or any number of possibilities. But it felt like something darker to me.

"How?" I asked.

"That I don't know, Mr. Hub. I only see what I see."

"And what about these little bumps?"

Zola hesitated for a moment before answering.

"This is all trouble, Mr. Hub. And it all comes at once, like a tornado. And it is soon."

It was enough for me. In truth, probably too much. Had I not been warned by Jesus and the others?

"I think this is all I want to know, Zola. May we stop now?"

"And you will travel to a far-away country of a thousand shades of green. It will be dangerous but you will return and many won't."

"Let's stop."

"Yes, Mr. Hub, we can stop now."

I stood up from the table and I actually felt a little light-headed. The feeling you get when you've been knocked to the ground and your buddies are standing over you asking if everything is *okay* and you sit up too quickly and feel faint.

"Mr. Hub," Zola said, "before you leave, I need to show you one more line."

"I think I've seen enough. More than enough." I started to walk away when she implored me to let her finish.

"It's good. You need good."

"Okay," and I returned my hand to her palm.

"This line here is your life path. See how it swings up?"

"Yes."

"When you find what it is you do, you will do it for a long time and it will make you happy."

"That's the only good thing I've heard so far."

"It will be with people. A large number of people and you will change lives. You will make people whole again."

"Like a doctor?'

"I can't see those things. But it's in you, Mr. Hub. That, I can see."

Though I tried, Zola refused any money and that was a big surprise to me. But the biggest surprise was her opening line, *You will see the cowgirl again.* That's what made me take notice and that was what made me offer up my hand. That was the litmus test of Zola's reading. If I saw Lacey again, I might actually believe what she said. Otherwise, it was nothing more than Zola practicing her trade.

Back at the pick-up truck, I ate some saltine crackers and a tin of smoked oysters. Then, I pulled out the journal my sister had given me, read her words in the inscription and began writing.

Chapter 29

I woke up early, my neck all kinked from falling asleep in an awkward position, the journal splayed out alongside my sleeping bag that I was half in and half out of, and I'd been devoured by mosquitoes. I could smell coffee in the air so I unfolded myself, threw on my boots and followed the scent over to Frenchy's trailer by the Ferris wheel.

After my initiation into the carnival, I didn't need to ask if I could have a cup. I greeted Frenchy, grabbed a tin cup, slipped on the pot glove and poured myself a cup and then topped off Frenchy's. I offered him a cigarette, which he took, and lit his then mine.

"Merci, beaucoup," Frenchy offered up in his Cajun accent.

"Bientot," I responded, remembering the phrase from my sister, who by the 6th grade spoke fluent French.

"Sacre bleu, vous parlez Francais?"

"No, learned some French from my sister."

"It is the language of romance, kid. You should learn to speak it."

"I've got my hands full just speaking English, Frenchy."

"It's a distasteful language. It does not fit well on the tongue."

We sat together, enjoying the quiet, knowing full-well that by noon when we opened up the carnival, it would be madness.

"Is he back yet?" Frenchy asked.

"I haven't seen him," I replied,

"He will be exhausted, but he will be back."

I hesitated before I asked, "Do you know who she is?"

"It's none of my business and it's none of yours, kid."

"Sorry I asked."

Frenchy rolled his own and lit up second smoke. I wanted to retract my question about Jesus and the mystery woman but I thought I'd wait a few more minutes before excusing myself so it didn't look like my feelings were hurt. They weren't at all and Frenchy was right, it was neither of our business.

"Thanks for the coffee. I'm going to go get ready. Check the seats, pick up the cash box. You know, fire up the ride to make sure everything's okey-dokey."

"You are a quick study kid. Even Wacko's noticed. You do the shit we ask you to do and we don't have to tell you a second time. Trust me, it's rare."

"Thanks, Frenchy. Jesus is a great teacher."

I rinsed out my cup, placed it back where I got if from and headed over to the Baby Octopus.

"Kid," he called after me, "They belong together. It's the real thing."
I just nodded my head like I knew what he meant. He'd offered me a kernel of trust and I wasn't about to push it. Instead, I set myself to the task of doing everything Jesus had taught me

By the time we were supposed to open the gates, Jesus was nowhere in sight. People lined up, I sold them tickets and then closed the gate and seated them, checked the safety belts and went over to fire up the diesel and just like magic, Jesus was already standing there ready for my signal. I nodded my head. The diesel fired up on the first try and our customers launched off into space to the sound of high pitched screams and laughter.

"Thanks, Hub," Jesus said. "I appreciate it."

"You covered for me."

And that was that. We busted ass until closing time and I could tell Jesus was whip-ass tired. Heading back to his pick-up, he asked me if I'd had any lunch or breakfast. When I told him I hadn't and I was so hungry that I could eat my own shoes, he laughed.

"Now a smart man would eat his partner's shoes so he had his own to run off in."

"See, Jesus, that's why you're the boss and I'm a low-life carnie."

"Come on, we're going to eat well tonight, I've got a basket full of food."

I got the lanterns going while Jesus brought out a wicker basket full of more food than I'd seen for a month. It reminded me of the scene in in Dickens's *Scrooge* where the Cratchit family has the bountiful Christmas dinner with a goose with potatoes, greens and fresh mince and apple pie.

We sat on our coolers and when Jesus lifted back the red-checkered table cloth covering the basket, I almost died. It was packed with foods I could only imagine. Dried salami, smoked fish, blood sausage, a couple of bottles of red wine that actually had corks instead of screw tops, dried figs, canned salmon and mackerel, fresh fruit, big fat chocolate bars with names I couldn't pronounce, beef jerky, pickled pig's feet, thick, dense slab bread and a small pecan pie carefully wrapped in aluminum foil.

I waited for Jesus to lead us into this banquet. We both pulled out our knives and Jesus began by slicing a big chunk of greasy salami and then passing it over to me. He cut himself a piece of equal size and cut the casing and peeled off the skin that bound the salami together. I did the same. He cut us each a wedge of smoked cheese. He dropped those into his coffee cup and I did the same. Then he opened one of the bottles of red wine, took a good long swig and passed it over to me.

"Now eat the salami and cheese together and take another pull off the wine."

The deep flavor of the salami combined with the sharpness of the cheese and red wine might have been the most wonderful flavor I'd ever experienced in my life and there was still a full basket of delight ahead of us.

"Oh, my God," I said, a mouthful of food mangling my words, "this is unbelievable, Jesus."

"And we haven't even gotten started yet."

We spent the rest of the night gorging ourselves, taking a break to have the occasional smoke and just talking about our families and our dreams. By the time we'd finished up, it was pretty late. We cleaned up the camp and hit the sack. Inside my sleeping bag, I lay on my back studying the sky looking for shooting stars to make a couple of wishes.

I thought about my session with Zola and wondered what it all meant and I know Jesus had to be thinking of the mystery woman. But neither of us spoke about these things for our own reasons. These stories belonged to us and we would protect them in our own silent way.

The next three days in Rawlins were a repeat of the first and there was a mind sucking sameness about them that made me feel like I was trapped in a dream or a tune that gets stuck in your head and you can't shake it. My journal kept me sane, but the idea that Frenchy and Big Heavy and, for that matter, Jesus, could do this year in and year out was unfathomable to me.

On the night before we broke camp, I decided to try calling Lacey one more time. I'd made three previous attempts all of them ending up with me visiting with her mother and leaving a message that I'd called. This time, Lacy answered and it so caught me off guard, I didn't know where to begin.

"Hello, Hub, is that you?"

I had to think about it. "Lacey...I thought it was going to be your mother."

"I know. My mom was starting to like your phone calls. She thought you were sweet."

"We're heading out for Cheyenne in a couple of days. Do you think your parents will let you hit the circuit?"

"I don't know, Hub. I've been working on them but it's hard to tell."

"I wanted to apologize for not rendezvousing with you the last night we were in Evanston. I'm so sorry, Lacey."

"I thought you didn't want to see me again."

"It wasn't that at all..."

"But then you called...and I felt really good, Hub."

"If your parents don't let you go to Cheyenne, I'll write you. Give me your address and I'll send you a card from each stop. I can do that."

I wrote the address down in my journal. Then, probably because she'd thought about it and wanted to ask me, she said, "Have you had a chance to meet my brother yet?"

"No, I haven't. I'm kept pretty busy, Lacey."

"He's supposed to call tonight and I'll tell him to go find you."

"It's probably not a good idea, Lacey."

"Hub, you two would get along together really well. Seriously. I just know it."

It couldn't happen and, honestly, I knew I had to say something to Lacey about her brother that would be hard for her to hear.

"Lacey, we've actually met."

"Why didn't you say something, Hub?"

"Because it's not how you think we met."

"My brother didn't say anything either."

"He doesn't know we met."

"Make some sense, Hub. Where did you meet him? How?"

I took a deep breath knowing full well that this could be it for me. Her brother was her brother after all, and I was about to offer a different glimpse of a brother she did not know.

"Remember the story Billy told about the carnies that ran your brother and Donny off the road?"

"Of course."

"It wasn't like that. Not even close."

"How do you know?"

"Because, I was one of them."

"You were in the truck that tried to run them off the road?" Lacey asked, confused and suspicious.

"I was hitch hiking back to the carnival with groceries when they pulled up in Donny's truck."

"That was the day I met you right?" she asked framing the events in her mind.

"Yes. At first, I thought they might be going to offer me a ride. But the minute they got out of the truck, they started calling me some pretty horrible names and told me they were going to beat the shit out of me."

"This is hard for me to believe, Hub."

"But it's true, Lacey. I swear to God, it's the truth."

"Maybe they were going to give you a ride."

"They were headed into town and when they passed me they flipped a u-turn."

"How did you know they weren't going to give you a ride, Hub?"

At that point, I wish I hadn't said anything to her in the first place. But, I had to because I wanted her to stop trying to get the two of us to meet.

"I was pretty damn sure they would have hurt me. Donny had a bat and was coming from one side of the truck and your brother from the other. I pulled out my knife and that stopped them in their tracks."

"A knife?"

"Yes, Lacey, I pulled out a knife."

"Then what happened?"

"They were still going to try and get me. I knew it sure as hell. So, I got ready. I slid the backpack off my shoulder to block a blow from Donny."

"Would you have used the knife, Hub?"

"If I had to," I said quietly.

"But the other truck? Was that real?"

"Yes. It belongs to Jesus, the guy I work with. He happened to be heading into town to buy some parts for the Ferris wheel. He saw things unfold and he got out of the truck and asked your brother and Donny what was going on."

"What did they say?"

"That they pulled over to give me a ride and I tried to rob them."

I could tell this was difficult for Lacey to hear all this. For the longest time she didn't say anything and then asked, "What happened after that?"

"They didn't know Jesus worked with me and then Jesus said, *Gentlemen, I work with him and the best thing for you would be to get your asses back into your truck and get out of here.* Then your brother said, *Or what? What if we...* and before he could finish his sentence, Jesus punched him in the face and knocked him out."

"So, this Jesus guy attacked my brother? Just like that?"

What could I say to her? If you broke it down, Jesus punched Tad because things might have happened, could have happened. I wanted to tell her that her brother was a prick and that he was lucky that that was all that happened. They would have hurt me and that was a fact. And I would have done my best to hurt them even if it included stabbing one of them.

But this is where the law falls apart. Jesus threw the first punch and that's exactly how it would be played out. Open and shut as far as the police saw it. The carnies started it all.

What Lacey could never understand or know, was that both of us could not afford to be tied up with the police. If she could just replay my question to Billy about why her brother and Donny didn't report it to the police, she might be able to see them for the chicken shits they were. They were shamed by a single guy. Jesus. That was a lot to process.

It was quiet on the other end of the phone and then, when I thought she was going to say something, the phone went dead.

"Everything okay, Hub?" Jesus asked when I wandered back to the truck.

"Yeah, sure, why?"

"You look down in the dumps."

"Just thinking, that's all."

Jesus, put on a clean shirt, threw water on his face and combed his hair. "Come on, Mopey. Want to drive around town drinking some beer?"

"Thanks, but I think I'll pass."

"Suit yourself."

For a while, I did nothing but sit on the cooler in the shade and listen to the evening chorus of birds and irrigation sprinklers. The crowds were gone, the last of the horse trailers left earlier for Cheyenne and the carnival was buttoned up tight. By the time we left tomorrow, the County Fairground would be a ghost town until we returned again next year. The little lazy city of Rawlins would go back to being just that, a small little farming community and just one more stop on our circuit in the endless nomadic life of Wacko's City of Fun Carnival.

I thought maybe I should've gone with Jesus but, in the end, I thought I'd take time to jot down some thoughts in my journal.

True, I felt crushed about Lacey hanging up on me. On the other hand, I realized my own good fortune. I'd met her and that was a good thing. I was still alive and had a routine with the carnival that would keep me out and away from the trouble I'd left behind. Every stop on the circuit put miles between me, Officer Broadhead and the juvenile court system.

And, just as certainly, I knew, at some point in time there would be a day of reckoning. The thing was, I wanted to have some control over how it happened.

I'd snapped at my sister over the phone for pointing out that I couldn't run forever and that was wrong of me. After talking with Soup, I thought of the pain and embarrassment my parents were going through, not to mention my little brother. He'd be lost.

I filled up nearly six pages of the journal and I smiled, trying to imagine what Ms. Nelson my English teacher would think of this story on the first day in school when she'd have us write about our summer vacation. But most of all, the writing made me take stock of myself and of what truly happened. In the end, the only common denominator in this trail of trouble was me. And that was sobering. *You reap what you sow* was my grandmother's favorite expression and I'd been doing a lot of reaping lately.

Chapter 30

We broke camp early and began the drive to Cheyenne. This time Jesus took lead in the caravan followed by the ragtag collection of homemade trailers, concessions and games stacked on the flatbeds with heavy equipment at the rear. The tail gunner was Wacko and Angel's rig.

From the passenger seat looking out at the oversized side-mirror of Jesus' truck I could see the carnival rigs serpentining along the road.

I thought about Zola's life as a gypsy and imagined they must have traveled in much the same way across Romania and the Slavic countries, from small town to small town, hustling people in games of chance, telling fortunes, trading wares, circling the caravans, hawking elixirs, playing gypsy music around the campfire at night and dancing wildly under the stars. Perhaps she was a descendent of gypsy royalty or maybe the daughter of the King of Gypsies. Then, all of that stolen when the Nazi's began to exterminate her tribe. How had she escaped? How had she survived, and would I ever be able to hear her stories and find out about the tear drop tattoos on her cheek?

My mother's mother was a storyteller. Every Sunday evening, Grandma Rosy held court over corned beef and cabbage dinners in a damp hallway of the tenant building where she and my grandpop Wally lived. She'd invite the neighbors and her parish priest over for dinner and she'd tell the most magnificent stories about her Ireland, complete with tales of silkies and the tinkers, the *pavees,* as she would call them and I was fascinated by these nomadic travelers. Though these stories would frighten my sister, they held magic for me. After the stories, Rosy would walk with us to the small bedroom we shared and make certain we said our prayers and then, as she tucked us into bed, she would whisper to me that *I was the gypsy of this family.* Could she have known then that I would somehow be traveling with a caravan of misfits?

I wanted to know more. Against all warnings, I wanted to know more about Zola. I wanted to hear her stories and I resolved to find a way into that mystery.

"What's going on in that head of yours, Hub? Where are you?" Jesus asked.

"Nothing. Nowhere," I answered, realizing this was not our normal routine.

"You haven't said a thing all morning."

"I've been day dreaming. Thinking."

"Anything in particular?"

"Not really. Everything. Nothing."

I didn't dare tell Jesus I'd had my fortune told by Zola. Worse than that, was the fact I wanted to get to know her.

"I don't believe that for a minute," Jesus said, taunting me. "It's the cowgirl got you?"

"Kind of," and that was the truth, but it was a dead-end street and I understood that.

"Well? How so?" he continued.

I could tell Jesus wasn't about to let up on my silence, so I started talking.

"I was just thinking about my friends back home. How they would think being in the carnival would be all romantic and stuff."

"Ain't nothing romantic about this, is there?"

"No. It's hard work but they wouldn't see it that way."

"How would they see it?"

"As an adventure. Like something they'd read in a novel."

"Fiction, right?"

"I guess."

"Nothing fiction about any of this."

"I don't know. Maybe there is."

Then, I prattled on about how this could be seen as a novel.

"If you think about it, Jesus, it's all here at the Wacko's City of Fun Carnival."

"That's a bit of a stretch, even for me."

The whole idea popped in my head to avoid talking about what I was really thinking about. It began to take its own form with its own logic.

"The first part of the novel begins with a kid running away from the law because he's done something stupid and crazy, right?"

"Okay, why does that sound strangely familiar?"

"He's got to become invisible so he joins a circus."

"Carnival," interrupted Jesus, "we're not a circus."

"Who said it was me or Wacko's City of Fun?"

"Go on."

I could tell Jesus was intrigued and this was a great way to pass the time.

"The carnival follows around rodeos. Wherever the rodeo goes, the carnival sets up close by."

"Okay."

"The kid gets partnered up with this really GOOD LOOKING guy whose body is completely tattooed."

"Best part so far."

"The kid hitchhikes to town one day to get supplies and on the way back he is about to get jumped by a couple of cowboys when his partner, sensing trouble, comes to his rescue."

"You forgot something," Jesus said, adding, "the kid meets the love of his life. A cowgirl at the café, right?"

"Who's telling the story here? You or me?"

"But you did."

"But maybe I want the kid to meet another cowgirl later on."

Jesus surrendered, "Okay. Okay. Go on."

So, on I went and I kept adding layers to the story until it was getting to be a full-length movie with plot twists and really cool double crosses. But essentially, it was about a guy (me) and a cowgirl (Lacey) who are from two warring families (the cowboys and the carnies) whose love is forbidden but they can't keep away from each other.

Jesus was completely into it (and so was I) because his character was the enforcer and then there's a major fight between the cowboys and the carnies when the girl's brother (Tad) finds out his sister (Lacey) is dating a carnie (me). It's like this clashing of gangs and it's a brutal fight and they're just beating the shit out of each other.

"And then what happens, Hub?"

"I'm not done yet, Jesus! Jesus!!" And we both started laughing because I hadn't used his name as a swear word before.

I hated to get interrupted because I was on a roll and sometimes it's hard to get back into a story but in this case, it was pretty much writing itself.

"So, here's what happens. It's a rumble. People are going at it with anything they've got. The cowboys are trying to rope the carnies, but the carnies are too quick. And the carnie family (me and the carnies) have got midgets (Little John and Stretch) who are really bad ass fighters. They like sneak up behind the cowboys and cut their Achilles heels..."

"But the cowboys would be wearing cowboy boots, the cowboys would notice," Jesus interrupted.

"Okay, Jesus, don't be so nitpicky. Maybe they stuck them someplace else. The main guy (me) is about to get into a fight with the cowgirl's (Lacey's) brother (Tad) so I don't have time to keep my eyes on the midgets. Okay?"

"Okay…okay, take it easy."

I realized that I needed to work Jesus (the enforcer) back into the story just to keep it interesting.

"So, the cowboy (Tad) pulls out a big Bowie knife and comes at the carnie (me) and then the enforcer (Jesus) sees a bunch of other cowboys coming up behind the carnie (me) and he jumps into the fight and kicks their asses. And this gives the carnie (me) a chance to pull out his switchblade and they get into a fight. The carnie (me) gets sliced in the arm, so he's bleeding and it doesn't look good."

"How bad is he cut?"

I ignored the question because I was on a roll.

"But it's not that bad. In fact, because the carnie (me) has a bunch of adrenalin rushing through him, he doesn't even notice it. Then, the cowboy (Tad) tries to stab the carnie (me) with a full on thrust but the carnie (me) manages to catch the cowboy's (Tad's) hand with his left hand and then the carnie (me) stabs him in the gut."

"No shit!"

"And he twists the knife in deep and the cowboy (Tad) crumbles to the ground and dies."

"The son-of-a-bitch had it coming," Jesus added, nodding his head like the cowboy (Tad) deserved to die.

That part really felt good and then I realized I'd been borrowing a little bit from Shakespeare's *Romeo and Juliet* and even a couple of scenes from *West Side Story*. But not completely, because I'd managed to work in the cowboys and carnies so it wasn't like I plagiarized the whole thing. Plus, I wasn't about to let the Romeo character (me) and the Juliet character (Lacey) take poison and die. That was just the easy way out. I never liked that about *Romeo and Juliet*. At least with *Bonnie and Clyde* they went down fighting.

For a minute, Jesus just took in the story and finally said, "That's a pretty good story, Hub. You should write that down."

"Thanks. Maybe one day I will."

For a while we drove in silence. I think both of us were just replaying it over in our heads. It was action packed, no question about it. But it was also what I'd like to have done with Tad the day they jumped me. And I'm sure that Jesus was enjoying the fact he'd kicked all those cowboys asses.

"There's only one thing missing, Hub."

"What's that?"

"The cowgirl. What happens to her? To them?"

"She (Lacey) hung up on him (me)."

I hadn't even completed the sentence before Jesus caught the mistake.

"Where's the phone come in?"

I backpedaled quickly, "The cowgirl (Lacey) couldn't get over the fact that her brother (Tad) was killed by the carnie she loved (me). She (Lacey) was HUNG up on the fact, even though her brother (Tad) was a complete asshole and she knew it, he was still family, so she walks away from the carnie (me) and they never see each other again."

"All that for nothing?"

"It seems so."

"Then, what's the point?"

"Sometimes the good guy doesn't win."

"Well, that sucks."

"Yeah, it sucks."

Chapter 31

I was surprised when the next sign showed us only 15 miles out of Cheyenne. My story had dissolved the distance between Rawlins and Cheyenne into a blink of the eye.

"This is going to be one of the biggest rodeos we do," Jesus said, adding a cautionary warning. "Really big and there are a number of things that can go wrong."

"How so?" I asked, curious about the comment.

"There's another carnival that will be on the midway with us, and Wacko and the owner don't get along real well. Plus, every single cowboy from the country will be there."

"What's the deal with Wacko and the other operator?"

"He used to work for Wacko and then started his own carnival. Took everything Wacko taught him and found some big money to get started out on his own."

"That stuff happens."

"True, but Wacko's pretty sure the guy stole a bunch of money from him before he left."

"That would explain a lot."

"Wacko couldn't prove it because the guy just disappeared one day and Wacko couldn't make payroll so there is no love lost between them. I honestly think Wacko would kill this guy if he got a chance."

"That sounds like Wacko," I said, trying to imagine how things might go if a fight broke out.

"It's not only the cowboys we've got to be careful of, but the carnies are a bigger problem. We don't like them and they don't like us and it's pretty toxic. Once we get all set up, Wacko will get us together and give us a talk. Just wait and see."

"So what's the drill?"

"Same old, same old. We'll set up the Octopus and then head over to the Ferris wheel and help Frenchy out. But the schedule is a little different than the regular stops."

"How so?"

Jesus explained that we couldn't even start the rides until the evening because of the Frontier Parade complete with marching bands, the rodeo royalty, the Thunderbirds putting on an air show and the Mayor of Cheyenne making a big speech.

We pulled into our designated area and slowly the rest of the rigs followed suit. This was clearly a big deal and the rodeo arena was at least three times larger than either Evanston or Rawlins. The heartbeat of Cheyenne Frontier Days was the rodeo arena and fairground surrounded by an Old Frontier Village where cowboys staged gunfights, a couple of saloons, a historic village, and a couple of main stages for entertainment. Buck Owens and the Buckaroos and Roger Miller, the guy who wrote *King of the Road,* were the featured entertainment. There were chuck wagons offering up cowboy grub and about two dozen other venues. In a way, it reminded me of a Disneyland for cowboys.

The minute our flatbed pulled up, Jesus and I started setting up the Baby Octopus with the help of a couple of guys from Big Heavy's crew. We were at a point where Jesus and I didn't even have to talk to each other. He'd taught me well and we probably put the Octopus, the safety fences and ticket booth up in half the time it took on my first day with the carnival.

Both of us headed over to help Frenchy and his crew erect the Ferris wheel. I ended up getting paired up with Crenshaw again and he was already swearing under his breath at Frenchy, the carnival and Wacko. Pretty much anything that came into his vision.

I wondered if he had some kind of tic, something he couldn't control that flooded his head with stupidity or something. There wasn't one of us here that didn't have something we were hiding, keeping under the skin but, for the most part, all of us could control it. Crenshaw couldn't. Drunk, Crenshaw was fun to be around. He had great stories and was one of those *Hail fellows, well met* my grandmother would talk about. His problem was being sober. He was meaner than a junkyard dog, almost like the things he said he couldn't help saying. This could be a problem around Wacko, particularly here in Cheyenne with all the other bullshit going on. Cowboys, carnies, and the other carnies was a crazy concoction and then throw into the mix a 50-gallon drum of gasoline with a crazy man holding a zippo lighter trying to light a cigarette and that's how I felt about Crenshaw. That's how I felt about Cheyenne. It felt dangerous.

Jesus was on the guidewires, which meant he was standing on the axle of the Ferris wheel making adjustments under the direction of Frenchy. I wanted to work my way up to that job.

Frenchy fired up the diesel; he'd slowly rotate the wheel while Jesus adjusted the turnbuckles. To look at it, Jesus looked like he was a gerbil in one of those cages that ran themselves silly. Only real slow. When Frenchy was satisfied, Jesus would climb down and we'd attach the seats into the stirrups.

"We always get the shit jobs," Crenshaw mumbled under his breath.

"There are six other guys doing the same thing," I said, and added something that was a sort of standard response in the carnival, "It all pays the same."

We set down the gondola seat where Frenchy directed us to. I started to head over to pick up the next gondola when Crenshaw said, "Fuck you kid."

"What did you say?" I snapped back.

"You heard me, I said fuck you."

Crenshaw said it loud enough that the other carnies stopped what they were doing and looked over to see what was going to happen. To see who was going to blink first.

"Crenshaw, grow the fuck up. Let's get this done, okay?"

As far as I was concerned it was over but when I bent over to pick up my end of the gondola, Crenshaw shoved me backwards.

"Fuck you and this whole chicken shit operation. I'm sick of all of you."

I had no choice so I pushed him back hard. He stumbled and took a wild swing at me and I punched him in the face. It was on and some of the carnies came over to break us up but, before they could, Wacko came out of nowhere and smashed a fist into the side of Crenshaw's face. It sounded like somebody smashing a watermelon on the ground. Crenshaw went down like all the bones had been pulled out his body. He crumbled. He was out cold. It happened so fast. Then Wacko started kicking him. Hard.

Nobody moved to help Crenshaw and when Wacko went to kick him again I grabbed Wacko to pull him off Crenshaw.

"Stop, Wacko," I cried but Wacko threw me aside like a ragdoll and then turned on me.

I expected him to do the same to me.

"Don't you ever get in the way of me and my crew or I'll do the same to you!"

"Yes, sir," I said. I was scared to death.

He turned quickly and yelled at Little John. "Get Crenshaw's kit together and drag this piece of shit out of here!"

"Right boss," and he took off running to where Crenshaw kept his belongings. Wacko turned and headed back toward his trailer.

Jesus had dropped from the axle when he saw me punch Crenshaw.

"You okay?" he asked.

"I think so."

"Crenshaw had it coming."

"Not like that," I answered. The adrenalin was still flowing and I was shaking.

"Come on, let's get him up. See if he's okay."

We bent to pick up Crenshaw but he was like a ragdoll and kept flopping around. His face was pulpy and beginning to swell. Jesus felt his neck to see if there was a pulse.

"Nuts," Jesus yelled, "grab us a bucket of water. Quick."

"Is he dead?"

"No."

"It was my fault, Jesus."

"Bullshit, kid."

"I should have just let it roll off my back."

"Not here, Hub. He called you out. You did the right thing."

"It doesn't feel right."

Crenshaw groaned. Nuts returned with the water and Jesus had him throw a bucketful in Crenshaw's face. He coughed and spit out some blood and a couple of teeth.

Little John arrived with Crenshaw's kit. It was a bedroll and a canvas US Army bag with his name stenciled on the outside. It surprised me. How anybody like Crenshaw could have been in the army that was full of rules and regulations was beyond me.

"Get your hands off me," Crenshaw garbled, "or I'll kick both your asses."

"Shut the fuck up," Jesus whispered. "You're lucky Wacko didn't kill you."

"Like he could have," he replied indignantly. It was mush language.

"Hub saved your life, asshole. If it wasn't for him, Wacko might have killed you."

Crenshaw tried to focus in on me. "Like I owe you shit."

"Listen, asshole, we're going to drag your sorry ass out of here and I'd advise you hit the fucking road. Do you understand what I am saying?"

"Or you'll do what?"

Jesus didn't hesitate. He punched Crenshaw in the face and it was lights out.

"Grab him underneath the arms, Hub."

Jesus took Crenshaw's feet and we carried, dragged, him out to the frontage road. Little John brought his kit and we propped him in the shade of a tree and left him there. I didn't feel very good about any of this. I felt, in some way, responsible for him. Maybe Jesus was right. Maybe Crenshaw was just one of those guys who never knew when to keep his pie-hole shut.

It reminded me of a summer trip my sister and I took with our father. The old man was a traveling salesman and his territory was the western states; California, Nevada, Wyoming, Utah and Idaho. Mostly, it was just a lot of driving and we'd wait in the car while he made his business calls and then at night we'd stay in a motel, usually with a pool, and eat in a restaurant. This year, however, he promised to take us over the border into Mexico.

I loved Mexico because it was so completely different than anyplace we'd ever been. My sister wasn't keen on it but I loved the energy, the different smells, the street food and I had my first taco with a side of beans and rice. I thought I'd died and gone to heaven.

What interested me most was the notion that things, dark mysteries, were happening behind the doors of some of the cantinas. Smitty told me once that there were shows, naked shows, where women would actually have sex with a donkey on stage. I called bullshit on him but he swore he had a friend who had a friend that swore it was the truth. And another thing, you could also buy Spanish fly down in Mexico. The rumor was that it was made from dried

Spanish beetles and ground into a powder and if you put it into a girl's drink or milkshake she'd get so horny she'd rip your clothes off and then you'd be in for the time of your life. I kept my eyes open and, as we walked along the sidewalks, with vendors trying to hustle us and little kids begging for change, I tried to peek into the XXX rated adult shows. I also kept my eyes peeled for anybody selling Spanish fly.

One day the old man left us at the hotel we were staying in while he made a few business calls. The place was pretty grand compared to most of the places we'd stayed in on the trip. The rooms all centered around a beautiful courtyard that had a big fountain in the center and it was open to the sky. There were really cool wicker tables with chairs that swept up and looked like a throne. All the tile on the ground was shiny and around the courtyard these handmade tiles told stories about the history of Mexico. And red peppers?

It seemed like every five feet a bunch of dried, red chile peppers hung down from the rafters. I told my sister I thought they were to keep flies away but she gave me a lecture about peppers and how there were a gazillion types used daily by Mexicans in their meals and blah, blah, blah. We'd just ordered lunch when the old man showed up and he was pretty lit up. In a good way.

"Guess where we're going tonight?" he asked, reaching down and taking a corn chip and dipping it in some red spicy sauce.

"To see traditional Mexican dancing?" my sister asked.

The old man started laughing. "Better than that. Hub, your turn."

"To go into one of those cantinas?"

The old man gave me one of those looks.

"We're going to a real bullfight!" he said excitedly. "Javier, the guy I do business with down here got us some tickets."

"Do I have to go?" my sister asked, giving the old man her disgusted look.

"You both do," he replied, like we didn't appreciate the gift he'd been given.

"Cool, dad," I said with great enthusiasm. It just took a minute for it to sink in but I really thought it was the best thing that we could ever do. Better, in my mind, than Disneyland although we'd never been there.

Javier met us when we got to the arena and took us to our seats. He spoke very good English and when we were seated, he told us all about the history of bullfighting and how it was a very important sport all around the world. I asked a lot of stupid questions that he answered patiently. My sister was pretty quiet and when he asked her what was the matter, she told him she thought the sport was brutal and cowardly. Trust my sister.

I thought he'd be offended but he simply said, "Yes, some people feel that way, even in my country, but it is a tradition that goes back hundreds and hundreds of years. Today's matador is very famous and if he kills the bull quickly he might be awarded the bull's ears. Perhaps even the tail."

"What does he do with them?" I asked, thinking of my lucky rabbit's foot.

Javier laughed, looked over at my old man with a smile and raised eyebrows and said, "I really don't know."

Before the bullfight began, there was a parade around the arena of all the participants. First the picadors came out on horses that were covered in big protective blankets. They had long lances and their job was to weaken the bull by stabbing it. They were followed by guys dressed like matadors but they weren't. They carried these banderillas that kind of looked like small harpoons. These guys were *muy loco* because they had to stick the harpoons into the bull who was already pissed off. Oh, yeah, they didn't have horses. Then the matador walks into the ring and he's all dressed in glitter and silk with these very tight pants and a fancy tight vest. He's carrying his hat, that kind of looked like a tightly coiled black poodle, in one hand and a red cape that's slung over his shoulder with a sword that's kind of bent at the end that he'll use to kill the bull.

Once it gets started and the first picador stabs the bull, my sister pukes all over the place and my dad has to leave with her. So, Javier and I have a grand old time of things. He asks if my father allows me to drink beer and I didn't want to disrespect him so I said, "Yes, he does on special occasions."

"Would he consider this a *special occasion?*"

"Absolutely," I replied looking him in the eyes.

"Then, we shall have a beer with some roasted corn."

I'm sorry my old man missed the entire bullfight but I'm glad he didn't come back and get me because I thought it was pretty damn interesting. There were some very close calls and I've got to hand it to the matador. He had seriously big balls. When he finally killed the bull, the crowd erupted and people started throwing out flowers into the arena. Then he took off his hat and held it up in the air and walked over toward us and then looked up at the grand box seats where there must have been some important dignitary who did something and the crowd went insane because then some other guys went over and cut the tail and the ears off the bull.

Javier was screaming as loud as anybody else and he leaned over to me and screamed, "He is the very best."

A couple of guys came out with donkeys and hooked the bull up by chains a started to drag it out of the arena. That part made me sad because I swear, I think the bull was still breathing a little.

And that made me think of Crenshaw. How we'd dragged him out of the carnival and left him by a tree in the dirt. At least he was still breathing and he had both of his ears.

Chapter 32

When everything was set up and ready for our opening, Wacko called us all together. Word had made it around to all the carnies about Crenshaw and there was a somberness to the meeting. If Wacko was still angry with me, he didn't show it but a couple of the carnies nodded to me as if to say, *Good on you for keeping Wacko from killing him.*

There was something different about Wacko's presence this afternoon. It was an intensity in his body. He looked tense like a wound-up coil and tight as though he was ready to throw down against anybody or anything. Like a number of the crew, he usually wore a blue denim work shirt, the shirttail left untucked, and a pair of Duck work pants but today he had on a tight black t-shirt that accentuated his muscles, tight Levis and a pair of motorcycle boots. It looked as though he was expecting to rumble. I'd never seen him in a short-sleeved shirt before and I couldn't help but notice how big his forearms were. And his tattoos. On his left arm a heart with wings and a dagger through it. On his right arm a skull, cross-bones and cobras coming out of the eye sockets. He was foreboding. Not the sort of man you'd want to cross under any circumstance.

"Listen up, all of you. For those of you who have been here before, you know the drill. If you get some free time, which you probably won't, don't head off without anybody with you. A fuck-of-a-lot can go wrong here in Cheyenne and we want to avoid it. Think before you act. We got the cowboys and we've got the other carnival to contend with. And ladies and gentlemen, I can sure-as-shit guarantee that we are not on either one of their Christmas lists."

A few of the carnies laughed softly.

"We won't start anything but if somebody is crazy enough to start something with me, we will end it. Any questions?"

Nobody's hand went up in the air. There wasn't anything to ask. Wacko was plenty clear. I saw Angel for the first time in a while and she offered me a smile and a nod. I'd purposely stayed as far away from her as I could. Jesus and I headed back to the truck when he asked me if everything was okay.

"What do you mean?" I asked, knowing he was referring to Crenshaw.

"About Crenshaw?"

"It's just I didn't get why you punched him in the face, that's all. He wasn't going to hurt anybody when we dragged him off."

"As insurance."

"What does that mean?"

"If he would have gone on five more minutes with his bullshit, I think Wacko would have killed him."

"Seriously?"

Jesus didn't answer because for him it was over and he was probably right about Wacko.

"It's about that time of the month to take a shower. Let's grab our stuff and head over to the public swimming pool. They've got pretty good showers and they let us take one for a quarter without paying the swimming fee."

"I could use a shower," I replied, smelling under my armpits.

"That's why I suggested it," Jesus replied, giving me a big old grin.

"A couple of the other guys want to go in to see the big parade. You interested?"

"Sounds good to me."

We grabbed our toilet kits and towels and headed into town.

"So, why the serious pep-talk today?"

Jesus considered the question carefully before answering. "A couple years back one our guys got killed."

"No shit," I replied quietly. "How?"

"An old-timer. Everybody love him. Stabbed to death from the back. It wasn't a robbery. Still had his billfold on him. Nobody knows why."

"Didn't the cops investigate it?"

Jesus laughed. "Are you kidding? If they did, it wasn't much of an investigation. They just went through the motions. It went down as an unsolved murder."

"Any reporters interview you guys?"

"No. Here's the reality. If it would've been a cowboy or a local they would have been all over it, but it was just a *carnie.*"

"His name was Hooker. Clarence Hooker and he was about the nicest guy I've met since I've been working for Wacko. He and Wacko were good friends and Wacko took it pretty hard. Hooker had no next of kin that anybody knew about, so Wacko put up the money and held a big wake and service for him. He's buried here in Cheyenne so this place carries some heavy weight for Wacko."

"Did Wacko have any idea who might have done it?"

"He has his suspicions. Thinks it was somebody from the other carnival."

"Any particular reason?"

"His gut instinct. That's all."

The pool was jam packed with kids swimming, cannonballing off the diving board and hanging out. I saw some really good looking girls about my age in a cluster talking and giggling. When we walked by the chain link fence toward the entrance they looked over and one of them must have said something funny because they started laughing.

"Just ignore them," Jesus said, not even glancing in their direction.

"I would, but they're pretty good looking."

"Good point," he said, turning toward the girls and blowing them a kiss.

That sent them into a giggling fit. I thought how I'd like to be in my bathing suit and be hanging out at the pool, meeting some new girls and some kids my own age. To tell the truth, it made me a bit homesick. I'd turn 17 in a couple of days and even if I could just up and go back, I wouldn't be the same as I was before. I'd seen a lot and felt much older and less naïve. I wondered if I'd have anything to talk about with my classmates back home. Sweet Lindsey was a lifetime ago. And Lacey, the saddest thing of all. I was sure I'd never be going through Evanston again. Maybe things are just supposed to happen the way they do and we can't do anything to change it.

The shower was the best quarter I think I've ever spend in my life. I felt like I'd washed the Crenshaw off of me. When we got back to the carnival there were about six carnies waiting for us. I was surprised to see Big Heavy and Frenchy standing around by our campsite smoking. Darnelle and the midgets were there, plus Nuts and the Ghost but the biggest surprise was Annabel and Zola standing off to the side away from the others.

"You've got to be kidding," Jesus whispered. "I can't believe the witch wants to go."

"She's not a witch, Jesus. I already told you that."

"Well, she's not riding with us. That's where I draw the line."

There was some discussion as to how we would get everybody into town. Jesus' truck could fit all of us in and then we were only looking for one parking spot. When everybody agreed, Big Heavy and Frenchy were the first to get into the bed and everybody else followed except Zola who went over and stood by the passenger side. I nearly split a gut trying not to laugh because I knew how uncomfortable Jesus was with the idea of having Zola tag along. I was already in the back of the truck.

"Hub, why don't you ride in the front seat with Zola and me."

"Done," and I jumped out, looked over a Jesus who gave me the snake-eye and then walked around to open the door for Zola.

"Let Zola have shotgun. You take the middle."

"Hello, Zola," I said, looking her directly in the eyes.

"Hello, Mr. Hub," she answered.

"It's your lucky day. Shotgun is the best spot."

"I don't know the shotgun," she replied.

"The window side," I said, looking to see if she was putting me on.

"Why is it called shotgun, then?"

I thought for a moment and realized I had no idea how it got the nickname.

"Jesus, do you know?"

"When stage coaches used to cross the country carrying money for the banks there was always an agent with a shotgun who sat by the driver. He carried a shotgun in case they got attacked by bandits."

I climbed into the cab and slid next to Jesus and Zola got in next to me. Annabel climbed into the back.

"Thank you, Mr. Jesus for allowing me to ride with you."

That flustered Jesus because here he was sitting in the cab with somebody that, I think, scared him.

"You're welcome," he replied without looking over at Zola.

We drove along in silence that became uncomfortable. Finally, Zola spoke.

"Mr. Jesus, you don't need to fear me."

"I don't," Jesus said curtly. "I'm not afraid of anything."

"Yes, Mr. Jesus, I believe this is true in a physical world but there are other worlds."

Jesus didn't say a thing and I watched as his grip on the wheel tighten. "I am not an *adivino* or a *bruja*, Mr. Jesus. That is all I want to say to you. Mr. Hub already knows this."

Great! This is just what I didn't need. To be brought into the conversation because Jesus would want to know why she said that and he'd weasel it out of me sooner or later.

We pulled into the dirt parking lot of Frontier Town and drove around looking for a spot. Big Heavy pounded on the roof of the cab and yelled, "Two rows over Jesus. A guy's pulling out."

Jesus gave it some gas and the barrels rumbled and we cut around a corner quickly almost throwing Big Heavy from the back of the truck.

"Just one thing Zola," Jesus said.

"Yes, Mr. Jesus."

"Why are you here? Why did you come today? You never join us."

"To tell you that you both are good men. And to tell you that you must be careful and watch out for each other. That is all, Mr. Jesus. That is all."

Jesus pulled into the parking spot and the crew piled out of the back. Before Zola opened the door, she said, "And Mr. Jesus, you don't need to give me a ride back. I will find my own way."

Then in a twinge of guilt or whatever, Jesus said, "It's a long way back. I'll give you a ride back."

"I have made you uncomfortable Mr. Jesus and that's not what I intended. I will be fine."

With that, she opened the door and we joined the crowd.

"Okay," Jesus barked, "remember, we all stay together. If we get separated, meet back at the truck by 4:30 pm. If you're not here, we leave without you." Everybody mumbled their agreement and people promptly split up into small groups and took off in every direction. I looked around to see if Zola was with us and she was gone. She'd vanished. We hadn't even gone 500 steps and it was as though she disappeared into thin air.

I nudged Jesus. "Do you see Zola?"

Jesus stopped, turned around and after surveying the crowd in the parking lot, looked back at me. "She's gone, Hub...I can't see her." He had a quizzical look on his face but didn't say a thing.

We headed up Pioneer Avenue that would take us to the state capitol where the parade would be starting soon. The street was packed with people in folding chairs, babies in strollers, kids waving little American flags and people pulling beer and soft drinks out of coolers.

"You want to tell me how that happened?" Jesus asked.

"How what happened?" I asked knowing full well he was referring to Zola.

"That she showed up and rode with us."

I wasn't interested in getting into it with Jesus. He was pissed off and how was I supposed to know why she showed up. Carnies were heading into town and she was one of them. One of us. I finally just said, "I have no fucking idea," and then tried to dump it off on him. "You let her get into the truck, not me. If you didn't want her to, you should have said so."

"But you said *Hello* to her. What was I supposed to say?"

"And I said *Hello* to every other person coming with us. That didn't mean anything. It was just courteous. That's all."

I felt like I was in the beginning of a fight with my sister. Jesus was picking at me, trying to get me to make sense of Zola's appearance and I wasn't going to bite.

"What about the bullshit she said in the cab, huh? *You are good men and you need to be careful...*and the part about *Mr. Hub knows.* Huh, what about that? Why did she say that? What is it you know, Mr. Hub?"

I knew exactly what she meant but I wasn't about to tell Jesus that I'd actually let her tell me my fortune. He'd warned me about talking with her and I sure as hell didn't want to tell him about it. That would be like adding fuel to the fire and things had already heated up with Crenshaw. *Let sleeping dogs lie* as my grandmother would always say. Today, this made sense.

"You said it yourself, Jesus. She's bat shit crazy."

The crowd let out a roar. You could hear them before they arrived. the

Navy's Blue Angels were specks in the sky but we could see them far in the distance closing in tight formation. Six of them in a 'V' formation with two each releasing funnels of red, white and blue smoke. When they ripped over us, you could feel the ground shake. On the second pass over the crowd they flew mirror images of each other. Three jets flying low in a small 'V' formation, and the other three flying upside down, directly over them. It seemed they were only feet apart from each other.

"Holy shit!" a kid, about 11 years old shouted and his mother shook him by shoulders and threatened to wash his mouth out with soap. Jesus and I started laughing because it was exactly what we were about to say.

The parade was fantastic with its marching bands, chuck wagons, stage coaches, riders dressed in period costumes, Cheyenne Indians on beautiful mounts in full tribal regalia and old fire engines. This was ten times better than the Macy's Day parade my dad took us to once where we watched floats and big helium balloons of Mickey Mouse and other cartoon characters from a store-front window of a barber shop. I'll never forget that because it got really hot and my sister threw-up all over the place and then we had to leave.

After the parade, we walked around and watched a shoot-out in Old Frontier Town, ate a barbecued pulled-pork sandwich with baked beans and coleslaw at the Sidewinder Saloon and washed it down with a couple of iced cold beers. Then we walked through the Indian Village where a drum circle was going on between a group of different tribes and on the way out, Jesus asked if we could stop and look at some Indian jewelry. While he looked at some turquoise bracelets, I looked at arrowheads and Indian dolls. I thought about buying a handmade Indian doll of a mother carrying her baby in a papoose and some arrowheads to send to my sister and brother. At the last minute, I decided not to do it.

Jesus bought a really beautiful bracelet with this intricate beading and when I asked who it was for he just said *A lady friend of his* and left it at that. I suspected it was the lady in the Cadillac but didn't push it.

As we headed back to the truck, I thought what a wonderful afternoon this had been. Jesus and I were just hanging out like two brothers would do. It was such a welcome relief from the pressures of the carnival. No looking over my shoulder worried about the madness of it all. It felt like I was normal again.

By the time we arrived at the truck, everybody was already waiting for us. Everyone except for Zola. Jesus, looked around nervously to see if he could see her anywhere but I knew she wouldn't be there. I knew where she was. She was back. Back at the carnival.

Finally, I looked over at Jesus and said, "Let's go. She's not here."

"Right," he said, checking his watch. "She'll have to find her own way back."

"She's already there."

Jesus nodded his head and we loaded everybody up and headed back to the madness of Wacko's City of Fun Carnival.

Chapter 33

Cheyenne was not the *same old, same old* as promised. Opening night, following the parade, was nonstop robot work. *Sell tickets, take tickets, place people into the seats, buckle the seat, turn on the ride, stand with a glazed look on my face, unbuckle the safety belts and reload and do it all again.* I only laughed once when I had a young family of four from London, England who were visiting the *wild west* on their vacation. After snugging up the belts on his two children the father said, *Thanks for snapping the lap strap chap.* I don't know if he was trying to be clever but it sounded so funny with his accent and all that it got me chuckling and so I started using the expression on people when I strapped them in. The thing about an English accent is everything they say sounds so smart.

By the time we finished opening night it was close to 2 a.m. and both of us kind of dragged our asses back to the truck and hit the sack. Usually, Jesus and I would have a smoke, visit and turn in. Most nights I'd write some stuff in my journal about the goings on at Wacko's but I didn't even have the strength to keep my eyes open let alone write something thoughtful down.

Day two, the same. Day three the same. Day four, my 17th birthday, started out the same way except for one very special thing. Around 7ish, I was going through the motions, not even trying to be clever with the *lapstrap* thing, when I heard this woman's voice ask if she could get a free ride. I was all ready to lash out because I was sick and tired of people trying to cut so they didn't have to stand in line like the rest of the stiffs.

When I turned around to rip into her, there she was! Lacey Dalton in the flesh!!! Lacey Dalton, the one and only Lacey *Barrel Racing* Dalton of Evanston, Wyoming. Lacey Dalton who broke my heart. Lacey Dalton, the one who got away. Lacey Dalton who I never thought I would ever see again.

There were a million things that went through my mind. Things I wanted to say if I ever saw her again. Things I had written to her. A journal full of apologies and promises. And now, here in front of me and all I managed to get out of my mouth, in this moment, was, "Hey."

Lacey laughed and said, "Is for horses."

"What?"

"Hay is for horses," she said, smiling that big wide sky Wyoming smile. And then she said it again, slowly so I could connect the dots. Slowly. "Hay... is...for...horses," and she threw her arms around me. Nothing, nothing in the whole wild world could have been a better birthday present. And she was more beautiful than I remembered her.

"Wait, here," I said, "stand here and don't move."

I loaded the Octopus and fired it up. I hopped over the fence and went to the ticket booth were Jesus was making change and started yammering to him about a million miles an hour.

"She...cameback...thegirlfromEvanston...thecowgirl."

"Speak English, Hub. What the hell are trying to say?"

I took a breath and told Jesus what had happened and he came out from the ticket booth and I dragged him over to meet Lacey and I could tell that he was pretty impressed. And Lacey said all the right things to him like how I'd talked him up and such things (which I had) and finally Jesus, God bless his soul, told me to take a half-hour break and he could manage.

I grabbed Lacey's hand and pretty near dragged her over to the pickup truck. We climbed up into the bed and I started asking her a bunch of questions, like what was she doing here and how did she get here and did her parents let her ride on the circuit or did she just run away like I did and on and on until she finally stopped me by leaning over and giving me a kiss. And it was a good kiss. A soft kiss. A long kiss that made me want to curl up in her arms and just hold her tight and not let go of her until the medics came to peel me away from her. And my heart slowed down. And the world righted itself. And I felt whole again.

Lacey talked and I listened, holding her in my arms. She was on the circuit and her parents actually agreed that she needed to barrel race. They hitched up the family horse trailer and even drove her to Cheyenne to support her dream. It was too much to believe and then it wasn't.

"My parents are going to stay here and see how I do."

"Oh," I said weakly, "that's great."

"Don't worry, Hub. My folks are staying with some friends so we'll have plenty of time together."

Then I was happy again. "When do you ride?" I asked because I wanted to see her ride because Lacey was really good.

"In about an hour and a half," she answered. "Do you think you can get free and come watch?"

"Not a chance, Lacey. It's the last night and we won't be done until almost midnight."

"Will you meet me afterwards?"

"Wild horses couldn't keep me away." I thought I was pretty clever with the rodeo line but Lacey just smirked at me like, *Ha, Ha, Ha.*

"My mom wants to meet you."

"Why? Does she know I'm a carnie?"

"Not really, but she said you were really polite over the phone and that's pretty rare with the guys I've dated before. So, she's curious."

"And that's what killed the cat."

"I knew you were going to say that."

"If you knew that, what's next?"

"You're going to try and kiss me."

And I leaned over and did just that.

"I've got to get back, Lacey."

She pouted.

"But, I'll meet you later on tonight. I promise."

Lacey walked me back to the Octopus and then gave me another kiss in front of everybody and some people hooted but she didn't care and neither did I.

"Good luck tonight. You'll do great, Lacey, Queen of the Barrel Racers."

"Thanks, Hub. I'll be thinking about you when I ride."

I let out a howl.

The rest of the night seemed like it was in slow motion. It reminded me of the last day of school where you sat in class with nothing to do but watch the clock slowly close in on the last three minutes before school let out and you ran into summer.

Just before we took the last load of stiffs on the Octopus, I looked over to see Angel talking with Jesus. It seemed strange to me that she'd drop by and I watched as Jesus nodded his head up and down like he understood or was agreeing with what she was saying. It didn't really make any difference to me because as soon as the last ride finished, I was out of here and on my way to meet Lacey.

Jesus tallied up the cash box while I cleaned up the garbage inside the gate and then he came over to speak to me.

"Wacko wants to see all of us back at the trailer when we're done."

"Why? What's up?"

"It's not good. A bunch of cowboys jumped Little John and Stretch."

"What the fuck."

"They're beat up pretty bad."

"Are they going to be okay?" I asked. I couldn't believe it. Seriously, what kind of assholes would jump Little John and Stretch?

"Angel's patched them up but she said it was ugly."

"Did they know who did it? Who jumped them?"

"Stretch couldn't talk. His jaw's broken and Angel's going to drive him in to emergency and I don't know about Little John."

"What does that mean that Wacko wants to see us?"

"Payback."

Jesus and I walked over to the truck where he locked up the cash box. He climbed up onto the bed, opened up his tool box and pulled out a pipe wrench.

"You got your knife on you, Hub?"

"I do."

"Good. You might need it."

Chapter 34

By the time we reached Wacko's trailer there were about a dozen carnies gathered around, all of them carrying something. Some kind of weapon. Everything from baseball bats to brass knuckles and nobody was talking.

Wacko came out of the trailer followed by Little John. Little John's head was bandaged up and he looked like he was wearing a zombie costume for Halloween with a bunch of dried blood on the outside of the bandage. He was holding a cold compress to his left eye. He was not recognizable. His face was all mashed up like hamburger. Somebody brought over a log for Little John to sit on. Wacko's face was all camouflaged up except for his mouth that was painted in a freaky red smile like the Joker in Batman comics.

Even the toughest of the carnies were choked up seeing Little John. Wacko raised both hands in the air for silence. He climbed up onto an Eskimo cooler and spoke.

"Cowboys did this," Wacko said, plain and simple. "The two guys that started it were a team. A tall goofy looking guy and a smaller mouthy guy. They ambushed them. There were others too. They mumbled something like, *I told you assholes it wasn't over.*"

Shit. I looked over at Jesus and we knew who it was. Goddamnit. Lacey's brother Tad and his stooge sidekick. Really? Now? The worst of all possible times?

"We're going after them. Now. The buck stops here."

There was a murmur of approval from the carnies.

"This is not in your contracts so, if you don't want to go, you don't have to and I won't hold it against you. Plain and simple."

There wasn't a sound from us.

"If you're on the fence, just ask yourself this: *Would Little John and Stretch come to your defense if you were getting your ass stomped?*"

"Hell yes," somebody cried out and I thought I could see a sliver of a smile from Little John.

"Any questions?"

"How will we know who they are?"

"We show up ready to kick ass and somebody will point the finger. They're cowboys not carnies."

A cheer came up from the carnies.

"I'm passing out some black Kiwi polish. Paint up in case it gets real crazy so we don't beat the shit out each other."

When the shoe polish got to me I hesitated for a second. Jesus noticed it and whispered, "You don't have to go if you don't want to. I'll cover for you."

"No way in hell," I said adamantly, "I was just trying to figure out what to put on my face."

But that was a bold-faced lie. I really didn't want to do this. Not with the possibility I might get caught and get sent back. Or worse, I could get seriously hurt, maybe even killed. Or double-worse, I'd never see Lacey again.

Jesus smeared three middle fingers into the polish and made three parallel lines from my nose to my eyes and then did the same for himself. If I looked half as bad ass as he did, I was ahead of the game because I was scared shitless. When Jesus passed the Kiwi to the next guy, he whispered to me again.

"Your girlfriend's here, Hub. Nobody would blame you for a lot of reasons."

I'd been there long enough to know the carnies wouldn't say anything but I'd be on the outs. Outside the family and what would be worse, I'd be a leper.

I looked to where he was looking and Zola was staring straight at me.

"Hell," Jesus joked, "Zola won't even need to put on any war paint. She's painted already."

Something made me walk over to her. When I got up close, she stuck two things into my hands.

"Take these, Mr. Hub. One if for you and one if for Mr. Jesus. They will protect you." I quickly looked into my hand and looked up to thank her and she was gone.

"One other thing," Wacko said. "We go over there in twos and we stay in the shadows until we reassemble. We attract less attention that way. Twelve guys in war paint will attract attention. Not only from the cowboys, but the other carnies."

"Where should we meet?" Nuts asked.

"By the flats just to the south of the arena. That way we can head on down by the chutes where the cowboys hang out."

"Let's go," Frenchy bellowed and we took off.

"Stay close, Hub. Stay alert."

"Here, take one of these."

"It's from Zola to protect us."

"I'm not into her bullshit, Hub."

"Do it for me." He took the amulet and shoved it into his Levis pocket and we headed out.

My grandfather was a Golden Glove champion boxer and actually boxed for the Navy when he was young. He taught me how to box but it was my uncle, Uncle Bill, who taught me how to fight and how to fight dirty. He was a bad ass special forces guy who drove fast cars and dated beautiful women. *Never square up. Stay low to the blow. Strike first and strike fast. Be the first one in and the last one standing.* I thought about this while heading over with Jesus. I felt surprisingly calm. Focused. I knew things would change the minute we got there and moved in. It's that crowd thing. Maybe Wacko, and probably Jesus, would call the two chicken shits out and it would be two on two. Truth was, I knew it wouldn't happen that way. Anybody who would lay in wait to jump a couple of guys like Little John and Stretch were chicken shits and wouldn't admit to it. I had another thought I bounced off Jesus.

"Maybe the rest of the cowboys on the circuit know what kind of assholes they are and they'll give them up."

It kind of made sense to me. Why would you want to step into a shit storm for a couple of low-lifes?

"It'll never happen."

"Why?"

"The same reason that we would have jumped in to bail out Crenshaw if he'd been beat up by cowboys."

"No, because we beat him up ourselves," I said sarcastically.

"Don't be an asshole now."

"I'm sorry. I get it."

We moved along quietly staying to the outskirts of the arena. The rodeo was over and I knew Lacey would probably be finishing up and visiting with her friends. This wasn't the way I expected my day would finish up.

"Jesus, how do you think this will go down?"

"Your guess is as good as mine."

"Do you think it will be a two-on-two. The cowboys against you and Wacko?"

"It can't be Wacko, Hub."

"Why?"

"Because he'll kill one of them. If he fights and kills one of those shit kickers, he gets thrown in the clink for murder and we're all out of work."

"So, who will it be? You and Frenchy?"

"Nope. He's too slow."

"Then who?"

"Us. We've got a score to settle."

Now I was scared and suddenly, my throat got dry and I was glad Jesus couldn't see me shaking. I think Jesus felt it and spoke softly.

"We hope for a two-on-two which means we've got to call them out."

"Why us? I mean, why wouldn't we let Wacko call them out?"

"I just told you. Because if he does, he's in and all bets are off."

I thought about the cowboys and about how those guys who rode were crazy. Did it translate into fighting? Could they get as bat shit crazy as Wacko? I could hear my uncle's voice, *Don't overthink things, just do it.* I wished he was here with me now.

"Another thing," Jesus added, in a cautionary voice. "Keep your knife hidden. Only pull it out if they've got something. It's important."

"Got it."

We reached the agreed meeting spot and Nuts and a couple of other carnies were already there. Wacko and Frenchy were right behind them and pretty soon we had a dozen carnies. Then, walking up from the back of arena, backlit so we couldn't tell who it was came this limping figure. We all tensed up and as it got closer somebody said, "It's Crenshaw."

"Jesus Christ, it's Crenshaw," Nuts said.

Crenshaw walked up the knoll like the living dead. He looked worse than the Little John and Stretch, but he was walking. I'll give him that. When he saw Wacko, he didn't hesitate. He walked right up to Wacko and apologized. He told Wacko he'd come back to the carnival to apologize but when Annabel told him what was going on, he headed right over here.

I watched Wacko's face. All painted up like the Joker, it was hard to tell what he'd do or say. Finally, Wacko stuck out his hand and shook Crenshaw's.

"It takes a big man to apologize," Wacko said seriously, "and if it gets nasty, it'd be good to know you're with us."

"Thanks boss," Crenshaw said, though it was hard to understand him all bashed up like he was. Then he slid into place with the rest of the carnies.

"Okay, gentlemen, listen up. We don't know who these two cowboys are but we'll give them a fair chance for a fair fight. If not, we'll pick the two biggest pricks out of the lineup and give them something to think about. Got it?"

I stepped forward and addressed Wacko. "I know who they are," and then corrected myself. "Jesus and I know who they are because we had some trouble with them in Evanston."

Wacko looked over at Jesus who nodded his head in agreement and then he looked back at me.

"Kid, you're pretty young to get involved in this, so just point them out to me and Jesus and I will take over."

And then, for some unknown reason I opened my trap and the following came out of my mouth, "I can't let you do that Wacko. It's my score to settle and if I don't take care of it here, and I let somebody else fight my battles, I won't be able to look myself in the face."

If anybody could understand that, it was Wacko. And maybe if I lived through this night he could explain it to me after this was all over.

"Let's go," he said and we spread out to look like a bigger group and moved down toward the chutes.

We were about three-quarters of the way there when one of the cowboys noticed us and said something to the others, because they got real interested in a hurry. They gathered around in their own group and none of them ran off. They knew something was coming, but they didn't know what.

One of them looked at Wacko, who was out front with Jesus and me and called out, "What the hell do we have here? An early Halloween party?"

What a stupid son-of-a-bitch, I thought to myself because Wacko was going to put a hurt on him. At best, it would be a three-on-three because Wacko had just been dealt in.

"Over on the right," I breathed to Jesus, "the two cowboys."

Jesus nodded his head slightly and then I called them out. By their names. In front of everybody.

"You two chicken shits beat up a couple of our guys and we're here to settle the score."

"Bullshit," another cowboy said. "Why would we do something like that?"

"Well, asshole," I answered, "why don't you just ask Donnie and Tad?" and I pointed directly at them.

The cowboy was stymied for a minute because I'd called them by their names. The right move would have been to let us go at those two. Just the four of us and who knew what would have happened. It would have been the smartest play.

The cowboys looked at Donny and Tad. Then, Tad realized who we were and, before I could call the two of them out to fight just Jesus and me, he sneered and called out, all big ass and tough, "Well, if it isn't Spic and Span."

Before we could propose a two-on-two it all ignited. The cowboy who was doing all the talking came after me but Wacko was already on him and then somebody threw a shoeing hammer to Tad and he came after me. Jesus went after Donny with his wrench and all hell broke loose.

Fights are a blur and all I can remember is this: Tad cocked back to bash my skull in with the hammer but I closed the gap quickly and when he went over his head I kicked him in the balls as hard as I've ever kicked anything in my life. He immediately doubled over and dropped to his knees and I kicked him in the side of his head.

Somebody sucker punched me and it dazed me but didn't knock me out so I went after the closest cowboy. I don't know if he was armed or not but I stuck him anyway. What was I supposed to do? Ask him to wait while I put my blade away. He yelped like and grabbed his arm to cover the bleeding and

I punched him in the throat. Another cowboy jumped on me and grabbed me around the neck and tried to strangle me. I stabbed that son-of-a-bitch in the leg and that got him off of me. I started to look over and see if Jesus was okay and then I felt a jolt. A bolt of lightning lifted me off the ground and I floated away. Somewhere. Into the white.

Chapter 35

First there is light. Then silence. And it doesn't fit. Then I am gone again and I drift. I am floating on pillow clouds. Somewhere in the universe. In the sky above the beyond, and I'm buoyant. As light as a feather on the wisp of wind.

Then there is wind. A whirring sound and a moving breeze. It moves along my body like fingertips lightly touching.

The sound amplifies slightly and rearranges itself. Slight at first but they carry words I recognize.

Then there are sentences. Short and to the point.

"Mr. Walker. Can you hear me?"

The voices are calling to my father. My father. My mother. My brother. My sister. The voice calls to my father but he is not here. He is away.

"Mr. Walker. Hub. Can you hear me?"

Then there is memory. It's slipping down a slide and fills my head. So much I search to find the space before it spills out.

Then blinding light and splitting pain. Then exact and pinpointed focus. Then sound. The sound of a voice. It is mine and it speaks.

"The light hurts my eyes," it says.

There is shuffling and the light softens.

And then a face. A woman with a paper hat looking closely at me. Bending to me. "Can you hear me, Hub?"

"Yes."

"Do you know where you are?"

"Heaven?"

"Do you know what day it is, Hub?"

"My birthday?"

"Do you know what state you're in?"

"Confusion."

She smiles. I've said something that makes her smile. She has deep emerald eyes.

"Wyoming?"

"Do you know who the president is?"

"LBJ."

"And the year?"

"1966. I think."

"I'm nurse Lowell and you're in the Cheyenne Regional Hospital."

"Why?"

"Because you were in an accident."

"No," I answer.

It bothers me because the pieces have been clicking into place. Stacking Legos on top of each other. Building long runways and reassembling quickly into houses.

"It was a fight. A fight."

I reach up to rub my eyes. They feel sandy and crusty. My hands are stuck. I can only move them slightly.

Her eyes signal alarm.

I shake my hands like I'm trying to flip water. I shake them hard and the bed rattles.

"Hub," she says, ever so quietly. "You need to calm down. You're going to be okay." She touches my arm.

I lift my head up suddenly and it feels like it's splitting in half. I am restrained. My hands are secured in leather straps that loop around safeguards attached to the bed frame.

"Unstrap me," I demand.

"I can't do that, Hub."

Louder this time. "Unstrap me! Please." It hurts my head.

Her voice changes. It is a fog horn. A warning.

"Hub, you need to settle down."

This time, there is no soft smile. I strain to sit up. She puts her hand on my chest and her voice changes again. Imploring me.

"Hub. Please try to calm down or you'll hurt yourself."

I realize, I have no control here and it's dangerous.

"I can't protect myself." I beg her, "Please, at least one hand in case they come at me."

"Nobody's going to hurt you, Hub." Her voice is soothing and I almost believe her. "You're safe here, Hub." And then again so I understand. "You're safe."

Safe. The word is soft the way she says it. And I begin to cry and I can't stop. Safe. And I think of Sunday mornings when I was little and my sister and I would crawl into bed with my parents. Safe. And I carried the New York Times like it was an ancient treasure of immeasurable value. Safe. With covers pulled up high while my father would read us the funnies.

"Nurse Lowell," I say between tears, "I'm not safe here. Really. I would like to go home."

I've asked her nicely and I see her weighing things in her mind. Like she's thinking that she might let me go. But I know. She won't.

She finally inhales through her nose and sighs, puffing out her lips slightly. Truth. The truth, nothing but the truth. It's coming. I can see it in her eyes. She's torn about telling me. Nurse Lowell takes another deep breath.

"Hub, you're under arrest."

I feel sharp jolts.

"Even if I wanted to, I can't unstrap you."

I start kicking violently and swearing loudly.

"Get me the fuck out of here. Now!"

The bed is shaking and if I shake hard enough I know it will fall apart.

Nurse Lowell goes to the sink, pushes a button, fills up a syringe and returns.

"Don't stick that fucking needle in me," I scream. "Don't you dare stick me with that! Please."

I am sweating profusely, trying to shake away from her, twisting, turning, tying myself in knots. I am bucking. I am a fucking bucking bronco.

"Shhh...shhh," she begs of me. She pushes the needle into a plastic tube inserted in my vein and gently pushes the poison through the syringe but I keep bucking. Bucking hard and fast. Bucking to throw her off my back until I am finally gone again.

Chapter 36

This time, when I return, I am back. Back in the real. I know where I am and why I'm strapped to the bed. It is my reckoning. A doctor stands to the side of my bed with a chart in his hands. He is studying it and doesn't notice I'm back.

"Hello," I say.

He looks up and introduces himself. "Hub, I'm Doctor Sharp and I'm the attending here. How are you feeling?"

"Like I've been beat up and run over by a train."

"You've got part of that right," he answers, pulling up a chair next to the bed. He takes my hand and feels the pulse then scribbles something down on the chart.

"I'm just going to check your vitals, Hub. To see if all the parts work. Is that okay?"

"I don't have much of a choice, do I?"

"Not really," he says semi-smiling. "I'll begin by checking sense of humor. That's still there."

He stands, takes a little pen light out of his top pocket and looks into my eyes asking me to follow the movement. He clicks off the light and makes a note on the chart. Next, he puts a cuff around my arm and pumps it up until it feels like it will burst, then releases the pressure. Again, he scribbles notes. A thermometer under the tongue and while he's waiting, he talks to me.

He begins by telling me I've suffered a concussion but that I suffered no serious internal damage. The concussion has concerned them. He asks if I've had any blurred vision, headaches, loss of memory, problems with walking in a straight line (like I could answer that all strapped down), nausea, etc., etc.. I shake my head appropriately. No. Yes. No. Question mark. Dr. Sharp withdraws the thermometer from my mouth, holds it up and reads it, jots down the information and then shakes the thermometer several times and drops it into a small dish filled with alcohol.

"Temperature's normal and that's good."

"Great, can I get out of here?"

He disregards the question for the moment. "You've got 27 stitches over your right eye, 32 over your left and a dozen under your left eye on the cheek but no broken bones."

"When can I leave?" I ask, trying a different approach.

"I'd say you're a pretty lucky young man, Hub. It could have been worse," and then asks me about my balance. "Any difficulty walking a straight line? Balancing on one foot?"

"It's hard to tell. Unleash me and I'll give it a try."

Dr. Sharp gave me the look. The kind of *nice try* look I'd get from my parents when I'd propose something outrageous.

"I'm afraid I can't do that Hub. I think you know that."

"Take a chance Dr. Sharp. You've got to face the fear," I said, laughing.

"Well played, Hub. Very quick witted." He folded up the clip board and spoke again. "I think you're going to be okay. A little beat up but you're a healthy young man."

It was a great relief to hear him say that.

"Do you feel like you could have some visitors?"

"Absolutely."

"Good. There are some people that want to talk to you. I'll have Nurse Lowell bring them in."

"Thank you doctor."

It was the first good news I'd had since being here. I couldn't wait to see Jesus and the other carnies. Hopefully, Lacey. To find out if everybody was okay. If anybody got hurt. I needed answers to fill in the blanks. There was a knock on the door.

"Come in," I said cheerfully.

Nurse Lowell opened the door slightly and came in by herself. I felt horrible seeing her.

"Nurse Lowell," I began, "I'm sorry about the trouble I caused and I'm even more sorry about swearing at you."

"Apology accepted, Hub. How are you feeling?"

"Not bad at all. A little banged up but Dr. Sharp said I'd live."

"That's good to hear."

"I've got a favor to ask. Can I get rid of this bed pan and maybe get up and freshen up before my friends come in? I swear I won't try to run away."

"Okay," she replied and that shocked me. She took out the infusion and put a bandage over where the drip went into my vein, unstrapped me, and offered to help me stand up. I declined her offer.

"Let me just give you my arm to steady yourself."

No sense *looking a gift horse in the mouth.* I sat up for the first time and was surprised at how light-headed it made me. I didn't dare say anything to Nurse Lowell because she'd scribble something down in her notes.

I swung my legs over the side of the bed. She slid a hand under my armpit and when I stood, she steadied me. It was a shock. I don't know how long I'd been in the hospital but I felt very unsteady. She walked with me a few steps and then slipped her hand away from me and I had to concentrate hard not to stumble.

I wanted to freshen up, brush my teeth and throw some water on myself before seeing Jesus and the crew. And, just in case, I wanted to look my best if

Lacey had come to visit me, but I wasn't betting on that considering what had happened with her brother. I hoped he was okay. I'd settle for alive. The crew would have to fill me in and the possibility that I might have killed somebody made me lightheaded.

I flipped on the light and stared into a mirror for the first time in a long time. I was shocked. I did not recognize the face staring back at me. Holy Mother of God, who was this person staring back at me? Whoever it was had no eyebrows. Both had been shaven clean with stitches that made him look like Frankenstein. His eyes were sunken and the cheekbone on the left-side had an uneven series of stitches that looked as though somebody had taken a can opener to his face. His crewcut had grown out and looked like fuzz. Most alarming to him was that this face had thinned out and his eyes were without sparkle. He looked gaunt. Lifeless.

Gaunt. That was a perfect word for what he saw.

"Nurse Lowell, may I use the shower?"

"Of course. Be careful. Try not to close your eyes. You might lose your balance. Do you want me to come in and help?"

"No thank you."

She turned on the shower, waited until the water was bearable. When she left, I climbed in letting the shower pound down on me. For a while I just stood there crying. *Get it out of you. Get it all out.* I lathered up and scrubbed as hard as I could being careful around the stitches and then just stood under the full-force of the water until I heard heavy knocking on the door.

"Hub, are you okay in there?"

"I'm just finishing up. Out in a second."

I could have stayed in that shower forever. It felt so good and it made me think how much I'd taken for granted at home. A shower, a real shower, everyday, not once a week if I was lucky. Exhausted from the shower, I climbed back into bed without a fuss. Didn't make a peep when Nurse Lowell strapped my wrists back into the cuffs.

"How did that feel?" she asked.

"I didn't want to come out. How long have I been here?"

"Almost a week, Hub."

Nurse Lowell could tell I was surprised.

"A full week?"

She nodded her head.

"Are you ready for your visitors?"

My spirits picked up.

"Let the madhouse begin," I said smiling. I was anxious to see the crew, to get a play by play run of everything that happened. Before she opened the door, she looked at me. I think she was trying to understand how I could be so excited to see the band of crazies that were about to visit me. And how could you explain these guys to anybody?

"They're safe. Just a bunch of carnies I've worked with."

"Hub, if it becomes too much just buzz for me and I'll have them leave."

"That won't be necessary," I answered softly. "Let them in."

I managed to shimmy myself up so I was actually sitting when they came in.

When the door opened, my heart sank.

Chapter 37

He filled the room when he walked in and it was clear that's not who I expected to see.

"Mr. Walker. I'm Federal Marshall Jack Winston and you are under arrest for being a fugitive from the law and charged with grand-theft auto, robbery, truancy, traveling under an alias and being armed and dangerous."

Shock. Flat out. Not that I hadn't done parts of everything he'd mentioned but I was shocked because I wasn't expecting this at all. Not here. Not now.

"My job is to transport you back across state lines and to the Federal Judicial Court where you will be tried and sentenced. This is the warrant. He dropped a pile of papers onto my lap. "I suggest you read this."

Honestly, I don't know if he was trying to be funny or not but I just looked at him and wiggled my arms to remind him I was locked in a harness.

"Nurse Lowell," he called out.

"Marshall?" she answered entering the room.

"I'm going to give you permission to remove the restraints."

"Thank you, sir."

"Don't thank me, Mr. Walker. Don't try to run off or I'll shoot you. Is that clear young man?"

"Yes, sir...perfectly clear."

"Do you have any questions, Mr. Walker?"

I wanted to explain or at least clarify a few things about the charges against me but this wasn't the place or the time. Instead, and because I felt something more was required of me, I asked him when we'd be leaving.

"As soon as the hospital releases you. Tomorrow afternoon at the latest."

"Thank you."

He offered no response. Not a *You're welcome* or *I'll probably drop you off in the desert somewhere and put a slug into you. Save the courts the trouble.*

"I will post myself outside of the door and nobody will enter without my permission. Is that clear?"

"Yes."

Moments later, Nurse Lowell came in and unstrapped me. I rubbed my wrists.

"I'm sorry I didn't say anything about Marshall Winston. I was instructed not to. You are under arrest."

"It's okay. I understand."

"You've got a couple of other people here to see you and they have been approved," she said, smiling at me. "I'll bring them in."

I couldn't wait to see the carnies. I sat up tall in the bed. When she returned, it was my mother and father. My mom gasped at the sight of me. My father's brow furrowed. My mom started crying immediately and my dad looked stunned.

"Oh, Hub. Hub. Hub. Hub," she came over to the bed and hugged me and I flinched.

"I'm so sorry, honey, did I hurt you?"

"It's all right. I'm okay," and then I started to tear up. "I'm so sorry about all this. I'm so, so sorry."

Then I lost it. Completely. My father, who was never a very affectionate man came over to the other side of the bed and tried to wrap his arms around me. It was awkward but I let him hold me anyway. I could smell the mix of cigarette smoke and Aqua Velva on him, a smell that took me back to my childhood when I'd hide in the closet during hide and seek and smell his sports coats. It was the smell of comfort and safety. Of home.

When we untangled ourselves, my mom opened up a basket she'd brought in and gave me some chocolate chip cookies Soup had baked for me and a drawing Sparky had made for me of a jet fighter. There was a chocolate layered cake, my favorite, and a couple bottles of Coke. It was warm but we could get some ice from Nurse Lowell.

I buzzed for the Nurse and she came almost immediately. My mother asked her for a couple of cups of ice and three paper plates with forks.

"Mom, make it four. Nurse Lowell has been great to me. She'll need a piece."

"Thank you, Hub, but I'm fine."

"I insist. Have it with your dinner but you can't miss tasting mom's cake."

She smiled broadly, "I would actually love a piece of cake, Mrs. Walker," and then added, "the food around here will kill you."

"Mom, was there anybody else out in the hall waiting to see me?"

"Why, were you expecting somebody in particular?"

"No, not really. Maybe."

"Like who?" my father asked.

I didn't like his tone. It was judgmental and suspicious.

"Nobody. I don't know. Maybe a couple of guys from the carnival."

"That would not be such a good idea. Haven't they caused you enough trouble?"

"Dad," I took a deep breath because I appreciated the fact they had come to see me. To be here for me. It took a lot given the way I left them in the dark. "They're not what you think. They watched out for me."

"Some job they did," he said sarcastically and I couldn't let that one go but my mom stepped in before I could say something stupid.

"Boys, stop it. This isn't helping at all."

She was right, but I knew the old man and I would be revisiting this. *The stupidity of his son.*

Nurse Lowell returned and mom cut pieces of the cake and passed them around. It was wonderfully moist and just as I remembered it. And the ice-cold Coke was like the nectar of the gods.

"That is delicious cake, Mrs. Walker. Really delicious."

"Thank you."

"And Hub, I forgot to give these to you earlier," she said reaching into her starched pocket and pulling out two envelopes.

"Thank you."

"I'll just put them over on the nightstand."

"If you like, I'll read them to you," offered my mother.

"It's fine mom, I'll read them later on."

Nurse Lowell actually stayed and ate the cake with us. At one point, I faked like I'd bitten into a file and mom and nurse Lowell laughed. My father even chuckled.

When Nurse Lowell left, we chit-chatted about insignificant things. Mom brought me up to speed on my brother and sister, and dad talked a little about work, but we all avoided the elephant in the room. When it was getting close to visiting hours being over, I finally talked about what Marshall Winston had told me.

Both my parents listened carefully and when I was done, my mother asked me something so sweet it made me realize the depths of the pain she, both of them, had felt.

"Do you think he'll let me ride back in the patrol car with you?"

"I don't think so, mom. I don't think so."

"Son," my father added, "We'll follow right behind you all the way home. If Marshall Winston stops for gas, we stop for gas. If he eats, you eat and we eat. Fair enough?"

"Thanks, it means a lot to me. Where are you staying?"

"Not far from here in a little motel. It's clean," my mother added, like that would be of great comfort me.

"Any idea when they'll release you?" the old man asked.

"Probably tomorrow morning."

"You're still a minor, so I'll have to sign a release for you. We'll be here at 7 a.m. sharp."

Both parents gave me a kiss on the head and then left. As glad as I was to see them, I was glad to have the room back to myself.

The first letter was from Jesus.

> *Hub,*
>
> *If you're able to read this letter, we hung around here until they kicked us out.*
>
> *Things got ugly but nobody got killed. If your head hurts it's because you got stuck with one of those electric bull prods. I got the guy good.*
>
> *Since they found out who you are, I can guess what happens now. I'm sorry I didn't steal your ID when we brought you to the hospital.*
>
> *I hope things turn out okay and you can make a great escape.*
>
> *From your friend Jesus*

The other letter was from Lacey and it was very short.

Dear Hub,

I'm really confused about this. My parents and I came to the hospital because Tad was really hurt. When they wheeled him into emergency I saw them wheeling you in too. My heart dropped.

I don't know what will happen to you but I truly hope everything works out okay.

I thought things might be different for us. Maybe it's because I'm a romantic. Honestly, I don't know if I'll ever see you again. I hope so, I think. Who knows how these things work?

Your friend,
Lacey

I read both of the letters again and then tucked them inside the nightstand drawer on top of a Gideon Bible. It wasn't exactly like I thought it would be. How all of this would amount to two letters.

I guess I thought the carnies, at least some of them, might have hung around which was really a fogged-up idea. The same with Lacey, the idea that she'd be hanging around all worried pacing up and down the hallway chain smoking Kents or something was preposterous. Maybe I'd watched too many sappy TV shows growing up, and in this one I was the hero. A young guy, a down and out carnie (me), who jumps into a fight of overwhelming odds to bring justice to a bunch of villains who beat up the midgets. And he gets beat up pretty bad and the docs say it's touch and go but the boss of the carnies (Wacko) and the entire crew decide to give up their next gig to wait and see if their buddy makes it out alive. And his girlfriend (Lacey) hears what the carnies are going to do so she passes up on riding the rodeo circuit to stay and take care of the hero.

But in this other world, the one I was in, it was nothing like my imagined world. The carnival moved on and so did my girlfriend. The hero wakes up to find his parents have come to see he hasn't been killed and outside his door a U.S. Marshall is waiting to take him to court for a gazillion offenses.

Marshall Winston came into my room at the crack of dawn followed by Nurse Lowell and my parents. He threw my clothes on the bed.

"Mr. Walker, put your clothes on. You're checked out. Don't bother putting your belt on. You can't wear it."

Nurse Lowell brought a wheelchair into the room and, after greeting me, my parents collected my stuff while I went into the bathroom and got dressed. I'd lost some weight so my Levis were almost falling off of me.

"Honey, we'll take all your belongings with us. Officer Winston said that it was fine."

I watched as she packed my journal into the duffel bag. I hoped she wouldn't read it. I thanked Nurse Lowell for being so kind to me and she gave me a hug and wished me well. She looked like she was going to cry.

Officer Winston came over and handcuffed me and shackled my legs in chains. My mother burst into tears and my dad challenged Winston for the need to take such measures.

"Is that necessary? Chaining him up like an animal."

"He's a fugitive from the law and he gets no special treatment."

And that was that. I left Cheyenne Regional in chains. I might have looked tough because I could see the staff sort of keeping their distance from me. I felt anything but tough. I felt small and stupid and lost.

Officer Winston pushed me into the back of his car where the doors had no handles or locks and I was caged from the front seat by a heavy gauged screen. And the son-of-a-bitch kept me chained up.

We made three stops on the 8-hour trip home. The first was a piss stop and a fill-up at a Texaco station in the middle of nowhere. Winston wouldn't let my dad go into the restroom at the same time as me. I guess he thought my dad was some sort of threat, and he actually stood behind me while I took a piss. I was really beginning to dislike Federal Marshal Jack Winston.

The second stop was for lunch. Officer Winston picked a truck stop and asked to be seated at a corner table where he could see everybody coming and going. And although the corner tables were taken, the waitress moved a couple of truckers to the counter so we could sit there. He sat with his back to the wall and I sat across from him. When the waitress dropped off the menus he just asked for coffee and I ordered pancakes with sausage and coffee.

Mom and dad came over to join us and were told to sit someplace else. My dad didn't like the idea and said so but it changed nothing.

I looked like a clown trying to eat the pancakes and sausage in handcuffs without a knife. People kept looking over at our table and would glance away when I looked at them. I'd probably do the same. Wondering what I'd done that warranted such precaution but Officer Winston was a stickler for rules. I kept wondering if he had any real life other than being a hard ass. Was he married? Did he have any children and, if so, I felt sorry for them.

I couldn't imagine what it would be like having a father like him.

Mom didn't eat any of her breakfast. She mostly cried quietly, constantly wiping her eyes with a handkerchief. Dad smoked one cigarette after the other and ground out the butts on his plate.

I didn't have to go to the bathroom so Officer Winston paid and we left. The marshal's car was boiling when we left and I asked him if he might roll down my window so I could get some breeze. Winston didn't acknowledge my request so I sat in the back, windows up, sweating like a pig.

Our last stop was another Texaco where I had to take a dump and that was really messed up. Officer Winston refused to take off my cuffs so use your imagination to figure out how that worked. And he made me leave the stall open while I took a crap.

"You want to tell me how I'm supposed to wipe my ass off with these on?" and I held up the cuffs.

The sadistic son-of-a-bitch laughed and told me to figure it out. A guy like Hitler would have loved Winston. He'd have made a good SS.

By the time we got to the Federal Justice building, it was early evening. My parents were allowed to come in while I was booked, finger printed, photographed and processed. Then I was taken into a small room, searched thoroughly and given a set of pajamas and some slippers and a blanket and locked into a holding cell where I'd await some sort of hearing.

Dad was at a payphone making a call to somebody and then, when they were moving me into another cell, mom came through the gate, even after Officer Winston told her to stop, and hugged me. A lady officer of the court rushed over and separated us.

"Hub, we love you," she called back to me. "Dad's getting a lawyer."

Winston signed off on delivering me and he went one way and I went the other. I really wanted to say something smart ass to him but couldn't think of anything.

I don't know what I expected. I figured since I was such a dangerous criminal, I'd be placed in a cell all by myself but that wasn't the case. I shared the space with two other criminals and none of us spoke to each other.

I didn't sleep much that night because I kept waking up hoping this was all a dream. Morning came and morning went. Around three I was taken into a small interrogation room where I was chained to a small heavy desk.

Pretty soon, a lawyer walked in and introduced himself to me. His name was Oliver Steele and I knew him. He was one of my father's friends. I think they might have served together in the war or something but we didn't chit-chat much and he got right to the point.

"Let me explain what's likely to happen, Hub."

"Okay."

"I've read the arrest affidavit and warrant and it doesn't look good."

"Meaning what exactly?"

"The charges are serious but taking into account that you're a minor there might be some wiggle room if we keep it away from a jury trial and you plead guilty."

"Will I have to go to prison then?"

"It all depends."

"On what?"

"On the judge."

Mr. Steele went on to explain the process. It seemed confusing and he used words like *initial appearance in front of a Magistrate Judge.*

"At the detention hearing, I'll try to see if I can get you released on bail pending a trial. There'll be an arraignment and that's where we present our plea."

"Will I be locked up the entire time?"

"Not if the judge allows us to post bond."

"How does that work?"

"Your parents would have to put up money for bail, and in this case, because the charges are so serious, the bail will be set high. They'll have to put up some sort of collateral like the equity in their house. But here's the deal, Hub. If they put up the money and you run off again, they'll lose their house."

I put my head down in my hands and thought of what I fuck-up I'd been. In all of it, my parents had my back. They never wavered, once.

"Hub," interrupted Mr. Steele, "what would you like me to do?"

"Find me a second chance, please. Find me a way to make this right."

"I'll do my best," and then he shook my hand, took his stack of papers and called the guard to let him out. Just before he disappeared, he said one last thing. "Don't give up hope, Hub. You're a minor and that works to our advantage."

Mr. Steele was a miracle worker and, even though I didn't completely understand the workings of the court in terms of how it pertained to me, I trusted him.

When I was released on bail, I felt like I'd died and gone to heaven. There were some very specific rules I had to abide by including not being able to leave our house.

"Look, Hub," he warned, "there is an officer of the court who can drop by your place unannounced at any time of the night or day. If you're not there, for any reason at all, your folks lose everything and you get locked up and they will throw away the key."

"I understand and I won't present any problems for anybody."

When I walked in the front door, Soup and Sparky threw themselves on me and pounded me with questions. I was overwhelmed and needed to catch my breath.

"What happened to your face?" my brother asked.

"I got in a fight with a super-villain."

"Did you win?"

"I'm here, aren't I."

"Cool," was his response and then he took off to play outside.

"Don't go too far. We're going to have lunch soon."

My dad brought in my duffel bag and dropped it off in my room and then had to take off for work. Before he left, he put out his hand and shook mine and told me he'd see me after work. The soft tender father I'd seen on the road now seemed uncomfortable with any outward affection. I shook his hand and then hugged him.

"Thanks Dad," I said, "for everything."

"I'd do that for any one of my kids, Hub. It's what parents do."

Maybe, I thought, but in our family, I imagined I was the only one that would ever put Mom and Dad in such a position.

Mom made the rest of us grilled cheese sandwiches with a thick cut of ham wedged on top of the cheese. Just the way I liked it.

Soup took my hand and walked me up the stairs to my bedroom. I dumped my kit out onto the floor. The clothes were filthy and probably needed to be burned. She picked up my journal and lightly feathered through it.

"Please don't," I asked her nicely.

"I'm sorry," she replied. "I'm glad you've been writing in it, Hub."

"It kind of kept me from going crazy," I answered, taking the journal from her and putting it over on the desk. "I think I'll keep working on it. Get it all down and see if it means anything in the end."

"It will, Hub," she replied earnestly, "I think you're going to be a writer one day."

That got me laughing. It was just such a random comment and so out of the blue considering all I went through. It was the first good laugh I'd had in a very long time.

She took offense, "I'm not trying to be funny. I'm serious, Hub. I really think you'd be really good at it."

"I'm sorry," I managed to get out between laughing fits, "it just sounds so funny right now."

I took off my shirt and went to the dresser to get a clean t-shirt.

"You've gotten so skinny, Hub. Didn't you eat anything?"

I glanced at myself in the mirror and had to admit Soup was right. I was mostly skin and bones but a couple of weeks of mom's cooking (because she would be cooking) would fatten me up.

"Does anybody know I'm home yet?"

"Not yet. But they've been asking, particularly since your arrest was in the paper."

"Let's keep it that way until I get my feet back on the ground, okay?"

"If you want, I can wash your clothes."

"That'd be really nice, but I can do it myself."

She picked up my clothes and wrinkled her nose. "This stuff smells like merde."

"Throw it all out if it's too gross."

With that she disappeared and the house was quiet. I decided to crash a bit. I still felt pretty weak. I lay on the bed but I couldn't get comfortable so I took my blanket, spread it on the floor and immediately drifted off.

Chapter 38

I've heard people lament about the judicial system. Old folks. Like it *takes too long* for the system to work and other such things but I'll tell you this; from the time I got home and my first appearance in the courtroom, it was only two weeks and I only wished it would have taken longer.

In those two weeks, I found myself missing the carnival, as crazy as that sounds. The carnies were solid. The kind of men and women that had your back if there was trouble. The night of the rumble was still foggy to me but slowly it started clearing up in bits and pieces. I remembered us gathering together with shoe polish war paint on and I remembered how it started. But when things got hot, got real, it was a blur. I couldn't put faces on the people that pounded on me but I could remember the guy I stuck, the look of complete surprise on his face. I got to thinking that maybe he recalled my face and the fact that, and I can't believe I'm going to say this, the fact that I probably would have killed him if it got to that. In the quiet of my home, that really scared me. Scared me because there was a darkness in myself that was, at that moment, revealed.

Mrs. Nelson, my English teacher was so cool in the way she taught us literature. When we read *Heart of Darkness* she didn't just talk about the book like most of my other teachers did. She would talk about the history of what was going on in the world and what experiences the author brought into their work. She told us that the power of Stephen Crane's work came from his keen observations of the human condition and that he didn't hesitate to write about such things honestly. *Stephen Crane was a realist and his work reflected that. He wrote about the things that burned his soul.*

I think I understand that now. I could have killed somebody. Somebody who was just like me. Somebody trying to grow up. Somebody who had an entire life ahead of him and was trying to figure it out.

And that bothered me. Deeply. It burned my soul.

Chapter 39

Finally, my day in court arrived. Mr. Steele had dropped by our house the evening before and explained how it would happen. Because of the seriousness of the charges, I was being brought in front of a judge in the adult system. Meaning all the advantages of being a minor vanished. I would not be accorded such a luxury.

In the preliminary appearance, Steele had entered a plea of not guilty and the date was set for me to appear in court. His approach was not to ask for a jury but to let the judge make the ruling with regard to my guilt or innocence.

My mom was visibly upset. "Why would we offer such a plea, Oliver? And why no jury?"

And my father, just to clarify, overlapped her question with his own. "But he's a minor. I thought that could work to his advantage. Right?"

"In some cases," he replied, calm and measured. "But what you have to understand is that, due to the nature of the events and the seriousness of the charges, he'll be tried as an adult in an adult court."

"My God, Oliver," she began and then stopped until all the pieces clicked into place and then continued, "In other words, if he's found guilty he could be placed into the prison system." It wasn't a question, it was a fact.

"Yes, he would."

The weight of that reality hung on us all and Oliver let it sit there for a moment.

"I'm not going to let that happen," he replied with conviction.

"But you don't know, Oliver," challenged my father, "you simply can't know, can you?"

"True."

"And why no jury?" I asked.

"We stand a better chance without one."

"Why?"

"Because, Hub, this is a conservative town and people believe in law and order. I don't think there would be any wiggle room. You did all those things."

"So, why would a judge be any different?" piped in my mother as she brought a pot of coffee and biscuits in from the kitchen.

"Because he might believe Hub's testimony. And Hub, I'm going to have to put you on the stand."

This came as a shock to me and but it was the last thing I wanted to do. "To say what, Mr. Steele?"

"To tell your side of the events."

"That's right. And the prosecution will jump all over your testimony. It will look like you're playing into their hands. Hopefully, it will give them a false sense of the narrative."

"Meaning?"

"Meaning, my job is to then break down each part of the equation and show that comparing all the events collectively builds a case, a dark, apparently straightforward case, of a criminal kid bent on a course that should incarcerate him for the safety of society."

"Wouldn't that be playing into their hands?" quizzed my father.

"That's to our advantage," Steele replied, leaving us all guessing.

"Hub, I believe your story of the events. All of it."

"I don't understand how that helps," I said with an edge to my voice.

"Take Jake's for instance..."

"What about it?'

"Before Jake sold his place to the Collier family, any minor could buy liquor if they followed the rules. Right?"

"Yeah, but what's that got to do with it?"

"You followed the rules, correct?"

"Yep. To the letter of the law."

"It's, *Yes sir*, Hub. Don't get sloppy with your language in court. It counts."

"Yes, sir."

"I've subpoenaed Jake."

I laughed. Like Jake would confess to selling liquor to minors.

"That'll be the day," I said, shaking my head like if this is my defense I'm in serious trouble.

"You're right, Hub. He won't. He'll take the 5th Amendment so he won't incriminate himself."

"Help us out here, Oliver," my mom began but he cut her off.

"He won't but 12 of your friends, all of them from your school, will testify to having bought liquor from Jake's Gas-o-Rama just the way you said."

The three of us just sat there slack-jawed.

The judge isn't stupid. Regarding that count against you, my guess he won't even consider it. There's more than a reasonable doubt that you actually *robbed* a liquor store. Because you never even left Jake's. Flip a coin with a jury though."

"What about the other two counts?" asked my father.

"Grand theft auto. Not as easy, Hub. Because you did take it and did some damage to it."

"And the armed and dangerous part?"

"I think I can make it circumstantial. You never drew the shotgun out. It was in the cruiser. Standard issue in every cruiser. No intention of use."

"Right," my father said, nodding his head, "but he did take the cruiser."

And he looked at me, like I didn't already know what I'd done. I didn't say anything although I wanted to.

"Unfortunately, there's no way out of that one I'm afraid."

"But he told me he left them a note apologizing. Doesn't that count?"

"I'm hoping so. Cold-hearted criminals don't leave apology notes for the police."

"What do you think the sentence'll be?" I asked because something was coming. I knew it. I just didn't know what.

"Unfortunately, Hub, you've had a few run-ins with the system before. It shouldn't pertain to this case but you can bet the prosecution will bring it up. I'll object. The judge will sustain the objection but it will be out there. He'd instruct the jury to disregard, but it would be on their minds. I didn't want to take that chance."

Steele was good and I think we all finally realized just how seriously he'd taken my case. How carefully he'd built a defense. For a moment, we just took it all in. My father finally broke the silence.

"But he's going to have to pay for the cruiser, right?"

That was it for me and I jumped on his comment this time.

"Jesus, dad. We get! Leave it alone for God's sake. Don't you think we get it?"

My father was about to respond when Steele cut him off.

"Gentlemen, stop it. There's no *get out of jail free* card I'm afraid. You've all got to be together on this. It's important. Let me finish." He waited until we'd settled down. "But I've got one more card up my sleeve."

"What's that?" I asked.

"Character witnesses. People who will testify to your character."

"It'd have to be a short list," I said in jest.

"It's a little insurance just in case."

And with that sentence hanging in the air, Oliver Steele bid us all a good night and disappeared.

Chapter 40

The day I was to appear in court, I got up early, took a shower and then got dressed up in the new suit my mother purchased for me at JCPenney. Surveying myself in the mirror, I hardly recognized the image I saw in front of me. I knew it was me, but it wasn't how I saw myself. I'd thinned out a bit and although my scars had healed up, I was somebody else. Not the punk, angry and reckless kid that left home. And that was probably a good thing. I looked older, maybe more respectable. Mom was right, the suit makes the man.

It was quiet around the breakfast table. Mom made my favorite breakfast of flapjacks and bacon with coffee and fresh orange juice. I was too nervous to eat so I just poked at my food until she asked me if I was done. No guilt attached this morning. No, *You really need to eat something. Breakfast is the most important meal of the day* crap. She just picked up my plate and scraped it into the garbage.

We drove to the courthouse in silence. My father was nervous and smoked cigarette after cigarette while my mother worried.

Oliver Steele greeted us on the courthouse stairs as we approached.

"Good morning. Hub, you look good. Are you ready?"

"I think so," I replied. What else was required at this point?"

"Just be yourself on the stand and I'll do my best to cover the rest."

"Okay."

"We've got a good judge. I couldn't have chosen a better one. He's new to the court but he's got a reputation for being fair."

"Oliver, that's so good to hear," my mom said nervously.

"We'll see," he said and then he suggested my parents go into the courtroom and take a seat. Before we did, he gave me some advice on how to handle the cross examination. "Hub, so much of this hinges on how you handle yourself under pressure. The attorney for the state is tough and she'll do her best to fluster you. You can't let her. Understand?"

"I do."

"Don't elaborate or offer more than she's asking of you. Okay? And it's yes ma'am or no ma'am. Not yep or nope. Be respectful above all things."

"Yes, sir."

"And don't look around the courtroom. There will be people there you know but don't acknowledge them. It will come off like you're not interested in your own trial. Pay attention. If you need to say something to me I'll have a legal pad in front of you and write it down. Legibly."

"Yes, sir."

"Okay, let's go in."

Chapter 41

From the moment Judge Harold McNamara entered the courtroom and the bailiff called, *All rise,* and read the charges, it was all business. The prosecuting attorney made her opening statement and when she was finished I was pretty certain I'd end up in an adult prison serving my time.

Oliver then stood up and thanked the court and began to lay out his version of the very same story but it sounded so completely different that I wondered what the judge was thinking. Steele admitted that the events had, indeed, occurred but that was not the real story and then he began to tell the court our side of the story. He was deliberate and thorough and reminded me of the movie version of *To Kill a Mockingbird* where Gregory Peck defends Tom Robinson, a black field hand accused of raping and beating Mayella Ewell, a white woman who lived with a drunkard bigot of a father.

Steele was impressive and I truly felt confident about him until I remembered the jury found Tom Robinson guilty when he was clearly innocent. My heart sunk. This could be me.

After he was done, the prosecuting attorney, Victoria Stratton, called her first witness.

"If the court pleases, I'd like to call my first witness to the stand. Officer Don Broadhead."

I could feel my heart sink. Broadhead looked a lot bigger than I remembered. And he looked like the law incarnate. With his crisply pressed dress uniform, his hat held in his arm, and his chest full of shiny medals, he was clearly impressive and I thought this was the end of me. Honest to God, I'd believe anything he had to say. After being sworn in, Broadhead took the stand and Stratton had him recount exactly what had happened. And he did just that.

When she asked him to point to the defendant he pointed directly to me and his arm seemed so long I thought his forefinger would snatch me up and beat me to a pulp.

Broadhead had clearly been in a court before. He showed no signs of disdain for me, he just simply told the story and it was pretty accurate. If I was sweating and nervous, Steele wasn't. He calmly took notes on a legal pad. Every so often, Stratton would stop Broadhead and ask him to clarify or elaborate on a point or two. Steele never objected to a thing even when I thought she was leading Broadhead. But here's the interesting thing. Broadhead never once mentioned how disrespectful I was when he talked about Jesus saving me and some other crap I'd said. That puzzled me. Maybe he'd forgotten but I seriously doubted it.

When it was Steele's turn to cross-exam Broadhead it was something else. Something I could never have imagined. First, he asked Broadhead if I'd actually been charged with the theft of whiskey from Jake's Gas-o-Rama. If he'd actually filed any papers at all.

Broadhead looked perplexed and he looked over toward Stratton to see if she could maybe give him a signal on a *Yes* or *No* answer.

Steele picked-up on the hesitation and asked him again.

"Officer Broadhead, was there a formal charge made by the owner of Jake's Gas-o-Rama?"

Broadhead hesitated and then said, "Not to my knowledge."

"Is that a *No* Officer Broadhead? Let me put it another way, Officer. On the evening in question, you took the defendant into your custody at Jake's Gas-o-Rama and then took him down to the station. Is that correct?"

"Yes."

"And then what happened?"

"I tried several times to call his parents to come pick him up."

"And then what?"

"I couldn't reach them so I had him sit at my desk until I could."

"Why didn't you book him at that point?"

"Things got out of hand. We had to deal with a couple of drunks, a husband and wife that started fighting, and I had to help break up the ruckus."

"So, in your opinion, Mr. Walker wasn't a threat and the event at Jake's Gas-o-Rama wasn't a serious enough issue to book him."

Stratton immediately objected citing the fact that Steele was leading the witness.

The judge sustained her objection. But Steele didn't miss a beat. He kept after Broadhead.

"Had his parents answered the phone, would you have sent Mr. Walker home with them?"

"Yes."

"Because, Officer Broadbent?"

"Because, he hadn't committed a crime."

There was a murmur in the courtroom. Judge McNamara banged his gavel and called for order. I turned around for the first time and saw my mother who offered a slight smile to me. My father remained stoic. I couldn't believe how many people were there. Jake looked relieved he hadn't been called to the stand. Behind him sat a bunch of my friends. Smitty who gave me a thumbs-up, a bunch of kids from Pershing, basically the upper parking lot gang. I guessed they were witnesses Steele would have called to testify to having purchased booze at Jake's. And then, I saw Lindsey sitting next to Bullet. She smiled and Bullet just gave a simple head nod.

Ohhhh, Lindsey. How I wanted to get up and go talk to her and apologize. I wanted to tell her I was really sorry for making her life uncomfortable. And I wanted to tell her how much her care package meant to me and that Bullet was probably the right guy for her.

I was so fixated on her I almost didn't notice Mrs. Nelson, my English teacher, sitting in the courtroom. Seeing her snapped me back into the courtroom. Why would she be here? Her of all people. It just didn't make sense and then I thought of what Steele's final words had been.

Character witnesses. People who will testify to your character.

It touched me that she was here to speak on my behalf if Steele needed her to do so.

Steele had finished working on Broadhead and Stratton almost flew to the front of the courtroom to re-examine. The first three questions she asked Broadhead were objected to by Steele citing the question had already been asked and answered. Judge McNamara ruled in his favor.

It seemed to me that Stratton's case was falling apart quickly. Jake's was a non-issue and she needed to gain some ground so she asked Broadhead what happened next.

Officer Broadhead then told the judge how, when he noticed I'd walked out of the station, he immediately went outside and saw me opening the door to his patrol car. He then recounted how he'd called after me to stop and I disregarded him, jumped into his vehicle and tore off into the night.

Steele made no objection and Broadhead went on to describe how he'd slammed on the alarm switch that activated the front gate and that I'd roared through it busting off the side mirror. Then he proceeded to tell the judge how several patrol cars had taken off in hot pursuit.

I looked over at Steele who was scratching notes on his legal pad. Stratton was allowing Broadhead to paint a pretty big car chase right out of a TV series while the judge listened attentively and occasionally made some notes. Steele was cool as a cucumber until Stratton finished up with Officer Broadhead and then he cross-examined.

Honestly, Broadhead told the story pretty much the way it happened so there wasn't much I could disagree with in his account. Putting it out in the world like that made me look pretty gangster and it concerned me. I could only imagine what the judge was thinking. He didn't offer any inkling of how he saw this but it certainly couldn't have been favorable.

"Officer Broadhead," Steele began, "why do you suppose Mr. Walker took your vehicle?"

"Objection," Stratton interrupted, "the defense is calling for a conclusion Officer Broadhead can't make."

"Overruled," Judge McNamara said. "Go ahead and answer the question, Officer Broadhead."

"Could you please repeat the question?"

"Of course," Steele replied and then presented the question again, "why do you suppose Mr. Walker took your vehicle?"

"I think he panicked. I think he was scared."

"Objection."

"Overruled."

"So, Officer Steele, did you think he intended to take the patrol car?"

"Objection."

"Overruled," McNamara replied instantly, "please answer the question, Officer Broadhead."

"No, I don't think Mr. Walker intended to steal my patrol car."

"Your honor, I object to this entire line of questioning," Stratton challenged.

She was upset. Judge McNamara called her to the bench. When she approached, it seemed to me like Judge McNamara was annoyed. He sort of pointed at her and then she said something turned and sat back down at her table. She was shaking her head.

"Your honor, I have no further questions for Officer Broadhead," Steele said and then thanked Broadhead for his testimony.

When Broadhead walked by me I swear he gave me a small wink. That got to me. Here I was thinking Broadhead had been a real prick and now, I'd seen him in a completely different light. If there was a prick in this equation, it was me. He was just doing his job and I was such a little punk. I was embarrassed for the Hub Walker I had been. The pseudo punk high school kid who thought he was tougher than he actually was. I was ashamed for everything I'd done and all the chaos I'd caused in so many people's lives.

Judge McNamara ordered an hour recess and then we would return to the court to continue the trial.

When we recessed, Steele had us gather together in a small anti-chamber to walk us through the next part of the trial. My mom hugged me.

"I'm pleased with the way things panned out in this morning's session," Steele said. "But what happens this afternoon is what the entire case hangs on."

"So, Oliver," my father asked, "what happens next?"

"I'm certain Hub will be called to the stand and the prosecution will try to discredit him."

"Meaning what?" mom asked.

"Jake's gas-o-Rama won't play into the judge's decision. The prosecution is down to their last straw so Ms. Stratton will attempt to rattle you, Hub. And you've just got to stay calm and not give her any ammunition."

"What's she going to ask me?"

"Officer Broadhead's testimony didn't help their case at all. She's going to try and paint a picture that you knew exactly what you were doing when you took the patrol car and took off."

"Okay," I replied, "but I did take it."

"Yes, we can't dispute that but what we can continue to point out is that Officer Broadhead said, under oath, that he didn't think you meant to do so."

"It was the truth. I still don't know why I did it. I was scared."

"That was clear to the court. But Ms. Stratton will probably bring up some of your past brush-ins with the system."

"But you said," interjected mom, "that the..."

"I'll object immediately and the judge will overrule but she'll come at you in other ways trying to get you to lose your cool."

"Okay, but what should I do?"

"Be polite. Answer the questions she asks. Don't give her anything more than she asks for even if you want. It might be difficult."

"I'll do my best."

"Anything I feel you've said that weakens our case, I'll come back to you in such a way that you can clarify. Is that clear?"

"Yes, sir."

"And then what?"

"I'll finish up with you and she might call any other witness to the stand that might help the state's case but I don't think so."

"Like who?"

"Honestly, I don't think she has any surprises up her sleeve. If I feel like we've done all we can, I'll not call any other witnesses to the stand."

"And if you don't?"

"I'll bring up some character witnesses who'll speak on your behalf."

"Like Mrs. Nelson?"

"Yes, like Mrs. Nelson."

Chapter 42

Steele was right. Stratton came after me with guns blazing. I could feel her trying to box me in. Get me to answer questions that made me look bad. Steele objected to almost every other question and the judge would overrule her. Still, I was starting to get confused.

She'd ask what seemed like a simple question like, "So, Mr. Walker, you never intended to steal Officer Broadhead's patrol car?"

A simple enough question and I gave a simple answer.

"No."

"Then why did you do so?"

"Because I was afraid?"

"Afraid of what? What were you afraid of?"

"I don't know."

"Does that happen a lot to you?"

"What?"

"Being afraid?"

"No, not really. No more than any of my friends I guess."

"Have any of your friends stolen cars when they were afraid?"

"Objection!"

"Sustained."

"Let me put it another way, do you think being afraid gives you permission to steal a car? A police car no less?"

"No."

"Objection."

"Overruled."

"But you know how to hotwire a car don't you, Mr. Walker?"

"Objection."

"Sustained."

"Have you ever been in front of a Juvenile Court judge?"

"Objection your honor. Objection."

"Sustained."

"You had a choice to make Mr. Walker and your choice was to steal the patrol car, wasn't it?"

"Objection."

"Overruled. Answer the question Mr. Walker."

"Yes."

"I have no further questions, your honor."

I felt as though everything Steele might have gained through Officer Broadhead's testimony had been negated with mine. The way Stratton kept coming after me, and the need for Steele to keep objecting, really spun me around. I didn't know if I was coming or going. It reminded me of those lawyer shows like Perry Mason where the guilty guy comes apart on the stand and finally confesses to the crime.

When Steele started to question me things started to right themselves. He carefully had me walk through the moment I left Broadhead's desk to the time I got into the patrol car and took off out of the compound. Then he turned his attention to the reason I actually climbed into the vehicle and turned over the ignition.

"Mr. Walker, what made you get into the patrol car?"

"I was afraid."

"Why did you leave the office?"

"Because it was getting really late and I was just sitting there while the police officers were breaking up a brawl between a drunk husband and his drunk wife."

"Is that what scared you?"

"No. Not really."

"Then what were you afraid of?"

"Getting in trouble with my parents. It was way after my curfew."

"But why didn't you just walk home instead of taking the patrol car?"

"I was going to walk home. That's why I left Officer Broadhead's desk."

"Please explain to us how you happened to take the patrol car then."

"Well," I began and then took a moment before answering. "I heard the Officer yell at me from the back door."

"What did he say?"

"He yelled, "Lynch! Get your sorry ass back in this building you ungodly piece of shit!""

"Who was Lynch?"

"It's the name I gave him when I got picked up."

By the expression on Steele's face, this was news to him. If it threw him off he didn't show it.

"And you used a phony name because?"

"I didn't want to get my parents involved and I didn't want to get in any trouble."

"Did you feel like you were in danger from Officer Broadhead?"

"Objection, your honor. The defense is leading the witness."

"Sustained. Mr. Steele, rephrase the question."

"Did you feel in any danger?"

"Yes. I thought Officer Broadhead was going to beat me up."

"Thank you, Mr. Walker. Your honor, I have no further questions."

"Ms. Stratton, do you have any further questions of the witness?"

"No, your honor."

"Mr. Steele, do you have any other witnesses you'd like to call to the stand?"

"Only one. I'd like to call Mrs. Julia Nelson to the stand."

That caught me by surprise. Was he calling Mrs. Nelson to the stand because he felt I'd hurt myself during the testimony. I thought he said that was his last straw, to call a character witness.

Mrs. Nelson was sworn in and took the stand. Steele took her through a carefully guided series of questions that began to paint me in a different light. In Mrs. Nelson's eyes she saw me as a bright, curious young man who full of promise and possibility. And then she said that of all her students, she thought I had the greatest potential and I could go to any college I wanted. Then she emphasized the word, *any*.

Mrs. Nelson actually thought I could go to *any* college I wanted. The only other person that I ever heard say that I had any potential was my sister, Soup. And she was my sister. Hearing that from Mrs. Nelson made me want to hug her. And thank her.

Stratton had no questions for Mrs. Nelson and she said the prosecution was done and ready to make their closing remarks. Steele, in turn, said they were ready to make theirs.

They were ready but I wasn't.

Chapter 43

Mrs. Stratton was good. She made a powerful argument about my having a choice to choose good over evil and she almost beat to death the fact that I failed to walk away. Not only had I stolen a car but it was a police patrol car and that chaos had followed trying to find me. Maybe we could excuse a joyride in a neighborhood car but not a police patrol car. These were the very people that swore to protect us and I had undermined that trust. That evil had triumphed over good and there had to be a consequence for committing grand theft auto. To let me get away with this would be a travesty of justice.

So compelling was her argument, I almost agreed with her.

When Mr. Steele talked, he argued that in a moment when I felt my life was in danger, I'd made a terrible choice. He invoked the testimony Mrs. Nelson had just given. He focused on her sense that I was a student of great promise and possibility and he closed with the suggestion that to not allow me a second chance would be a greater travesty of justice.

After both sides made closing remarks, Judge McNamara recessed the court for an hour and gave us instructions to return for his ruling.

I remember very little about that hour sitting in the same room with my parents and Oliver Steele. I sat in the corner of the room on a hard-back chair sipping Coke through a straw. Mom and dad were in whispered conversation with Mr. Steele and, frankly, I was just exhausted. I just wanted it to get over. To get on with my life whatever that meant.

The bailiff returned and escorted us back into the courtroom. We all rose when Judge McNamara arrived and stayed so until he sat down.

"Will the defendant please rise."

I did.

"In the case of the State of Utah vs Hub Walker, the court finds Mr. Walker innocent of attempting to rob a liquor store. In the charge of grand-theft of a police patrol car, the court finds Mr. Walker guilty."

I heard the verdict. I heard my mother gasp.

Since both the prosecution and defense agreed that the sentencing would be revealed following the completion of the trial, I heard Judge McNamara continue.

"Mr. Walker, in this unusual case, due to many circumstances, your sentence will give you two options: you will become the custody of the state in the state school for a year where you will complete your final year of high school or its equivalent. Or, if you should so choose, you may enlist in any branch of the United States military where you will serve your country for a tour of active duty. Do you have any questions Mr. Walker?"

"No, your honor."

"Son, you have 24 hours to make your decision and you then will report your decision to the court."

With that, Judge McNamara lifted his gavel and pronounced the court dismissed.

Chapter 44

On the drive home, I said nothing. My parents were clearly upset by the sentence. They were talking to each other in a way I hadn't heard in forever. And it was about me. As though they'd forgotten about me sitting in the back seat.

My father, who, all along, I felt, wanted me to feel the swift arm of justice was singing a different tune now. In his book, neither of those choices fit the crime. I was still a teenager.

"Maybe we could appeal the verdict, honey," he said to my mom.

I don't remember my father ever using that term of endearment with my mother before. I'm sure he did but this was a first time I've ever heard him do so.

"That's exactly what we should do," she said emphatically. "Oliver said we could."

"We'd have to pay him this time," dad said, "but we can take a second mortgage out on the house."

"No," I said. My voice was firm. My mother turned around.

"Oh, Hub," she began.

"Mom and Dad. I'm not going to let that happen. I can't."

"Listen, son..."

"No state school for me, dad. It'd kill me. I'm going to enlist."

"Jesus, Hub," my mother, who never swore, said, "there's a serious war going on."

"I know. I'm aware."

When we got home, Soup and Sparky were waiting at the door for us.

"What happened?" Soup asked before we got inside.

"I'll tell you later on," I answered, "not now."

"Give us a bit of time sweetie. We need to talk with Hub alone."

The three of us sat at the kitchen table and picked up where we left off in the car. Mom was adamant that I go off to state school and complete my last year of school.

"Just think of it as a private boarding school, Hub."

"Okay, mom, but it's not."

"Listen son, you have to be 18 to enlist and you just turned 17," said my father as he lit up a smoke.

"If you sign for me, dad, I can enlist."

"I don't think I can do that for you, Hub," he said, choking up a bit. "I'd never forgive myself if anything happened to you."

That killed me. The fact my father was really concerned almost made me cry. I mean, I had been nothing but trouble for them in the last couple of years. Parents, seriously, I just didn't understand how they could care about me...not after the things I'd done.

There was an ashtray full of butts by the time I finally convinced both of my parents to let me enlist. My father kept bringing up the fact that the war, the Vietnam war, wasn't like his war. It was a bloody mess. It made no sense to him at all.

In the end, I talked them into it. Tomorrow, we'd go back into the court and tell the judge I would be enlisting in the military. And the next day, with the permission of my family, I would go down to the enlistment center and sign on the dotted line.

Vietnam.

Vietnam. A thousand shades of green or so I'd heard.

What could possibly go wrong?

Vietnam.

Acknowledgements

This novel would not have survived had I not had such great support from the following people:

To John Alley and Anne Holman for their sensibility in giving grand advice.

To Ron Carlson, Sylvia Torti, and Jeff Zentner for their very generous blurbs.

To Chris Thompson for such a spectacular cover.

Finally, a special thanks to Joanie Packard for pulling the book together.

Last but not least to The King's English for their bravery in publishing this novel. May there be more.

Jeff Metcalf is Professor of English and the Director of Humanities in Focus documentary film program at the University of Utah. An award-winning writer, teacher and journalist, Metcalf lives in Salt Lake City and teaches literature and playwriting in the English Department and in the Honors College at the University of Utah.

Metcalf has been the recipient of the 2019 Cathedral of the Madeleine Award for Literary Arts, the 2017 Surel's Place Artist-in-Residence Award, the 2016 Taft-Nicholson Artist-in-Residence Award, the 2014 University of Utah Distinguished Teacher Award, the 53rd Utah Arts Council Award for Creative Nonfiction (*Requiem for the Living*, University of Utah Press), the 2008 University of Utah Career Teaching Award, the Huntsman Award for Excellence in Education, a Fulbright Memorial Scholar Award, the National Council of English Teachers Award, the Lifetime Advocacy Award from Writers@Work, grants from both the Utah Humanities Council and the Utah Arts Council and numerous other teaching awards.

When he is not writing, teaching or filming, Metcalf can be found fly-fishing the great trout waters of the West.